Algonquin Sunset is a fantastic book! Incorporating accurate historic knowledge and language into the trilogy makes the books not only a great story but also an excellent learning tool.

MARTI FORD

Area 3 Superintendent

Frontier School Division

Manitoba

Revelle writes in a very oral style reminiscent of the storytellers of old: engaging stories combined with traditional teachings. Algonquin Sunset is a good read!

WILLY BRUCE

Oshkaabewis

Aboriginal Veterans Autochtones

To demonstrate the importance of the past so nicely depicted in your novel Algonquin Sunset, *we would like to make this analogy: A gymnast has to take many steps backward to jump higher; so it is with humanity. To us it sums up your message. This is why it is so important not to forget where we come from, who we are, where we want to be, and what we want to leave for future generations. In most aspects of life, if we want to make the right decisions, we have to step back, analyze, and anticipate the potential results and consequences prior to jumping forward. Your novels* I Am Algonquin, Algonquin Spring, *and* Algonquin Sunset *have opened our eyes to this.*

ANNIE SMITH ST-GEORGES AND

ROBERT SMITH ST-GEORGES

Algonquin Elder, Traditional Practitioner, and Home Elder; Métis

National Arts Centre

Ottawa

In this installment of the Algonquin Quest Series, we are given a stark description of how life centred around teaching and learning skills associated with personal and tribal survival. Rick shows us the challenges of child-rearing in a time when a balance had to be established between looking after our children and teaching them while at the same time protecting our communities from the ever-present dangers. Rick also gives us a glimpse into how enemies were dealt with and the cruelty of these bloody conflicts. He reminds us that survival is never easy and sometimes is deadly to communities. This makes us better by helping us to understand the conflicts in our own world and to avoid the human destruction of life, as well as all our relations on Mother Earth.

ROBERT THIBEAU, CD
President
Aboriginal Veterans Autochtones

Reading this saga of what might have been prior to contact is very thought-provoking, and whenever I walk in the woods, I wonder if something like that might have happened along where I am walking. I just love it.

JOE WILMOT
Mi'gmaq Language and Cultural Coordinator
Listuguj, Quebec

I enjoyed reading our Lakota language in this novel, along with the ancient ways of my people.

ROB HER MANY HORSES
Substance Abuse Counccllor, Outreach Worker, and Coordinator
Lower Brule Lake Sioux Reservation, South Dakota

AN ALGONQUIN QUEST NOVEL

ALGONQUIN SUNSET

Rick Revelle

DUNDURN

TORONTO

Cover image: 123RF.com/sergwsq
Printer: Webcom

Library and Archives Canada Cataloguing in Publication

Revelle, Rick, author
 Algonquin sunset : an Algonquin quest novel / Rick Revelle.

Issued in print and electronic formats.
ISBN 978-1-4597-3702-0 (paperback).--ISBN 978-1-4597-3703-7 (pdf).--
ISBN 978-1-4597-3704-4 (epub)

 I. Title.

PS8635.E887A643 2017   jC813'.6   C2016-906776-9
                                           C2016-906777-7

1 2 3 4 5   21 20 19 18 17

  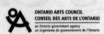

We acknowledge the support of the **Canada Council for the Arts** and the **Ontario Arts Council** for our publishing program. We also acknowledge the financial support of the **Government of Ontario**, through the **Ontario Book Publishing Tax Credit** and the **Ontario Media Development Corporation**, and the **Government of Canada**.

Care has been taken to trace the ownership of copyright material used in this book. The author and the publisher welcome any information enabling them to rectify any references or credits in subsequent editions.

— J. Kirk Howard, President

VISIT US AT

dundurn.com | @dundurnpress | dundurnpress | dundurnpress

Dundurn
3 Church Street, Suite 500
Toronto, Ontario, Canada
M5E 1M2

To my friend, Rob Her Many Horses, may your Lakȟóta aíčhimani bring many rewards in this life

and

To my mother, Iona Revelle, a feisty little Native woman who lives life to the fullest

and

In memory of the Dakota 38

AUTHOR'S NOTE

Both the Lakȟóta and Ojibwe languages are like the Algonquin language in that they are spoken less and less by their people. In this novel I have introduced these two languages, hoping that maybe just a little bit will stay with readers.

In the following pages of this Author's Note, I give thanks to the people and organizations that enabled me to bring the pronunciations of each Native dialect to this book. I will always remain appreciative of the work put into saving these languages on the World Wide Web for future generations to educate themselves. I ask readers when they find the time to please have a look at the *Ojibwe People's Dictionary* (http://ojibwe.lib. umn.edu) and the *Mi'kmaq Online Talking Dictionary* (www.mikmaqonline.org). Both are very informative and educational.

Unless we were physically involved in producing the two aforementioned websites, we could never know how much research, people hours, money, and discussion went into such endeavours to get the end results we see today. Both of the websites are continually updated.

Once readers see the Anishinaabe-Ojibwe language, they will notice many similarities to the Algonquin language in spelling and meanings. However, there are enough differences between the two that I have included them as separate glossaries at the end of this book.

When I couldn't find a certain word either phonetically spelled out or pronounced on one of my talking dictionary sites, I didn't provide a pronunciation guide for that word. I will never put in print any of the pronunciations of the Native dialects I use in my books without first hearing the words sounded out or seeing them phonetically spelled.

When different tribes met and conversed, they used sign language along with their oral languages. Throughout this novel, whenever two or three different linguistic nations talk together, try to picture that they are using sign language along with their oral languages. Native tribes that were allies quickly learned each other's languages, and even enemies were able to converse because many times, they had captives from each other's villages who became part of the tribe and acted as interpreters.

This book is fiction; however, the ways the characters live, hunt, harvest, and wage war are as accurate as I can find in all the research I have done, along with the many hours of reading other writers' works about the Ojibwe and Lakȟóta Nations. Conversations with Elders and young people of the Native nations I write about have led me in the proper direction.

Many of the experiences I write about that take place in the woods and while canoeing are related to events I have encountered myself. Although I'm not a hunter, when I was growing up, members of my immediate family took me hunting and fishing. Friends such as Larry Porter and Al Whitfield, who are good storytellers and hunters, gave me the foundation to write about some of their present-day encounters that are generational in practice.

As always, I would like to thank my Mohawk friend, Eddie Maracle, for his knowledge of two important subjects that aided me greatly in the writing of my novels. His skill with computers as an IT expert and his knowledge of his ancestral Mohawk language were immensely helpful in my writing.

Garth Firth, a close friend who travelled with me to Manitoulin Island in the spring of 2014, couldn't figure out why I would give up four days of golf to visit every museum on Manitoulin Island. Now he knows!

As in my two previous books in the Algonquin Quest series — *I Am Algonquin* and *Algonquin Spring* — the Algonquin family of Mahingan (Wolf) plays a major role in this novel.

In *I Am Algonquin* and *Algonquin Spring*, I didn't include phonic pronunciations for Native words. For *Algonquin Sunset*, however, I now had the capability to do so. In the two previous novels, I didn't have research materials to allow me to break down the pronunciation of a word for all of the Native languages I used. So I made the decision that if I couldn't do the phonic separation of a word for all the languages, I wouldn't do it for just one. It was a matter of being consistent in my approach to these Native languages.

As of September 2016, by way of all my research findings, I now have the ability to address the pronunciation hurdles of the past. The first time a Native word or name appears in this novel, the pronunciation and meaning follow it; after that, when the word occurs again, it doesn't have this information but those details can still be accessed in the glossaries at the end of the book. There were still words that I was unable to find pronunciations for and in those cases I didn't guess in print how to sound them out. Such words appear without pronunciations.

For the Lakȟóta language I used three sources. The first source and the one seen in the main body of the novel is the *English–Lakȟóta Dictionary* compiled by J.K. Hyeriand and W.S. Starij'ing of the University of Pittsburgh. The Lakȟóta words from that dictionary are easily pronounceable due to by the separation of syllables and the use of phonics. The second source I used is the *Dakota Dictionary* by John P. Williamson, a missionary on the Santee Reservation who lived from 1835 to 1917. He produced his dictionary in 1902. The third resource I used is the *Lakȟóta Dictionary Online*. Its Lakȟóta words aren't as easily pronounceable at first glance, but when the Hyeriand and Starij'ing dictionary words are placed alongside, pronunciation is straightforward employing their method. Further encounters with these words can be accessed in the glossaries for reference.

For the Anishinaabe language, I used *A Concise Dictionary of Minnesota Ojibwe*, produced by John D. Nichols from the Department of Native Studies, Department of Linguistics, University of Manitoba in Winnipeg, and by Earl Nyholm from the Department of Modern Linguistics, Bemidji State University in Minnesota. I also referenced the *Freelang Ojibwe Online Dictionary* and the *Ojibwe People's Dictionary*. For the Anishinaabe language, I added phonetic pronunciations when I could find the spoken word from the *Ojibwe People's Dictionary*, which has an online talking dictionary. The pronunciations are my interpretation of how I perceive the words to be spoken by Anishinaabe speakers.

For the Mi'kmaq language, I also added phonetic pronunciations taken from the *Online Listuguj Talking Dictionary*. Again the pronunciations are my interpretation of how I perceive the words as spoken by Mi'kmaq speakers.

For the *Ojibwe People's Dictionary*, to the staff and students at the University of Minnesota College of Liberal Arts, American Indian Studies Department, my heartfelt congratulations on such an excellent job of preserving the Anishinaabe language!

For the *Mi'kmaq Online Talking Dictionary*, I would like to thank the people of the Listuguj community in the Gespe'g Territory of the Mi'kmaq along the Restigouche River on the southwest shore of the Gaspé Peninsula for such a wonderful gift of the Mi'kmaq language to all the peoples on Turtle Island and beyond. As

I went from just seven words and two sentences in 1997 to what you see now, the hard work of Sean Haberlin, Eunice Metallic, Diane Mitchell, Watson Williams, Joe Wilmot, and Dave Ziegler will forever be appreciated by this author.

For the Algonquin-Omàmiwinini language, I have used three main sources for my Native words. The first one — the *Algonquin Lexicon*, prepared by Ernest McGregor for the Kitigan Zibi Education Council in 1994 — has been with me for all three Algonquin Quest novels. To be able to pronounce the words, I accessed two websites: *The Algonquin Way Cultural Centre*, administered by the Algonquins of Pikwakangan First Nation, where some of the words are pronounced but all are phonetically spelled out (see www.thealgonquinway.ca); and a talking dictionary produced by the Algonquins of Golden Lake and the Renfrew County Roman Catholic Separate School Board in 1997. The words were spoken by the students at St. James School in Eganville, Ontario (see www.hilaroad.com/camp/nation/speak.html). The third resource was created by Wayne Campbell with the assistance of Suzanne Polson, Gene Cada, Carol Bob, Mike Porte, and Valerie Smith.

Special thanks go out to John Beheler, the executive director of the Dakota Indian Foundation in Chamberlain, South Dakota. Also thanks to two wonderful Lakhóta friends and acquaintances: Jera Brous-Koster and Rob Her Many Horses from the Lower Brule Sioux Reservation in South Dakota. Their guidance and responses to my questions always led me in the right direction.

I also want to thank Judy Harbour of the Lake of the Woods Ojibway Cultural Centre in Kenora, Ontario, for help with some translations of the Anishinaabe language.

Thanks also to Wade Miller, who works for the Parks and Trails Area of the Minnesota Department of Natural Resources. Wade was able to give me the information I needed about the junction of the Crow Wing River and the Mississippi River. The information he provided me with about water flow and the surrounding landscape at this confluence was invaluable to me for a pivotal part of this novel.

My deepest appreciation goes out to two young Anishinaabe women who in 2015 were Grade 6 students at Walpole Island Elementary School, where I visited in February of that year to talk about *I Am Algonquin*. Tymmiecka Johnston and Jaelyn Black Bird asked what my Native name was. When I told them I hadn't yet been given one, they smiled and said that they would come up with one for me. Later, in the cafeteria that day, they came to me and honoured me with an Anishinaabe name and clan. I was now part of the Ma'iingan–Wolf Clan and my name was Mashkawiz Mahingan Inini, pronounced *mash-ka-we-zee ma-hin-gan in-in-e*.

The two young ladies live on the Walpole Island Reserve–Bkejwanong. The school, Walpole Island Elementary, is full of bright, smiling, and energetic Native students guided by a dedicated group of teachers in a spotlessly clean environment. All the students are fed breakfast and lunch each day free of charge, and this is all done with $4,000 less (2015) per child than for a student in the public school system.

I am deeply indebted to Michael Carroll, my publisher's editor for *Algonquin Sunset*. His passion made this book a much better novel than I could have imagined. He understood the "Native Way" and acknowledged the traditions and cultural aspects of my writing.

Lastly, I want to thank my local Kingston editor, Anne Holley-Hime, who had to put up with almost three hundred pages of hard-copy manuscript each for *Algonquin Spring* and *Algonquin Sunset*, which I handed her, asking her to make me look good. The first time I met Anne she asked me to email her the manuscript, and I replied, "I don't work that way from the first draft." So thanks, Anne, for braving the world of paper cuts and page turning from the last century. But in the end she was able to experience all these new Native languages. Good editors are hard to find, and she is good!

During the early 1300s, two migrations took place that began to reshape the Native map in the Great Lakes region of North America. Coming from the east and the present-day Gulf of St. Lawrence, a group who called themselves the Anishinaabe, which means the "Original People," settled around what is now Sault Ste. Marie. Another faction during that time migrated from the Lower Mississippi Valley toward what is currently Minnesota. They called themselves the Lakȟóta, which means "Friends."

Over the next five hundred years these two great tribes became two of the largest and fiercest in the Midwest and Great Lakes areas. The histories of both

Canada and the United States were boldly shaped by the leaders of these celebrated Native nations. Much blood, both Native and white, stained the lands they lived on before the Europeans wrested their territories from them with war, intimidation, coercion, and lies.

The Anishinaabe are known as the Chippewa in the United States and as the Ojibwe in Canada, names given to them by the French. In this novel, for clarity, they are referred to as the Anishinaabe. After the Anishinaabe settled around Lake Superior, they broke off into three distinct tribes in later years, with the Ojibwe-Chippewa remaining in the Lake Superior region and the Odawa settling around Manitoulin Island, in Southwestern Ontario, and in northern Michigan. The third group, the Potawatomi, moved into the Lower Michigan Peninsula.

After the split from where they had originally settled in the Straits of Mackinac, these three tribes remained allies and fought many future wars together. They became known as the Council of Three Fires. When the French arrived on the continent, the Council was their ally until the French surrender to the British at the end of the Seven Years' War in 1763. The British then used the Council as a buffer against the Americans. During the War of 1812, these three nations were the main reason Canada didn't fall into U.S. hands. The British had neither the military force nor the ability to defend the country, the Natives supplied the needed warriors to win the war, but in the end they still lost their lands to the bullying and deceit of the land-grabbers of the British Empire.

The Lakȟóta, also known as the Dakota and Teton Sioux, settled in the lands next to the Anishinaabe and became their merciless enemies for hundreds of years. Strangely enough, even though Dakota translates into "Friend" or "Ally," they were neither to the Anishinaabe. The Lakȟóta were known as the Nadowessioux (Snake) to the Anishinaabe, while the Lakȟóta called the Anishinaabe the Ȟaȟátȟuŋwaŋ (*ha-ha-ton-wan*).

In the late seventeenth century, the Anishinaabe obtained firearms by trading with the French and the Hudson's Bay Company. During this time, the French began to settle in the Lakȟóta lands. The combination of French settlers and the Ojibwe obtaining guns became a focal point that caused the Lakȟóta to start an exodus into the plains of the Midwest. During this time, all the Plains and Woodland Natives depended on dogs as beasts of burden for hunting and as sentries, with some families owning as many as forty to fifty dogs. Then, in the 1690s, the horse appeared in the Plains Native culture with the southwestern tribes, the Apache and the Comanche, who stole horses from the Spanish. They called this animal the "sacred dog." The coming of the horse changed Lakȟóta life immensely, creating a thriving horse culture around 1730. Once that occurred, the Lakȟóta overcame the powerful Arikara (Sahnish), who had been weakened by smallpox epidemics between 1771 and 1781, reducing their strength from thirty villages to two. With this powerful new animal, the Lakȟóta drove the Cheyenne (Tsžhéstáno) and Crow (Apsáalooke) from their traditional lands and were able to control most of the other Plains tribes. The Lakȟóta split into seven groups and became the dominant horse society force of the Great Plains, and it took all the might of the U.S. Army to defeat them in the late 1800s.

The seven bands of the Lakȟóta were the following:

- Oglála: They Scatter Their Own or Dust Scatters
- Sichángu or Brulé: Burnt Thighs
- Húnkpapa: End of the Circle
- Minicônjous: Planters Beside the Stream
- Sihásapa or Blackfeet: Note — not the commonly known Blackfeet/Blackfoot tribe of the northern U.S. Plains and Canadian Prairies
- Itázipaco or Sans Arcs: Without Bows
- Oóhenupa or Two Kettles

When the Lakȟóta migrated west, they became a lesser threat to the Anishinaabe. Starting in 1695, the Anishinaabe turned their military might against the Haudenosaunee (*ho-de-no-sho-nee:* Iroquois Confederacy) and began driving them back into New York State. This war was the direct result of the Haudenosaunee massacre of the Ouendat (Huron) allies of the Ojibwe (during this era, Ojibwe became synonymous with Anishinaabe) and the takeover of their lands in 1649. In 1701 the Iroquois were forced to sue for peace because they feared the Ojibwe might wipe them out as the Iroquois had previously done to the Huron.

Now that we have a short historical synopsis of these two nations, let's go back to their early beginnings around the shores of Lake Superior, known as Anishinaabewi-gichigami to the Anishinaabe. There, these two nations made a life for themselves until the coming of the Europeans, when guns, furs, and horses created a different kind of life and warfare, changing their lives forever.

Did the bad blood between the Anishinaabe and Lakȟóta begin in a place now called Crow Creek, South Dakota, around 1325? If so, why?

Some interesting facts about pre–European contact Native people have been uncovered at the Crow Creek Massacre site, one of which dispels the fallacy that scalping was introduced by Europeans. Archaeologists, in fact, discovered that Natives of that era did scalp their enemies. The bodies unearthed at the site revealed marks of scalping and ritual mutilation during the massacre, some of the remains showed indications of previous scalp and battle wounds that had healed, and prevalent in most of the bodies were signs of malnutrition.

As a writer, I have had a few things said to me that have made me proud of what I have written, but none so much as what one man said in passing to a friend of mine. In Yarmouth County, Nova Scotia, there is a Métis lobster fisherman named Alvah D'Entremont who told my good friend and his brother-in-law, Larry Porter, something that made writing *I Am Algonquin*, *Algonquin Spring*, and *Algonquin Sunset* so worthwhile that it brought a tear to my eye.

You see, Alvah never had time in his fifty odd years of life to read. He was too busy trying to make a living for his family hunting and fishing. Alvah had never read a book until Larry gave him *I Am Algonquin* to read. Among other things, Alvah told Larry he was totally amazed at what I had written and how I was able to put him right there in that time frame in the woods and that he couldn't put the book down.

Alvah has read all my books and has said they are the best he has ever read in his life — the only two, in fact, until he reads this third one.

For me, as a writer, that has made everything worthwhile. Thanks, Alvah!

If we looked at a map in the 1300s to see where the Lakȟóta and Anishinaabe lived pre-contact, we would find that the Lakȟóta held the territory west of Leech Lake and the junction of the Crow Wing and Mississippi Rivers. Everything east of that was Anishinaabe territory, to Lake Superior and then to the north of Superior.

To the southeast of Lake Superior, other tribes began to settle after being driven west by the European incursion three hundred years later. These tribes soon learned the might of the Anishinaabe and their powerful warrior societies.

The story that is about to unfold takes place in the Upper Great Lakes region of the lakes Gichigami (Lake Superior), Mishigami (Michigan), and Misi-zagging (Huron). It begins around 1342, a century and a half before the way of life of the people on Turtle Island was pelted with a raging storm they could not find refuge from, a storm that did not abate until all the peoples of Turtle Island were diseased, slain, beaten, or demoralized enough that they became prisoners in their own lands for life eternal.

PROLOGUE

TWELVE YEARS HAVE passed since the Omàmiwinini (*oh-mam-ih-win-in-e:* Algonquin) and Mi'kmaq allies clashed with the great Haudenosaunee (*ho-de-no-sho-nee:* Iroquois Confederacy) force of the Kanien'kehá:ka (*ga-ni-enge-ha:ga:* Mohawk) warrior known as Ò:nenhste Erhar (*o-noss-tay air-har:* Corn Dog) and his friend, Winpe.

I, Anokì (*uh-noo-key:* Hunt), and my sister, Pangì Mahingan (*pung-gee mah-in-gan:* Little Wolf), had grown into young adults. After I came through the Wysoccan Journey to enter into Omàmiwinini manhood, the decision was made to keep my childhood name because of the relevance of its meaning at the time of my birth. The Elders have always told me that I was a chosen one because of the birthmarks on my buttock and my hairline. I had yet to experience anything special in this life, but there were more years to live.

After that brush with death those twelve summers ago, the Omàmiwinini and their ally survivors had taken a different outlook on their lives. We became even more of a nomadic group than previously, wintering with the Mi'kmaq, the Ouendat (Huron), our own people, and a new ally to the north beyond the Nipissing, the powerful Anishinaabe. With these new friends we also gained a new and fierce enemy. The Anishinaabe called them the Nadowessioux. They called themselves the Lakȟóta.

With the powers of Mitigomij, Glooscap, Elue'wiet Ga'qaquj (*el-away-we-it ga-ah-gooch:* Crazy Crow), and the warriors allied with us, we became a group of people without any real ties to one community. The main family core of the group has always stayed together. Depending on where we travelled or what we took on, there were always other warriors coming and going to and from our band to aid us in whatever our undertaking was at that time.

The other nations started calling us the Piminàshkawà (Pursuers or Chasers) because we were always chasing something or someone and helping our friends and allies in times of war, strife, and hunger.

It is the only life that my sister and I have really known. We have been raised in the way of the warrior, to respect our family, and to be wary of our enemies. Each new day is an adventure, and Pangì Mahingan and I have been taught by the best, our Uncle Mitigomij (*mih-tih-go-mihzh:* Red Oak) and our guardians, Kìnà Odenan (Sharp Tongue), and Agwanìwon (*uh-gweh-nee-won:* Shawl Woman). Taking it upon themselves to be the protectors of the

Elders and orphans, Kìnà Odenan and Agwanìwon are looked up to by all of the Omàmiwinini, Ouendat, Anishinaabe, Mi'kmaq, and allies, plus feared and respected by our enemies, who have witnessed their powers in battle. Along with our mother, Wàbananang (*wa-ba-na-nang*: Morning Star), this pair of two-spirited women helped raise my sister and me.

1

THE CANOE

ANOKÌ

"How long should I make this boat, Anokì?" asked Ki'kwa'ju (Wolverine).

"Depends," I replied. "How many people, dogs, and supplies do you want to carry? Also, if you use it for hunting, you need a good-sized canoe to carry back a moose or an elk."

"Three lengths of the measuring stick?" Ki'kwa'ju asked.

"Yes, that will work. That's the length of three men. It will give you a good-sized canoe."

Ki'kwa'ju was a Mi'kmaq name, except Wolverine wasn't born a Mi'kmaq. He had been captured by the Mi'kmaq in a skirmish with people they called the Eli'tuat (*el-e-do-what:* Men with Beards). Wolverine was perhaps only twelve summers old at that time. The Mi'kmaq gave him this name because he fought them like a wolverine as they captured him and because his light-coloured hair matched the hue of the wolverine's light-shaded stripes of fur.

Ten summers ago he was brought to our group by a close Mi'kmaq friend and fierce warrior named Elue'wiet Ga'qaquj (*el-away-we-it ga-ah-gooch:* Crazy Crow). The woman who had reared Crazy Crow, Nukumi (*no-ko-miss:* Mother Earth, Grandmother), also raised Ki'kwa'ju. She and the Mi'kmaq Elders decided that the boy should come farther inland and live with us. The boy enjoyed living the Mi'kmaq life, but Nukumi was worried that the Eli'tuat would someday return and take him back from them. So the decision was made for Wolverine to come and live with my group of Omàmiwinini. In his time with us, he has proven to be a fast and eager learner and a brave warrior and is now my brother-in-law since marrying my sister, Pangì Mahingan.

Wolverine had picked a tree with no branches within the three lengths of his measuring stick. Branches created holes in the skin that took a lot of time and effort to close up. A tall, straight tree with very few skin blemishes was what we needed. We had prepared ahead of time an akwàndawàgan (*a-kwon-da-way-gan:* ladder), and using the stick to measure three times as he scaled the ladder, Wolverine arrived at where he had to make his final mark. Here he cut around the trunk of the tree and then made a slit all the way down to the bottom and again cut around the trunk. Then Wolverine started to peel the bark away from the tree, using a rigid wedge of bark to help with prying the skin off the trunk.

"Ki'kwa'ju, do you hear the noise of the bark peeling away from the tree?" I asked. "That's the tree telling us it's giving its coat to us as a gift. Once we have the bark, we'll make a tobacco offering of thanks to the tree. Now roll the bark up and we'll tie it in a bundle to make it easy to carry. Fill the inside with ferns to help take the moisture away. Now you have to go and pull up spruce roots. You'll need at least fifty roots and then you have to split and soak them."

"Anokì, are you going to help me?" asked Ki'kwa'ju.

"How will you learn if I do the work?" I asked. "Achie (White Ash), come and help us. We need an extra pair of hands if you can tear yourself away from whatever you're doing."

Achie was an Ouendat warrior who had fought with us against the Haudenosaunee chief Ò:nenhste Erhar (Corn Dog). His brother, Öndawa (Black Ash), had been slain in that battle along with another Ouendat friend, Tsou'tayi (Beaver). Since that time twelve summers ago, he and another Ouendat who had fought that day, Önenha' (Corn), had become part of our group.

Walking out of the surrounding forest, Achie said, "Anokì, I've been watching something entertaining that you and Ki'kwa'ju should come and see."

We followed the Ouendat up a treed embankment to a small plateau overlooking a narrow gorge. Beneath us a small stream flowed through the valley. Peering down, we eyed a nòjek (*now-shek:* female bear) and her two makons (*mah-koon:* cubs) as they foraged along the shoreline. The mother made a meal of the berries lining the stream, while the cubs wrestled on the shore, tumbling into the current and chasing each other through the water, all the time squealing. Every once in a while they roamed a little too far, and the mother grunted her dissatisfaction. Upon hearing her, the two stood up on their hind legs, sniffed the air, and then ran back to their original area, where once again they renewed their play.

The three of us stood downwind enjoying the goings-on. Bears had poor eyesight, so we were safe from being sighted. Yet, if the mother caught our scent, she would charge at us to defend her cubs. Then we heard a sound that shook the air around us. The cubs reared up and looked downstream, while the mother stood with her nose quivering and the hair on her mane standing on end.

Glancing toward the source of the noise, we watched as a huge nàbek (male bear) splashed through the stream toward the cubs at a full run, muscles trembling and mouth frothing. As his massive body drove through the water, the force of the animal caused water to spray upon his black coat, which glistened in the sunlight. His deafening roar as he approached the defenceless cubs echoed through the forest, sending all the roosting and ground-feeding birds into a noisy departure and adding to the imminent mayhem.

From the opposite end the mother bear loped in huge strides to defend her cubs. A full-grown makadewà makwa (*ma-ka-de-wa mah-kwa:* black bear) could run very fast and could overtake a fleeing warrior in a very short distance. These two bears below were running at top speed with only one thought in each of their minds:

the male to kill the cubs, who in the future would threaten his existence; and the female to protect them from his fury.

The nàbek reached the cubs first and grabbed the closest one by the neck, shaking the defenceless animal until its neck snapped. As he turned to chase the other cub, the nòjek hit him at full stride. She was no match for this enormous male, but when it came to her cubs, there was no fear in her body. The two roared, bellowed, clawed, and bit, and the stream became a froth of churning water reddened by their blood. In the end, the male crushed the female's skull with his massive jaws. He stood over her, bloodied and with chunks of hair missing from his wet and glistening coat where she had bitten and clawed him. The male then reared up on his hind legs, turned his head sideways, and let out a massive roar. Turning, he limped away to recover from his wounds. Once he recuperated, he would carry the scars of this battle for the rest of his life: bare spots where she had torn out the hair and maybe the loss of an eye where it appeared the female had raked his face with her sharp claws.

Stunned, we looked down at where just a short time ago we had been entertained by the young makons. The stream was washing away the redness of the battle. The remaining cub, which had run and hidden in the woods, returned and stood over its mother, bleating a sad lament.

Achie broke the silence by saying, "I'm going down there to capture the makon. It will never survive by itself in the wild. Wolves or the male will end its life in a few suns. Once I've secured him, we'll prepare the two carcasses. The hides and the meat won't go to waste."

Glancing at Ki'kwa'ju, I saw the sorrow and shock in his eyes. Walking past him, I said, "Come, we have work to do."

As we made our way down the face of the cliff, the noise of our descent startled the remaining cub, which took off into the underbrush. Achie, seeing the little one take flight, sped up, causing him to tumble end over end onto the floor of the gorge. Quickly jumping to his feet and not seemingly suffering any ill effects from his fall, he continued after the young bear, crashing through the undergrowth on its trail. Ki'kwa'ju and I looked at each other and laughed. The sight of Achie plunging down the slope and then getting up and racing into the brush to pursue his quarry was just too funny.

"Ki'kwa'ju," I said, "blow that horn you carry and let's hope Kìnà Odenan, Agwanìwon, and Kànìkwe (No Hair) are within hearing distance. We can use their help to carry this meat out."

Ki'kwa'ju sounded the horn in one long, mournful tone. Besides the clothes he had on when captured, the horn was the only thing Ki'kwa'ju had that was his. When he came to us, the Mi'kmaq had given him an axe made out of material we had never seen before, a leather shield, and an item Ki'kwa'ju called a sverð (sword) that could cut off a man's head with one powerful swing. The Mi'kmaq had captured these items from Ki'kwa'ju's people during a battle years previous and had gifted him with the items when they sent him to us.

If the three of them were close by, they would be here soon. Since my father's death, the two women had been our leaders. Kànìkwe was their constant companion. He told everyone he met for the first time that he was their àbimì (*ah-bih-mee:* guard), which created a roar of laughter from all who knew them, including the two women. Kànìkwe feigned insult when that happened, but all who were familiar with him and the two Warrior Women knew that the women had no need of a protector. The three of them were ruthless in battle, and Kànìkwe owed his life to Kìnà Odenan and Agwanìwon from many years ago.

As long as I could remember, the Ouendat had always kept orphaned animals as pets in their large villages. Unlike my people, the Omàmiwinini, who travelled with the seasons, the Ouendat stayed in one spot for ten or fifteen years and in doing so tended to collect these animals when the beasts were young and to raise them as village pets. These past few years when I visited the Ouendat villages, my first impressions upon entering were the smells of my newfound surroundings: the pungent odour of meat and corn being cooked, the aroma of cedar, pine, and maple wood burning in their cooking fires, and the stale scent of close to two thousand people in a local area. Then there was the whiff of the numerous dogs that ran around, defecating and urinating wherever they pleased.

If you had been with me, after the jolt to your sense of smell, your sight would have suddenly taken over and you would have begun to view the spectacle going on around you. More times than not, you might have seen a full-grown bear that had been reared from a cub, either tied to a stake or begging for food, with a child holding it on a roped tether. Or you might have witnessed a young deer walking around, nuzzling up against the women and children as it tried to get handouts. The deer would have had the run of the village, and once they had grown older most would have left. It was different with the bears, though. When they were no longer cubs, they had to be tied up or else they would have raided the food stores of the village and gorged themselves. In the end the bears usually met an ill fate.

This past winter the longhouse I lived in had a pet wàgosh (wa-*gosh:* fox) that kept the mice down. He was definitely well fed, and when he had hunted all the mice where he was staying, he moved on to the next dwelling. I figured out early in my stay that this animal would make a warm bedmate, so I took a little food to bed with me each night and trained him to come and get it. Once he was there, I stroked and cooed to him as the animal fell asleep inside my fur covering. Even when he was off mousing in other quarters, he always came back to my sleeping area every night for his treat.

Ki'kwa'ju and I were working steadily at our task, skinning the bears at the bottom of the cliff, when off to our left two bodies crashed out of the bushes. Glancing up, we saw a very irritated bear cub and a cut and battered Achie. Again this prompted another round of laughter from Ki'kwa'ju and me. Achie peered at us, then looked at the bear, and he, too, started to laugh.

"This young bear will make a very fine pet for the village," Achie said. "He has the grit of a true warrior. I'm going to call him Tindee Anue, which means Two Bear in our language, to remind everyone that he had a twin."

We were just finishing cutting up the two bears when our three other companions and their dogs trotted down the small valley. They stopped and smiled at us.

"Good hunting, I see, Anokì," said Kìnà Odenan.

"A gift from Kije-Manidò (Great Spirit)," I replied, then told them the story of the bears.

The ten dogs they had were able to take most of the meat and the bear pelts on pole sleds we made from the available saplings in the area. The rest of the meat was carried by the three companions. Achie had his hands full with the cub, and Ki'kwa'ju and I had retrieved the rolled-up birchbark for his canoe and had loaded it on our shoulders to carry to the shoreline of the lake. We would start making his canoe there tomorrow.

That night, as we huddled around the fire to ward off the night chill, the forest sounds intermingled with the young cub crying for its mother and the dogs whimpering because of the distressed noises of grief from the bear cub.

Achie had dug up some roots, gathered berries, and vainly tried to feed the little one. Finally, the animal settled down, and everyone in the camp was able to sleep.

The next morning Achie took some of the bear meat and left for his nearby village along with Kìnà Odenan, Agwanìwon, our dogs, and the bear cub. Kànìkwe stayed with Ki'kwa'ju and me to help build the canoe.

We steamed the wooden cedar ribs in hot water for five days as we worked on soaking and making our spruce rope. Then we lashed and fastened the gunwales. Once we could bend the ribs we fastened them to the birchbark and the thin cedar sheathing that strengthened the boat. Now all that was left to do was the boiling of the resin to seal the seams. Right from the start Ki'kwa'ju didn't listen and forgot to wet his thumb to spread the resin. As a result, Ki'kwa'ju's finger stuck to the seam he was covering, and Kànìkwe walked toward him while removing his knife from its scabbard.

Ki'kwa'ju looked at Kànìkwe and asked, "What are you going to do with that knife?"

"Well, the only way I can get that thumb free is to cut it off — unless, of course, you want to go around the rest of your life dragging a canoe on the end of your hand."

Ki'kwa'ju's face paled as white as the birchbark, and he stammered as Kànìkwe bent over and worked the knife around the thumb, freeing it from the resin. Sighing deeply with relief as the colour returned to his features, Ki'kwa'ju held his thumb up, brandishing the clump of resin on the end. He glanced at Kànìkwe and laughed nervously.

Kànìkwe chuckled, turned to me, and winked. Gazing over his shoulder at Ki'kwa'ju, he said, "Maybe the next time you'll listen when we instruct you in the ways!"

It took Ki'kwa'ju a few hours to pick the resin, plus a layer or two of skin, away from his thumb, but it was a lesson he would never forget.

After working on the canoe for six suns, it was ready for Ki'kwa'ju to try out the next day. I had been working on a canoe paddle for my friend, fashioning it from an ash tree. The wood was strong and smooth to the hand. After our evening meal, I gave Ki'kwa'ju the paddle as a gift. He thanked me with a hug and a gift of tobacco.

The morning sun rose in an orange fireball, and the bay was ripple-free, enabling us to see the sun and surrounding trees in the reflection of the water. It was as if there was another world below the stillness of the lake. Ki'kwa'ju ate the early-morning meal with us and then shoved off to paddle to a small island and back. As he left, the wind increased from the south, causing the waves to reach up and push the canoe and occupant effortlessly along.

"Anokì," inquired Kànìkwe, "has he ever paddled a canoe by himself in the wind?"

"No," I replied, "and neither did he take any weight for the front of the boat."

We looked at each other and smiled.

Ki'kwa'ju had no problem sitting in the back of the canoe going toward the island with the wind at his back, but once he reached the shoreline and began to come back, things got tricky for him. The wind had picked up and blew into his face, and because of the lack of weight in the bow, the boat sat up in the air. With Ki'kwa'ju in the back and no extra weight in the front, the wind and waves pushed against his efforts to paddle, causing the vessel to spin in a circle and propelling it back to the island's shore. After this happened a couple of times and Ki'kwa'ju pushed off the rocks with his paddle, he moved to the middle of the canoe.

"Anokì, are we going out to help him?" asked Kànìkwe.

"No, this is a good lesson for him. He never asked any questions before he went out onto the water. Besides, he's from a people who have lived their whole life on water. He has good balance and will figure this out. Kànìkwe, I'll bet you three of my best arrows he'll make it back to shore without tipping the canoe."

"I'll take that bet, Anokì, and I'll match your wager with three of my arrows. Just in case, though, I'm going to get an Ouendat canoe from its storage spot and ready it for when our friend tips his canoe. I won't have him drown. Your sister, Pangì Mahingan, would skin both of us alive if that happened!"

Turning our eyes back to the water, we watched as Ki'kwa'ju made small gains into the wind, but for each advance the wind caught him and the canoe in its grasp and spun them in a circle backward. Finally, he crawled to the front of the boat, weighing it down, and proceeded to paddle as quickly as he could. With the end of the canoe sitting in the air and the front now weighed down, he was able to get to the shore.

Keeping a straight face as Ki'kwa'ju exited the boat, Kànìkwe asked, "How did the new canoe handle?"

Not saying a word at first, Ki'kwa'ju bent over, scooped up a handful of water, and sprayed both of us. "You knew, didn't you?"

When Kànìkwe and I burst out laughing, Ki'kwa'ju glared at us, then also hooted and chuckled. "The canoe handles beautifully," he said finally.

Kànìkwe put his arm around Ki'kwa'ju and said, "It cost me three good arrows. However, I'm happy you didn't drown. Plus now I won't have to face the wrath of Pangì Mahingan. So the day has ended well for everyone. I'll go hunt for our meal tonight to celebrate your new canoe and the experience you achieved today."

That night we ate a beaver Kànìkwe had killed. We roasted the tail over the fire and boiled the rest of the meat. What bear meat we had left was roasted on a spit. Tea was made from some berries I had picked that afternoon.

When I went to sleep, I dreamed once more of my father Mahingan's last days. The dream that had haunted me these past few years, the message of which I had yet to figure out, was one I would have to share with Uncle Mitigomij so he could help me find its true meaning.

2

THE DREAM

ANOKÌ

The dream started out as it always did: Nukumi, the Mi'kmaq Grandmother, had the children and wounded gather around her. She told everyone not to worry, that her son, Crazy Crow, and her guardian, Glooscap, would save everyone and that help would appear.

The sounds of battle drifted to our hiding place. Then, like magic, Uncle Mitigomij's big cat, Makadewà Waban (*ma-ka-de-wan wah-bun:* Black Dawn), and my father's wolf, Ishkodewan (Blaze), appeared among us. The panther had a young girl gripped in his jaws, carrying her like a dog would hold a newborn puppy. The wolf's muzzle was reddened by someone's blood. Nukumi took the girl, and the two animals disappeared back into the dim light of the forest.

Handing the girl to me, Nukumi said, "Anokì, this is your sister. Protect her."

While I clutched my sister, a crow swooshed through the air over our heads, then, out of the forest, a silent column of painted men emerged — Wolastoqiyik (*whoa-la-stow-key-ick:* Maliseet) warriors! There were over forty on my count, and once they passed through, five of them remained to watch over our small group.

In a short time the noise of the battle increased with the war cries of the Maliseet and then I heard the distinct war whistles of my father's friend, Pangì Shìshìb (*pung-gee she-sheeb:* Little Duck), an Omàmiwinini chief. Soon my ears picked up the whoops of his warriors.

Nukumi turned to everyone. "The battle has started to turn. We'll be safe now."

Two bodies crashed through the forest, startling us and our companions. They were Haudenosaunee trying to escape. Unluckily for them, they ran into the Wolastoqiyik warriors guarding us and met their fate quickly.

The din of the battle continued through most of the day. As the evening sun started to glow, the warriors of the Wolastoqiyik tribe returned to our site. They brought their wounded to our small camp, and Nukumi and the other women tried to do what they could for them. Of the thirty-five warriors who entered the conflict, seven never came back and ten were wounded.

Soon after, my father's people entered the camp. Mitigomij brought a woman to me and said, "This is your mother, Wàbananang."

My mother took me and held me close. "Anokì, your father, Mahingan, and Uncle Kàg (*ka-hg:* Porcupine) have perished. They died with honour. We were able to save their bodies from Ò:nenhste Erhar and his men and have given them a warrior's burial."

Tears appeared in my eyes: of joy for seeing my mother and of sadness for the loss of my father.

My mother told me that the Mi'kmaq warrior E's (*s:* Clam) had, with the help of the wolf and the panther, saved her life. Pangì Shìshìb came in behind Ò:nenhste Erhar and his men and drove them off before they could mutilate the bodies of Mahingan and Kàg.

When Uncle Mitigomij arrived in the camp, he told us the warrior the Mi'kmaq called Glooscap fought the wizard Winpe for a long time. They scarred each other but neither came under the axe of death.

Then, out of the forest burst the bellowing and blood-covered warrior Crazy Crow, rapidly gaining the attention of the camp group. "Today was a great battle. I feel like my body has received a boost from the Great Spirit, and that skirmish between the big one, Glooscap, and the so-called wizard Winpe was one for the ages. When Winpe left with his warriors, he turned to Glooscap and said, 'Watch over Nukumi and Apistanéwj, your little friend. I will be back for them!' That Winpe doesn't know when to quit!"

I will never forget the entrance Crazy Crow made, his one good eye glistening, his imposing stature, chiselled body, and bellowing voice. He was something to behold. Then I spotted my twin cousins coming into camp, bloody and in mourning for their father. Uncle Mònz (*moans:* Moose) walked beside them with his head hung down. Of the four brothers, Mahingan, Kàg, Wàgosh (*wa-gosh:* Fox), and Mitigomij, only Mitigomij was still alive.

Suddenly, my dream ended as I was shaken awake. Opening my eyes, I gazed up into the bright morning sun at two dark shapes between me and the early fireball. Rising from my sleeping spot, I soon realized they were my cousins, Kàg's twin sons, Makwa (*muck-wa*: Black Bear) and Wàbek (Bear).

"Come, Anokì, the Attawandaron (Neutral) and Tionontati (*tea-anon-ta-tay*: Tobacco) Nations have sent emissaries to the Ouendat with a mikisesimik (wampum belt). They need help. The Onöndowága (*oh-n'own-dough-wahgah*: Seneca) and their allies are preparing to invade the lands of our friends. An ally of the Attawandaron, a Wenrohronon warrior who lives near the Great Falls, brought the terrifying news. He said his people had captured an Onöndowága warrior during a skirmish as they were passing through their territory. Before he died in the fires at the stake, he said they were on their way to raid the Attawandaron and Tionontati villages for captives and tobacco. We must hurry and gather our forces to help them in this time of peril. The Attawandaron are a peace-loving people who depend on their allies for protection. They're no match for the powerful Onöndowága!"

3

READYING FOR WAR

ANOKÌ

The Tionontati Nation lived along the shores of what the Ouendat called Lake Attigouatan (Georgian Bay) and the Attawandaron resided on the shores of Erielhonan (Lake Erie). Both nations were planters of the soil, growing the Three Sisters — mandàman (corn), askoot-asquash (squash), and azàhan (beans) — and nasemà (*na-sem-mah:* tobacco). The Attawandaron also lived near the flint grounds where all the tribes in the area came to collect the material to make weapons. Because of this important resource, the tribe had a certain neutrality and freedom from being attacked. However, the Haudenosaunee warriors of the Onöndowága Nation rarely took this neutrality into account. They were also a people of soil tillers with immense orchards of apples, fields of corn, squash, beans, and tobacco. They often traded for what they needed, but they were, first of all, a warrior society, and would rather go to war and take what they wanted. The Onöndowága were powerful and liked to constantly weaken their neighbours by raiding them. They considered the Attawandaron and Tionontati to be weak and easily overpowered.

Both the Attawandaron and Tionontati Nations' warriors were heavily tattooed and gave off a fierce look. The truth, though, was that these two nations' warriors were more interested in farming, hunting, and fishing than warfare. Because they grew large fields of tobacco, considered one of our sacred medicines, they were always generous with their allies, who protected them, and were charitable with this plant in trade with us. The Ouendat grew small patches of nasemà beside their longhouses, but nothing to rival the two tribes to the west of them.

We sped back to the Ouendat village and found it bustling with activity. The men were preparing weapons and readying a war feast, while the women were gathering corn and dried meat from their storage areas to supply the warriors with food for their coming trek. They had also dug a hole and erected a wooden post. Here was where the warriors who wanted to go to war would strike their war clubs, affirming their desire to fight. The Ouendat were like all the other tribes: no one was ever forced to go off to battle; it was the individual's own decision. Most warriors would only follow leaders who they knew could give them brave and decisive leadership, a chance for glory, and the prospect of returning alive. A leader who didn't have a good record of doing these things rarely got a second chance at leadership in battle.

The Ouendat who had stepped forward to lead was known as Waughshe Anue (Bad Bear) in the Ouendat language. He wasn't a very tall man, though no one should have been deceived by his appearance. Waughshe Anue was a shrewd and brave warrior who had led many successful forays into Haudenosaunee territory. His face was tattooed with black streaks on each cheek, and he was an expert with the bow and war club. Waughshe Anue's head was shaved, leaving just a long braid at the back. The Ouendat people believed and trusted in his leadership.

Waughshe Anue relayed to us what the messenger had told him. The Onöndowága had over fifty canoes and three hundred warriors. They had last been sighted in their canoes on Erielhonan, and from there they were three or four days from reaching the villages of our allies. The enemy would keep away from the strong currents of the Big Falls and then come to shore once they were past that danger. There would only be at the most a hundred warriors in most of these villages they were targeting, not enough to defend against the warlike Onöndowága and their allies. The Attawandaron urgently needed our warriors to help protect them!

That night, during the feasting, Kìnà Odenan and Agwanìwon, the Warrior Women, gathered our small group together and asked if we wanted to aid the Ouendat in this fight. We all agreed and struck our weapons on the war post. Our group consisted of the two Warrior Women who led us; Kànìkwe; myself; the twins, Makwa and Wàbek; my Uncle Mònz; my father's sister, Wàbìsì (*wah-bee-see*: Swan); and Nigig (*neh-gig*: Otter) and his two daughters, Àwadòsiwag (*ah-wa-dow-she-wag*: Minnow) and Ininàtig (*e-na-na-dig*: Maple), who were married to the twins. Also there were my mother, Wàbananang; my sister, Pangì Mahingan; and Ki'kwa'ju, plus the two Mi'kmaq, E's and Jilte'g (*jil-teg*: Scar). The two Ouendat warriors, Achie and Önenha', had been with us so long that they would also follow the Warrior Women in battle with no concerns. Nigig's mother and wife were no longer with us; both had passed away five winters ago. There were now eighteen of us. Sometimes the group was more, sometimes less, always depending on what our pursuit was that year and who was available to follow the two Warrior Women. We were very lucky that the main core almost always stayed together.

Others who had travelled with us in the past had either left to return to their villages or had suffered death in one of our battles. The three Susquehannock brothers, Abgarijo, Oneega, and Sischijro, whom my father and I had saved from starvation those many years ago, had left us after the battle that had taken my father's life. Sischijro had also been slain during that battle, and his brother, Oneega, had been wounded. Abgarijo stayed by his wounded brother until he healed, and once Oneega was fit, they journeyed with us to the land of the Ouendat and from there were able to proceed safely to the lands of their people with the guidance of a group of Lenape (Delaware) who were allies of the Susquehannock and lived near their villages.

The Lenape had been on a trading journey among the Ouendat Tionontati and Attawandaron tribes for furs, corn, and tobacco. The Lenape lived alongside the big sea and brought sought-after seashells to trade with these tribes. Our hearts were saddened when the two brothers left, but they missed their homeland and had suffered much since their capture at the hands of Ò:nenhste Erhar and his men. Starvation and death had stalked them, but they had proven themselves to be tough and trustworthy warriors who had fought bravely at my people's sides. They had been gone almost ten summers now, and in subsequent trading with the Lenape we had been told the brothers had made it back safely to their home village and had grown to be strong warriors who valiantly battled their enemies, the Haudenosaunee.

The two Warrior Women were great leaders and fighters. They led with an immense degree of skill and strength and were always open to different ideas from the rest of us. The other women in our group weren't as skilled as the two leaders in hand-to-hand fighting, yet they were able to hold their own in battle with expert marksmanship with their bows, and Mitigomij had also taught them to use his main weapon of choice, the wewe-basinàbàn (*way-way-buh-sih-nah-bahn*: slingshot).

At this time there was also a group of Anishinaabe in the Ouendat village who had come to trade. They were led by two brothers, Zhashagi (*sha-sha-gee*: Blue Heron) and Omashkooz (*oh-mush-goes*: Elk), who had about fifteen warriors with them.

That night the celebration went on until the stars were high in the skies. When I woke the next morning and exited the longhouse I was in, I looked toward the war post. There, on top of it, was a crow preening itself. That brought a smile to my face because I knew that Crazy Crow, the famous Mi'kmaq warrior, had to be nearby.

I kept my thoughts to myself, just in case I was mistaken about the crow, though I very much had the feeling the man the Haudenosaunee called Tsyòkawe Ronkwe (*dio-ga-wee ron-kwe:* Crow Man) would make an appearance.

Later that morning the village became a noisy din of barking dogs anticipating their departure with the warriors, the nervous chatter of the men who were leaving, and the prattling of the members of the community going about their usual activities. Then the clamour suddenly subsided as the sentinels on the stockade walls got everyone's immediate attention when they roared that a small group of people was advancing toward us. The camp guards below opened the gates and warily approached the newcomers to see who they were. As they got close enough to the visitors to recognize them, they shouted a greeting. Both groups then merged, slapping one another's backs and talking and laughing loudly as they entered the village. Once in the village, the other warriors gave a huge welcoming cheer to the visitors. It was Crazy Crow, Glooscap, Apistanéwj (*a-bis-tan-ouch:* Marten) — called the Little One — and their dogs. With them were Nukumi and Uncle Mitigomij. My uncle also had my part-wolf dog, Nìj Enàndeg (*neesh en-nahn-deg:* Two Colour), the son of Ishkodewan, with him. There was no sign of the great black panther, Makadewà Wàban (Black Dawn), but everyone knew this ageless beast lurked somewhere in the nearby forest.

I had been forced to leave my wolf dog with Mitigomij when I departed last fall to come to the Ouendat Nation. He had been hurt in a battle with a bear, and Mitigomij had volunteered to keep him and bring him back to health. My dog's father, Ishkodewan, and Pìsà Animosh (*pee-shah an-ney-mush:* Small Dog) had both died of old age six winters ago. Nìj Enàndeg had been born about a moon after Ishkodewan had died, the only one in the litter, and I had raised him from a pup. He grew bigger than his father and was grey with a black head.

As was the custom of our people when visiting the village of an ally, Crazy Crow presented Waughshe Anue with an elk skin as a gift, ensuring that the recipient wouldn't refuse the visitors food or accommodation.

With the addition of these three warriors, I could see the spirits of the Ouendat fighters rise. The Anishinaabe visitors, the brothers Zhashagi and Omashkooz, though, didn't have the same awe-inspired expressions on their faces for the newcomers. The brothers were from the western edge of the big lake to the west, and the exploits of these three men might not have reached their ears. But Zhashagi walked up to Mitigomij and said, "Our friends, the Nipissing, have talked about a great warrior who walks with a limp, is an expert marksman, and is feared by all his enemies. It is a privilege now to meet the man behind those stories. Please honour myself, Zhashagi, and my Anishinaabe warriors as new friends and allies."

"Zhashagi, your reputation as a warrior has preceded you," Mitigomij replied. "I've also heard from our allies, the Nipissing, of your bravery, and I welcome the friendship of the Anishinaabe people, who I am told are a powerful nation of warriors."

I approached Mitigomij through the crowd that had gathered around him and his companions and shouted, "Uncle, I'm happy to see you and that you've healed my wolf dog!"

Nìj Enàndeg, upon hearing my voice, ran to me and stood on his hind legs. He put his forepaws on my shoulders, licked my face with his rough tongue, and gave me an earsplitting howl of welcome that almost knocked me over. I gave the big animal a hug and ruffled the fur on his head. He then dropped to the ground and stuck close by, not letting me out of his sight. There was a very strong bond between us. His father, Ishkodewan, had saved my life when I was a young boy, and I considered Nìj Enàndeg a gift from my father and Nìj Enàndeg's father, because when the wolf dog was born there were no other litter mates to confuse me in my selection.

The Ouendat warriors, upon seeing the dwarf Apistanéwj, rushed up and asked him to touch them. He took great pride in brushing each warrior on the sleeve of the arm that was held out to him. Dwarfs were considered War Gods to the Ouendat people, and if a War God caressed them as the Little One was doing now, it was a good omen that they would return victorious. If, though, he touched them on the forehead, they couldn't go to war without losing their lives. Apistanéwj wasn't tall enough to touch them on the forehead, so every warrior left happy and confident of the coming battle. The Little One enjoyed all the attention, even though he had no idea why the Ouendat warriors were so interested in him.

Apistanéwj and Glooscap made strange companions due to their height difference. Glooscap was over seven feet tall, and the Little One was only about four feet. Both of these men had become great friends and legends of the Mi'kmaq Nation and each was from a different island to the north and east of the Mi'kmaq. The two had constant companions in the dogs that had once been the property of what I had been told was a race of men with beards, unusual weapons, and huge boats. One dog was black and the other white; they seemed ageless and perhaps had hidden powers none of us could know. The dogs had been given the Mi'kmaq names Na'gweg (*nah-quik:* Day) and Tepgig (*dip-geek:* Night).

The final warrior in the group was loud, boisterous, and respected by all the nations and his allies for his bravery — and by his enemies for his skill in battle. Elue'wiet Ga'qaquj, or Crazy Crow, also had a mysterious past, since no one knew where he had come from. The Mi'kmaq had found him floating down a river in a canoe with only a crow for company. He had ended up being raised by a close friend of Glooscap: Nukumi, who travelled with this group all the time. Her common name was just plain Grandmother. Crazy Crow possessed the unique ability to talk to crows and constantly had one around him day and night. He was also at times a loner who would appear out of nowhere when needed. He revelled in warfare, especially against the Haudenosaunee, who had been trying to slay him for years without success.

The Ouendat women brought out containers of corn soup thickened with wood ash, pieces of cornbread, and chunks of greasy venison for the warriors to eat before they left. The war dogs were given fish and meat scraps to fight over. After eating, the men collected their medicine bags containing healing herbs, a few items for painting their bodies prior to battle, and other things that were sacred to them. Most of the articles used to make colours would be gathered on the trail for when it was time to paint ourselves. We used roots, berries, red clay, eggshells, charcoal, moss, and available plants relative to the season to colour ourselves. Each man was also given a pouch of corn and dried meat for the trail; eating a couple of handfuls of dry corn staved off hunger when washed down with two or three vessels of water. The water swelled the corn in our stomachs, taking away the sensation of hunger. When journeying to and from battle, speed was of utmost importance, and unless the warriors stumbled onto game or made an effort to hunt, they had to make do with what they carried.

The Wenrohronon warrior had brought the news to the Attawandaron people two suns ago and then the appeal had been sent to us for help. Our allies needed our group to get there in the fastest time that we could. To aid them was essential. The Ouendat leader, Waughshe Anue, stood at the gate, raised his club, and cried in his language *"A-yagh-kee!"* ("I go to war!") He then left the village at a brisk trot with his three war dogs running beside him and the rest of us following. There were fifty-two Ouendat, the seventeen Anishinaabe, and our group of twenty-three warriors, plus more than fifty war dogs.

Mitigomij disappeared into the forest to rejoin Makadewà Wàban, his panther. There he changed himself into Michabo (The Great Hare). This transformation enabled him to keep up with the column while staying in the shadows of the woodlands. We wouldn't see him again until the evening when the column stopped to camp. As for the panther, he was only seen when he wanted to be. Until then he remained in the gloom of the forest, but always close enough to aid his companion, Mitigomij.

Scouts were sent ahead and warriors, as well, ranged out on the sides to prevent any surprises from befalling us. Our Omàmiwinini group brought up the rear. The party followed a well-worn warrior trail that would take us to the Attawandaron main village. At the pace we were travelling it would likely only take us one sun and a bit to reach our friends.

As we raced through the forest, we were surrounded by the aroma of the pine and cedar trees towering above. We interrupted the silence of the woods with the swish of our feet on the pine-needled ground, the quick breaths of some, the occasional snapping of an animosh (*an-eh-moosh:* dog) when another dog came too close, and of course the shrill cry of a pikwàkogwewesì (*pick-wa-go-gwese-e:* jay) as it warned of our intrusion.

The Little One, Apistanéwj, took turns riding on the backs of the two big dogs, Na'gweg and Tepgig, neither of which ever broke pace when the small rider became their passenger.

Grandmother Nukumi stayed close to the Little One and Glooscap. The warriors who knew her always looked forward to stopping for the night when she was present. Her campfire was at all times an excellent place to visit for ample food and hot tea.

All of us had put whatever protection we could find on our bodies to combat the bugs. Grease, mud, and goldenseal were the popular choices. The mud, though, had to be constantly reapplied because it hardened and broke away from the skin when it dried. In the late spring and early summer, the bugs flew in swarms that entered the mouth, ears, and eyes. Sunlight and wind always seemed to be the best deterrent of all.

We stopped once at midday near a stream to rest and drink water. Some of the warriors had found a patch of berries and shoved them into their mouths for a quick meal. When they exited the berry patch, the other warriors who hadn't accompanied them started to laugh and point at them. Once I saw their faces, I also broke out in laughter. The men's faces were covered in the red juice of the previously enjoyed berry patch. The red-faced berry men soon realized what all the mirth was about as they wiped their faces and saw that their hands were the colour of the berries. A quick trip to the stream returned their features back to normal.

The dogs lay in the stream to escape the bugs, cool off, and lap up the water. Waughshe Anue, though, soon had us on the trail again, and we travelled until near dusk, when two of the six scouts came back and said they had found a place to rest for the night. One of the scouts was able to slay a deer, and the others had prepared fires to keep the bugs away and cook the venison. This inspired a cheer from everyone as the thought of fresh meat was a welcome respite from eating dried corn and smoked meat.

That night we ate, laughed, and smoked. We thanked our scout for his successful hunt and watched as he rolled up the pelt and secured it in a tree to pick up on the way back. Nothing went to waste in our world. Our people also believed that by wearing the fur of a slain animal we gained the power of that beast.

Many of the warriors then gathered at Nukumi's fire to drink her soothing tea before lying down for the evening.

At daylight everyone rose and ate a hurried meal. The eight scouts who left before camp broke were now accompanied by Crazy Crow.

With Waughshe Anue's leadership, the party made good time that morning toward our destination. As we left the enclosure of the forest and entered a beaver meadow, three of the scouts exited the forest from the opposite side of the field.

"We smell smoke in the distance," one of the scouts said. "The others have continued on while we returned to warn you that there might be problems ahead."

Waughshe Anue turned to the warriors. "It is time!"

Some of the warriors quickly went into their bags for what they needed to apply war paint. Others foraged around the site for roots and berries they could use. Most warriors painted previous war wounds, and many applied hand marks to their faces and chests that signified they excelled at hand-to-hand combat. Some painted their faces white with red or black masks like the features of raccoons across their eyes. Warriors adorned in red, black, yellow, and white jumped into my sight. Glooscap covered himself with red ochre; others, like him, painted their whole bodies, while the rest just daubed arms and faces with lines, swirls, and lightning bolts that indicated power and speed. Every symbol or colour meant something to each warrior. All were prepared to die a warrior's death in battle.

I painted red lightning bolts down both of my arms and streaks of black on my face. On my chest I put a black handprint. Taking some of the black dye, I put it on the deer horn that protruded from my battle axe. Then, after tying my hair in a topknot, I was prepared to go to war with my friends and family. Beside me, my friend, Ki'kwa'ju, painted his face half red and half black and then ran a white line from the left side of his forehead down to the right side of his chin, dabbing white dots along the line.

The two Warrior Women had painted their bodies yellow, which meant they were heroic, led a good life, and were willing to fight to the death. They gathered their warriors together.

Once everyone had applied their paint, sunflower oil was passed around to slick our hair. Kànìkwe took the oil and rubbed it on his bald head, which he had left unpainted. He looked at me and said, "Makes me slippery if anyone tries to grab my head." Then, laughing, he joined his close friends, Kìnà Odenan and Agwanìwon, whom he would die protecting if necessary.

I stood with my mother, sister, and Ki'kwa'ju, the man we called Wolverine in our language. He had the shield, axe, and big blade the Mi'kmaq people had given him when he came to us. The blade he kept in a leather sheath attached to a belt. The axe and shield he clutched in his hands. Over his back he had a quiver of arrows and a bow. The rest of us had bows, arrows, spears, clubs, and flint and bone knives.

I glanced around to see if I could spot Mitigomij, but to no avail. He wasn't with us. I knew, though, that once the fighting began, he would appear with the big cat and at that place death and the smell of death would surround both of them.

Then Agwanìwon spoke. "When the battle starts, we'll stay together as we always have, watching out for the person beside us and also those nearest to us. We have always achieved success fighting for one another. Follow me and Kìnà Odenan to victory. *Aye, aye, aye!*"

Her voice resounded through the open area, and the Ouendat and Anishinaabe warriors looked around at our group and then also took up the chant, sending the birds in the treetops to the heavens.

At that moment Crazy Crow came from the opposite side of the meadow. "It is time!" he roared. "Our enemies have already attacked and are now burning, killing, and taking captives." Then, turning to Waughshe Anue, he said, "Lead us, great warrior, to victory!"

4

THE LAND OF THE TATTOOED WARRIORS

ANOKÌ

Crazy Crow led us to the edge of a cornfield that surrounded the village. Once we arrived, we discovered that the five scouts who had stayed behind had two Attawandaron warriors with them. The faces, arms, and legs of both men were covered with tattoos. All seven of the warriors in turn were splattered with blood. The Attawandaron had been chased through the cornstalks by three Kanien'kehá:ka (*ga-ni-enge-ha:ga:* Mohawk) warriors who had met a sudden demise under the clubs of our scouts and whose bloodied bodies lay among the broken stalks.

Crazy Crow came to me and whispered in my ear, "These Kanien'kehá:ka warriors will have followed only one man on this raid — Ò:nenhste Erhar!"

"The wizard Winpe will also be with him," I said. "We must be careful of their presence. I'll let the others know.

Glooscap especially will be interested in the nearness of Winpe."

Waughshe Anue called Zhashagi, Kìnà Odenan, and Agwanìwon together to plan the attack. When the meeting broke up, Agwanìwon gathered our people and said, "Waughshe Anue has asked the Omàmiwinini to take the left side, the Anishinaabe will take the right side, and the more numerous Ouendat warriors will be in the middle." She then added, "When walking through the corn, try to stay away from the stalks. If the enemy sees the tasselled corn tops of the plants moving, they will suspect an attack, so walk carefully, my friends. We go on Waughshe Anue's signal."

Shortly thereafter, Waughshe Anue gave the hand signal and more than eighty warriors and their war dogs crept silently through the cornfield. Everyone bent over to stay below the corn tassels, weapons clutched in their hands, fierce dogs at their sides. The only sound that could be heard as we drew nearer was the faint rustling of the cornstalk leaves in the gentle breeze that blew from the south. As we closed in on the battle scene, the light wind carried to us the pungent smells and flying embers of the burning longhouses. One ember landed on my shoulder, and before I could sweep it off, it singed my skin. I noticed other warriors with the same problem, and even some of the dogs experienced hair-charring embers that their masters had to douse with handfuls of soil. The stink of scorched dog hair added to the stench around me.

We had almost approached the end of the cornfield when it started to rain lightly. The drops, though not numerous, were the size of peas, and when they hit the broad leaves of the corn plants, the noise they made was similar to the racket of stones thrown against the side of a longhouse by children as they play. Today, though, no children were playing.

Glancing around, I noticed the rain was splattering some of the paint on my companions' bodies, making their appearance even more ominous. As we neared the village through the cornfield, the sounds of the battle cascaded into our midst: the screams of victims, the barking and yelping of dogs, and the distinctive war cries of the Haudenosaunee attackers. Leaving the cover of the stalks, we came upon a heart-stopping scene. The heat and flames from the burning longhouses leaped toward me as if fuelled by my presence, reddening my bare skin. As I turned away from this fiery inferno, my nostrils caught the stink of death from burning bodies. Stumbling across corpses lying on the ground with stunned expressions on their faces and horrendous wounds caused a sudden gagging to rise in my throat. Then the sweet scent of burning nasemà from the village's storage hut gave me a false sense of calmness.

The din of the surrounding battle soon brought me out of my dreamlike trance. Hand-to-hand fighting raged throughout the village — individual battles to the death, spears jabbing, knives slashing, and the sickening crunch of clubs breaking bones.

Running a step or two behind my mother, Wàbananang, I watched as a lithe Kanien'kehá:ka emerged from the smoke and raised his club on the run to take a swing at her. Quickly bringing my spear up, I released it in one motion, hurling it at my mother's assailant agonizingly close to her right shoulder. The spear hit the top of the Kanien'kehá:ka's left shoulder, ripping a furrow through it and sending him spinning in a half circle. Then Ki'kwa'ju dashed in and took a two-handed swing with his axe at the man's back, breaking his spine and doubling him over backward to fall in a heap at my mother's feet. Simultaneously, two other Kanien'kehá:ka warriors rushed my mother and Ki'kwa'ju. In an instant, Wàbananang had two knives in her hands, and with the sweep of her right hand she cut one of the charging warrior's ears off, while with her left hand she buried that knife in his throat. The man's eyes bulged, and when he opened his mouth, no words came out, only blood.

I intercepted the other warrior, and with a two-handed swing of my round wooden club, hit him full in the stomach, the clout driving the air from his lungs in a huge gust from his mouth, the warmth of his breath hitting me square in the face so that I picked up the scent of what his last meal had been. As the Kanien'kehá:ka knelt to catch his breath, Kìnà Odenan swung her war club at his right side. The force of the blow was so powerful that it broke his neck and his head spun until it was opposite his chest.

There was no time to think about what had just happened. Our group was now being assailed by charging Onöndowága and Kanien'kehá:ka warriors. The battle was brutal. Myself, my mother, my sister, Kìnà Odenan, Mònz, and Ki'kwa'ju fought back to back, trying to keep a group of eight bloodied enemy warriors from killing us. Nìj Enàndeg was beside me snarling and snapping at one persistent warrior who kept lunging at me with a long-handled spear. The big wolf dog had finally had enough and pounced at the man in mid-thrust so that animal and assailant crashed to the ground in a screaming, snarling bundle. That action incited the remaining enemy warriors to make a headlong charge into our ranks. At that precise moment I heard the distinctive crack of a slingshot and watched as a man dropped at my sister's feet with a hole in the back of his head the size of a child's fist. Then there was the scream of a panther, and a black blur passed my head and collided with a huge man brandishing a vicious-looking war club. Man and beast hit the ground with a thud, and the panther finished his work as fast as I could bat an eye.

Once the Haudenosaunee realized Mitigomij had entered the battle, they all turned their attention to attacking him. Gaining the scalp of that great Omàmiwinini warrior would be the biggest prize of the whole conflict, and the man who killed him would become famous. But Mitigomij was a man who didn't die easily. Once these attackers turned their backs on us and diverted their attention to Mitigomij, we charged them from behind. Between my close family members, the wolf dog, and the panther, the battle quickly swung in our favour.

When we were done, four enemy warriors lay dead, we were covered with blood, and Mònz had a horrific facial wound. As we stood over our slain foes taking our battle souvenirs, I heard my mother gasp. Glancing at where she was looking, I saw the object of her sudden nervousness. Rounding a burning building in the distance was Mandàmin Animosh (*man-dah-min An-ney-mush*: Omàmiwinini name for Ò:nenhste Erhar or Corn Dog) followed by the wizard Winpe and a dozen warriors. They were headed straight to where Agwanìwon and the rest of our group were in a frantic battle for their lives.

Kànìkwe, Nigig, and Glooscap broke from the others to defend against Ò:nenhste Erhar and his approaching warriors. Nigig charged ahead of his two companions and made a two-handed thrust at Ò:nenhste Erhar with his spear. Ò:nenhste Erhar sidestepped him and hit Nigig in the middle of the back with a stone axe, knocking Nigig forward into Ò:nenhste Erhar's accompanying men, who clubbed Nigig to the ground and brutally beat him to death with their clubs.

"Mitigomij!" I cried. "Look!"

Spying where I pointed, Mitigomij turned to his panther. "Makadewà Waban, go!" Then, turning to my wolf dog, he roared, "Follow!"

Both animals took off, and the rest of us tried to keep up with them. The two dogs headed straight for Ò:nenhste Erhar.

Mitigomij shouted, "Ò:nenhste Erhar," as the canines raced toward their quarry.

Ò:nenhste Erhar turned and stared into the distant eyes of Mitigomij, then gazed at the rapidly advancing animals. He yelled back at Mitigomij, "You've picked a good day to die! Once I finish with your animals, I'll be coming for you! I don't believe you're as invincible as they say!"

Mitigomij reached into his shirt and pulled out a bone whistle hanging from his neck. Putting the whistle to his mouth, he let loose with three shrill blasts, immediately stopping the animals. With one more blast, the two beasts turned and went to the aid of our other family members nearby.

Then, from an unbelievable distance, Mitigomij released three arrows in rapid succession that struck the Kanien'kehá:ka warrior's chest. I was close enough to see the look of astonishment on Ò:nenhste Erhar's face as the first arrow hit him in the heart and he took a stumbling step backward. Then the next arrow struck him in almost the same spot, causing blood to trickle out of his nostrils. When the last arrow hit with a resounding thump, the famous Haudenosaunee warrior took a short step forward, released the grip on his war club, and let it drop onto the rain-soaked ground. Slumping to his knees, he tried to say something, but only blood issued from his mouth, which when mixed with the warm summer rain flowed down his chin to the ground, reddening the puddle of water he was kneeling in. In that instant, he toppled face first into the bloodied mud, dying a warrior's death far from his homeland.

Winpe and the other warriors watched as all this unfolded close by. The wizard stared at my uncle, and I watched as he grasped and re-grasped his club, his face and eyes contorted, the veins in his neck bulging. As I watched him standing there, I saw more hate in his face than I had ever seen before. His whole body trembled with rage. I knew Winpe wanted to take on Mitigomij, but after noting the distance my uncle had made those shots from, the wizard had to be rethinking his vengeance.

As Mitigomij made his way to my side, Winpe screamed, "This is not over!" He then turned and directed his companions to take Ò:nenhste Erhar's body away while the other warriors made menacing lunges at Glooscap and Kànìkwe. As they escaped with the body of their fallen leader, I noticed Winpe diverting his attention to something in the distance. Saying something to one of his men, the wizard then disappeared into the cornfield.

The rain was now coming down harder, and my war paint started to run, mixing the colours and symbols I had painstakingly applied previously. The Ouendat warriors led by Waughshe Anue were taking losses but gaining ground and driving the Onöndowága from the village. With the death of their chief, the Kanien'kehá:ka were leaving the field.

Nìj Enàndeg and the panther had come upon a pack of about twenty enemy war dogs covering their masters' retreats, and with the help of some Ouendat dogs were forcing them to withdraw. The two packs were a snarling, howling, bloody mess of teeth and fur. The panther had one huge dog in his jaws and was shaking the life out of it, blood and fur flying with each shake of Makadewà Wàban's head. Nìj Enàndeg, meanwhile, was in a struggle with two ferocious dogs, and to even up the odds, I let fly with an arrow that felled one of them.

The Anishinaabe, led by the two brothers and with the help of the Tionontati warriors who had arrived as our groups exited the cornfield, had also turned back the enemy they were struggling with and were able to recover some captives the Onöndowága attempted to take with them on their retreat.

With the battle's end, the Attawandaron women began to wail for their lost husbands and sons. The rain, now a downpour, put out the fires, filling the air with the pungent smell of wet, smouldering wood and the stench of the conflict. Our people and allies removed their losses from the field of battle. Wounded allied warriors lay in the field, moaning for the attention of the healers.

Enemy bodies lay in the forming puddles of water, while dogs emerged from the shadows to creep up on the corpses and snatch chunks of flesh to satisfy their hunger. From the sky, crows cawed and ravens croaked, wheeling in the air as they waited for their chance to take a piece of the dead. The aftermath of a battlefield wasn't for the faint of heart.

The enemy wounded sat up if they were able to, never uttering a word, no matter how horrific their injuries. This wasn't a time to show weakness to their adversaries, for they knew the worst was yet to come before they passed on to the other side. The healers would also come to them with herbs for their wounds and food; their captors would want them to regain whatever strength they could for the tortures that lay ahead. There was no sport in putting a weakened warrior through the coming agony. He needed all his strength to show his bravery!

I stood in the midst of all this carnage, thanking Kije-Manidò for watching over me and my friends this day, and made an offer of tobacco. My heart was heavy for the loss of Nigig, a great friend and Wàbanaki warrior who had died fighting to protect his daughters and their husbands, the twins. Mònz, my uncle, had a horrific facial wound, and if he survived, would be scarred horribly. The Anishinaabe and Tionontati had each lost five or six men, and a few more were disabled with wounds. The Ouendat had suffered several losses and wounded. The Attawandaron, though, had endured the most because they had been vigorously defending their village before our arrival. More than thirty of their warriors had been slain and another twenty or so were wounded, close to half their male fighters in all. The attackers had also slain seven women who had fought to defend their children. In the end, the invaders had gotten away with more than a dozen women and children to take back to their villages.

The battle had been devastating for all of the participants, both attackers and defenders.

The rain stopped and the surrounding air became cooler. As we stood near a fire with my people, the Anishinaabe brothers, Zhashagi and Omashkooz, joined us. Kìnà Odenan thanked them for their strong battle skills that day and told them that if they ever needed the talents of our Omàmiwinini group to send for us.

Zhashagi replied, "My people have a very powerful foe we call the Nadowessioux. They call themselves the Lakȟóta. Our battles with them have been going on for years, with many fallen warriors on each side. I foresee a time that we might need your help and skills, especially that of the lame one, Mitigomij. That man has powerful magic. The other, the one you call Crazy Crow, has no equal in battle. Your group is experienced and ruthless in battle. I'm happy to have your Omàmiwinini force as friends. You may very well hear from me in the future."

That night the remaining Attawandaron took their revenge on the Onöndowága and Kanien'kehá:ka warriors who had been captured or were too wounded to flee. Fourteen of the enemy were forced to run the gauntlet and were then put to the stake to die in flames. All of the men and women of the village participated, plus the allies who had come to their aid.

Walking into the firelight with three bloody scalps hanging from his large spear, along with three fresh notches on the staff, Crazy Crow spoke to the Warrior Women. "Kìnà Odenan and Agwanìwon, my friends, the crows have told me a terrible thing. Winpe the wizard has captured Nukumi and the Little One, Apistanéwj. Glooscap has left by himself to bring them back. I'm going to follow and help."

"No, Elue'wiet Ga'qaquj, this has been foretold," objected Jilte'g. "Glooscap has to do this himself. It is his destiny."

"So be it, my friend," replied the great Mi'kmaq warrior. "However, I'll have my sky friends watch over him."

5

THE RETURN OF A LEGEND AND THE MAKING OF A NEW LEGEND

ANOKÌ

After the battle in the land of the Attawandaron, we stayed a few days to prepare our wounded for the trip back to the Ouendat village. The decision was also made among the leaders of the Omàmiwinini, Ouendat, and Anishinaabe to transport our dead and bury them near Waughshe Anue's Ouendat village.

Our small group had lost the brave Wàbanaki warrior Nigig, who had been slain during the battle. His two daughters, Àwadòsiwag and Ininàtig, were married to my twin cousins, Makwa and Wàbek. Nigig's daughters were also skilled warriors who had fought bravely beside their husbands.

My Uncle Mònz had suffered a terrible wound at the hands of an Onöndowága's war club. Mònz had seen the weapon coming toward his left side at the last moment, giving him enough time to move his head slightly to avoid a crushing blow to his temple. The club had caught his face and torn his left cheek down to the bone. As the weapon had passed away from his face, it had ripped off the tip of his nose. Our two chiefs, Kìnà Odenan and Agwanìwon, were right there when the Onöndowága warrior had struck Mònz — unlucky for the Onöndowága, lucky for my uncle. Agwanìwon had impaled the warrior just above his breechcloth with her spear, while Kìnà Odenan had crushed the back of the man's skull with a mighty swing of her war axe. The man had dropped face first into the mud without making a sound, so quick and brutal was their retaliation. During this action, their friend, Kànìkwe, had grabbed Mònz and carried him to safety. Kànìkwe had tended to my uncle's wound, sewing the cheek back into place and covering it with honey, which he always carried in his medicine bag. Mònz had then made his way back alone to the edge of the cornfield. That was where we had found him at the end of the battle — dazed and pale from loss of blood. His wife, Wàbìsì, and my mother, Wàbananang, took him under their care and made sure he was watched over with food, water, and medicine.

When we departed, the wounded who could walk led the way, followed by the dead and more severely wounded carried by the warrior men and women on makeshift litters. It was slow going, but we were determined to get everyone back.

The Ouendat warriors had a different way of hauling wounded unable to walk. They strapped them to the backs of healthy warriors who took turns carrying them on the homeward trail.

As we made our way through the forests and meadows, we took a path along an escarpment that overlooked a dried-up beaver meadow. Mitigomij pointed out to me a line of wolves filing through the meadow.

"Anokì," he said, "take a close look out there and tell me what you see."

"All I see is a line of wolves, Uncle."

"Anokì, come now," he said. "There's much more there than that. Look deeper into the line's makeup."

"Yes, Uncle, now I see! The first four wolves are old and frail and are setting the pace for the rest. If they were left in the rear, they would fall behind and die. In case of an attack from another group of wolves, they would die in the initial attack, enabling the five that are the strongest of the pack, that are right behind them, to prepare to defend the rest of the group. In the middle of the pack, I see that the younger ones are being protected. Behind them are the next strongest six of the pack, followed at the end by the alpha wolf controlling everything from the back end. I see it now!"

"Anokì, that line position controls the whole group, deciding the direction they are going in and anticipating the attacks of enemies. The pack follows the beat of the Elders. The column is a sign of mutual help and not leaving anyone behind. Now look at our group. Where do you think our people learned how to walk in the woods? The wolf was our Elders' teacher for this lesson. Anokì, always look around you in the forest. The birds and animals will teach you the ways of life and survival. Never forget that!"

"I won't, Uncle."

The only warrior who didn't make the trip home with us was Glooscap, who had left to search for his friends, Nukumi, Apistanéwj, and the two dogs, Na'gweg and Tepgig, who had been kidnapped and taken away by the wizard Winpe.

Crazy Crow, the fearless Mi'kmaq warrior, had been told by Jilte'g that he wasn't to follow because this event had been foretold by the Elders, and Glooscap had to save them on his own.

Approaching me, Crazy Crow told me he couldn't let his friend and fellow warrior, Glooscap, go into the land of the Haudenosaunee to hunt for Nukumi and Apistanéwj without assistance. Even though Jilte'g had warned him that this event had been foretold, Crazy Crow couldn't allow any harm to come to his friends. Gazing up at the sky, he uttered the crow rally call: *"Caaawww, caaawww, caaawww, caaawww."* Then he disappeared into the cornfield, followed by his airborne friends.

I relayed this information to Agwanìwon and Kìnà Odenan. Agwanìwon replied, "Crazy Crow cares for his friends and will never see any harm come to them if it's within his power to protect them. We'll see him again. I'm sure of that."

The following winter I found myself in the Ouendat village of Ossossanè, sitting across a fire from the great warrior Crazy Crow, who was about to tell his story of the adventure he had just returned from four moons after leaving the battle against our Onöndowága and Kanien'kehá:ka adversaries.

Crazy Crow had come back with a story about his friend, Glooscap. The narrative he told to us became part of the Legend of Glooscap.

Crazy Crow's Story

The day I left, my crow friends led me on a trail straight to Erielhonan. I was on a constant run and still I couldn't gain on my large friend, Glooscap. After many hours, I became fatigued and had to stop to make tea and hunt for roots and berries to eat. I was intent on saving my corn and dried meat in my pouch and only using it under conditions of extreme hunger. My more immediate hope was to keep up with Glooscap and hopefully stumble onto small game during the journey.

After eating, I signalled my readiness to my feathered companions resting in the surrounding trees or on the ground eating insects and we again took to the trail. That first night I was so tired that I didn't even build a fire; a couple of handfuls of berries and some corn washed down with cool water from a spring nearby staved off my hunger pains. I cut enough cedar boughs to make a bed, caked myself with mud from the banks of the small stream to ward off the bugs, and crawled under a deadfall. The aromatic smell of the surrounding pine forest and the continual buzz of the insects as they tried to find bare skin on my mud-caked body gently put me to sleep.

Waking before dawn the next morning, I watched as an apalqaqamej (*a-bach-caw-a-mitch:* chipmunk) ran back and forth from his hole to the forest and then back again with his mouth full of nuts. The little fellow scampered so fast that he caused the leaves in his path to flutter. When he neared the hole, he dived into it. Starting to feel early-morning hunger pangs, I waited until the small busybody left his hole, then took my knife and dug into the storage area. There I was able to retrieve a handful of nuts that was enough to satisfy my immediate appetite.

Racing through the forest, I got to the lake just in time to watch from a hill as Winpe first assisted his wife and son into the canoe, then proceeded to roughly handle his captives in after them. Nukumi's and Apistanéwj's hands were bound, and the two dogs, Na'gweg and Tepgig, followed meekly.

Glooscap arrived in time to see the boat leave, so he called to Nukumi to send back his dogs. She cast a spell and shrank the animals to a size small enough to enable her to put them into a wooden bowl, even though her hands were bound. Then she pushed the bowl toward the shore where Glooscap received them unharmed. The big man took the dogs and put them into his medicine pouch for safekeeping.

After that, Glooscap strode to the shoreline and sang, bringing a bootup (whale) to the shore. He jumped onto the bootup's back and commanded the marine beast to follow Winpe and the others.

Having no song in my heart to call a bootup, I was able to find a hidden Haudenosaunee canoe and went after Glooscap. When I next caught sight of him, I watched as he came upon a lodge in the forest. Out of the lodge emerged a sorceress whose hair was filled with toads. Glooscap picked the toads from her hair, tricking the sorceress by pretending to kill them by cracking a cranberry branch between his teeth. Each time he made a cracking noise he released a toad to Turtle Island and freedom. The sorceress, realizing she had been tricked, exacted her revenge on him. Her attempt on Glooscap's life failed when he returned the dogs to their full size and they made short work of her.

After three more days of trailing Glooscap, I watched as he encountered another lodge, this one housing an old couple who were wizards. They sent their two daughters to slay Glooscap, and again the dogs saved their master.

Finally, after many suns, Glooscap came across Nukumi and Apistanéwj. The two were lagging behind Winpe, unable to keep up because of hunger and suffering. Nukumi told Glooscap of their capture and cruel treatment.

He could see by their appearances that they had suffered greatly and said, "I'll punish the wizard Winpe for what he's done!"

Glooscap caught up with Winpe and confronted his foe with a challenge. Winpe then summoned all his powers and grew in size to fight the battle. Glooscap, in turn, called upon his powers and towered over the wizard. Taking his bow, Glooscap tapped the top of Winpe's head with it and the wizard toppled to his death. Glooscap then turned to Winpe's wife and son and told them to leave and go anywhere they pleased.

When Crazy Crow finished telling his story, he stood and said, "Glooscap never needed my help." He then turned from the fire and disappeared into the darkness that night along with his Legend of Glooscap.

6

THE FEAST OF THE
DEAD AND THE OGÀ

ANOKÌ

After the story Crazy Crow told us, we received news
of Glooscap from an Innu band that came to trade with
the Ouendat. The Innu said they had met Glooscap on
their journey to us and had camped with him at the
rapids below the Kitcisìpi Sìbì (Ottawa River) on the
Magotogoek Sìbì (St. Lawrence River). Glooscap had
told them that Apistanéwj, Nukumi, and the two dogs,
Na'gweg and Tepgig, were returning to the land of the
Mi'kmaq. The messenger informed us that Glooscap
now realized where his permanent home was and that
he had a responsibility to protect his adopted tribe to
pay them back for taking him in and giving him shelter, food, and protection after they found him those
many years ago on Natigòsteg (Forward Land: Anticosti
Island). For that he owed them his life and his lifelong

devotion. He would stay there to defend them from all dangers and had asked the Innu to thank us for the adventures he had experienced and the friendships he had made with us. Glooscap wished us all well and hoped we would meet again someday before our deaths.

The message saddened us all, but we knew Glooscap was happy in the lands to the east and from there, to the best of his ability, he would also protect our people from dangers rising from the big ocean.

Zhashagi, his brother, Omashkooz, and their accompanying warriors had stayed another few suns after we returned from the Haudenosaunee battle, long enough for their wounds to heal so they could make the trip back to their people. Zhashagi told our female chiefs, Agwanìwon and Kìnà Odenan, that his people intended to trade with their friends, the Omashkiigoo (*oh-mush-key-go*: Cree), the following spring.

"If you ever need our help in the future, send us a wampum belt and we'll come to your aid," Kìnà Odenan said.

The winter spent with the Ouendat was uneventful. Mitigomij and his panther disappeared into the wilderness, Glooscap was gone, but my immediate family and my wolf dog, Nìj Enàndeg, were here in the Ouendat land to keep me company.

The Ouendat were proficient in growing corn, beans, and squash, so there was never any shortage of food. Kìnà Odenan and Agwanìwon made sure our Omàmiwinini band hunted and contributed our share to the supply of food for the community. The two Warrior Women were always leading hunting trips for moose, deer, and elk to help sustain the diet of the village with meat. My mother, Wàbananang, and the other women hosted feasts every ten to fifteen suns for the Ouendat with the game that our hunters brought back. When we weren't hunting, our time was spent repairing weapons and making new arrows, clubs, spears, and clothing from the skins of the animals we slew. We also assisted in the repair of the shelters, made pipes, and crafted snowshoes to get around in the snow. Some of the clothes we fashioned were traded with the Ouendat or given to our hosts to repay their hospitality.

The longhouses we stayed in were always smoky, even though there were holes in the ceilings to allow the smoke to escape. I and my fellow residents' eyes constantly watered and stung from the woodsmoke. To aid in the remedy of the irritation, the Ouendat women prepared a tea from goldenseal leaves that we used as eyewash. This helped to ease the inflammation but wasn't a cure.

The rodent problem in the longhouse was looked after by a resident fox that seemed quite well fed for his work. It wasn't the same fox I had befriended the previous winter, but another just as efficient at hunting.

The matter of head lice was another concern. Even though I had covered my sleeping quarters with cedar boughs to ward off the lice, the number of people and closeness of quarters aided these little pests to spread without any limits. Finally, I had to give in and shave my head like my Ouendat companions, leaving only a scalp lock on the top that I made stand up with an ample application of bear grease, next attaching three turkey feathers on the back to a braid of hair that I left long on the nape of my neck. The women would never shave their heads, so they took turns combing one another's hair, using very fine bone and wooden combs. This was usually done while sitting by the fire and flicking the bugs into the flames from the combs.

I said we spent an uneventful winter among the Ouendat, but there was one incident that created a stir that broke up the dullness. A little Ouendat girl decided one afternoon during a bright, unseasonably warm winter's day to search for dried berries while there was a crust on the snow, making her travels easier. She took a reed basket with a lid on it with her and returned to the longhouse after foraging for a good while outside the village walls. When she got back, I was sitting beside my cot eating corn and squash soup with Nìj Enàndeg at my feet.

There were about twenty men, women, and children sitting around a fire closest to me, eating, playing games, and laughing. The young girl sat unnoticed among everyone. Grabbing a wooden bowl, she reached into her basket to take her berries out, cleaned them in water, then tossed them into the bowl. All the time she did this she had a huge smile on her face, seeming very much like any other child enjoying her chosen task.

After a short time watching her clean the berries, I observed the basket lid move when she replaced it after taking some of the berries out. A small black nose poked out from under the lid, followed by a pair of eyes, then a head. A pair of feet with long claws emerged and grasped the side of the basket, knocking off the lid without making any sound. The lid rolled among the unconcerned and oblivious people gathered around the fire — until a sudden exodus of people took place as the occupants of the longhouse and the animal simultaneously recognized each other's identities, causing a sudden rise in the noise level. The stress level of the small animal then escalated along with its black-and-white tail, which shot into the air, releasing an aroma that quickly permeated the longhouse.

When I first spied the animal appearing out of the basket, I had dropped my soup bowl, startling my dog, and we both beat a hasty retreat. The two of us got to the door before everyone else, closely followed by a stampede of scurrying occupants laughing and screaming. Some of the slow-rising groups basking lazily in the warmth of the fire were the recipients of a disgusting odour that stung their eyes and marked their clothing with an unbearable stench.

It was many days before the smell left the longhouse. Some of the residents departed for a while to stay with friends while the men burned cedar and juniper to get rid of the stink. I could never figure out how that little girl got the shigàg (skunk) into the basket without it spraying her. Maybe it was hungry and the berries were the lure. It did break up the monotony of the village and was the talk of everyone for six or seven suns.

Once the warmth of the spring sun arrived, the people of the village decided to move in a day's time. They had lived on this spot for ten winters, and the soil to grow their corn, squash, and beans hadn't been as fruitful for the past couple of years. A judgment had been made to move when the snow disappeared. Community members were sent to the new place to clear the land, opening up areas to plant crops. My people lent their labour to aid in the work. We helped cut down the larger trees with sharpened bone and stone axes, piling the chopped wood for future use in fires. The smaller saplings and logs, along with split logs, would become building materials, and the peeled bark would be used for roofing and siding cover for the new longhouses. The underbrush was then burned off to clear the land, and the women planted seeds.

When an Ouendat village moved, the people had a celebration called the Feast of the Dead. Now that they had decided to move the village, their dead ancestors also had to be brought along and reburied before the spring hunt and planting took place. Other villages would be invited and gifts exchanged at this celebration.

The Feast of the Dead took place over ten suns. The first eight suns involved family members of the departed digging up the bodies in various levels of decomposition, cleaning the remaining flesh off the bones, and preparing them for burial at the new village. The bones were then wrapped in a set of beaver furs. Some men participated, but on the whole it was women who handled the task. At no time did any of the people performing the cleansing of the bodies show any revulsion toward the activity.

Once the bones were cleaned and wrapped, they were transported to the homes of the relatives where a feast was held in memory of the dead person or persons. Gifts and food were placed next to the fur packages, and visitors were treated to victuals and water.

The village leader then made the decision concerning when the bodies were to be moved. With so much to transfer, the number of people, and the mourning that took place, it required two days to reach the new village site. During the journey, the relatives carrying the deceased cried out in anguish until they reached their new homes. Once there, a burial pit was prepared and the dead were laid to rest with everyone gathered around to grieve their losses.

Our small band of Omàmiwinini participated as best we could during the ten days and were surprised to learn that when the village moved again after the next ten or twelve winters the whole process would be repeated in another Feast of the Dead with these deceased remains and any others who passed away in the meantime.

After our people helped the Ouendat relocate and assisted in building their new longhouses, Kìnà Odenan called a meeting of our small group. "Agwanìwon and I have decided we've imposed on our allies, the Ouendat, for too long. It's time we moved on and made our own way. Kànìkwe has told us that the ogà (*oh-gah*: pickerel) will be running at a waterfall of a river that empties into the 'place of the bay,' what the Haudenosaunee call Kenhtè:ke (*gan-da-gay*: near present-day Napanee, Ontario). We leave at sunrise tomorrow."

My sister's husband, Ki'kwa'ju, came to me and asked, "How long will it take us to get to this waterfall?"

"Six or seven suns," I replied. "Once there we'll spear the fish and use weirs to capture them, clean them, and then smoke them on drying racks."

The next morning our group departed. Kànìkwe led us on the trail followed by the twins, Makwa and Wàbek, and their wives, Àwadòsiwag and Ininàtig, the daughters of the dead warrior Nigig; my mother, Wàbananang; my sister, Pangì Mahingan, and her husband, Ki'kwa'ju; and me. Uncle Mònz and Aunt Wàbìsì were behind us. Mònz's face had healed and was now just a deep pink slashing scar across his cheek. His nose, where the axe had struck him, was now rounded where the tip had been severed. At the end of the column were our Mi'kmaq friends, E's and Jilte'g, and the Ouendat warriors who had been with us for many years, Achie and Önenha'. The two Warrior Women chiefs were on each side of our procession, guarding the flanks. Our family unit consisted of seven women, who were as much warriors as each of the ten men accompanying them. In fact, the women at times were fiercer and more skilled than the men in the act of war.

Each of us carried our own weapons, food, and water. The twenty or so dogs travelling with us carted our bedding lashed to their backs. Nìj Enàndeg, my wolf dog, was one of the exceptions. He and a couple of other fierce dogs were our sentinels on the trail and were unencumbered with burdens.

When we arrived at the big lake that the Ouendat called Ouentironk (Beautiful Water: Lake Simcoe), we found some canoes the Ouendat had hidden along the shore. We took five of their larger vessels and loaded the dogs and ourselves into them and made good time across the lake. Reaching the other side, we discovered a birchbark map on a split-ended stick that was left behind by a previous group who had ventured through here from the other direction. A circle on the map meant a day's travel and an overnight camp. Along with Kànìkwe's knowledge of the area from a past trip here many years ago and the guidance provided by the map, we were able to proceed quite easily.

On the fourth day, E's, Mònz, and my mother broke off to hunt for fresh game. They returned with a large wàbidì (*wah-bi-dee:* elk) and some added company to the delight of our group. Mitigomij and Crazy Crow had come upon them as they were gutting the animal. E's said they had celebrated the occasion by making a fire and roasting some of the meat. Surprising to them, E's also said, the big cat, Makadewà Wàban, had lain by the fire and eaten his fill before disappearing back into the shadows.

I was always amazed by the sudden arrival of Mitigomij and Crazy Crow after they disappeared for months at a time. Crazy Crow, I noticed, had a few more notches and teeth on his fierce-looking weapon that was a combined staff, spear, and club.

The decision was made not to go to the big lake Ontarìo (Shining Waters) to search for Ouendat canoes we had been told were well hidden and then paddle along the shore to our destination. Instead we stayed inland to avoid detection from any Haudenosaunee who might be on the lake. As we walked, I told Uncle Mitigomij about the recurring dream of my father's death.

"Anokì," he said, "your dream is a reminder being sent by Mahingan, your father. He wants you to hold the value of life dearly to your breast. He didn't get to choose the place or time for his demise. That's chosen by the powers of all the mysteries that surround us. He died knowing that his family was safe and would be able to go on without him. He wants you to know that he'll be watching over you, but you must give up your mourning for him and become a leader. Your birthmarks were chosen for you and are signs of the future. The one on your head is a sign of knowledge and the one on your buttock is a sign of travel to distant places. Mahingan has also come to me in dreams at times, but now he must move on because he has left us with the knowledge that he wanted to pass on."

"Thank you, Uncle. I understand now."

After eight suns, we reached our destination. The roar of the rapids could be heard before we saw the foaming white water. It was amazing: thousands of ogà and odawàjameg (*oh-duh-wah-shaw-megg*: salmon) leaped in the rapids, trying to make their way inland to spawn.

Since it was close to evening, we immediately set to work making three shelters for ourselves. The two Ouendat, Achie and Önenha', were tasked with scouting the area for any dangers. The dogs would alert us to anything out of the ordinary heading toward our encampment. Once the shelters were erected, fires blazed and Achie and Önenha' returned to join us in a feast of the remaining elk meat and some fish that were hastily speared before nightfall.

The next morning the women erected drying racks, half of the men constructed a stone fish weir, and the others stood in the cool, swift water spearing fish. Everyone was kept busy spearing, trapping, gutting, and filleting the fish.

Mitigomij came to my side and said, "This is a place of danger. With this much fish, others will know of the bounty of the waters here. I'm going to travel around the area to make sure we won't be surprised. Crazy Crow will stay with the group. We have powerful warriors here, but an ambush would weaken us quickly."

7

THE TREACHEROUS RIVER

ZHASHAGI

The sky was a magnificent blue in the midsummer that year, and the reflection of the sun's light bounced off the calm waters of the river, sparkling and dancing over the slow-moving stream, seemingly replicating evening fireflies in their mating ceremony.

Our canoe consisted of me, Zhashagi (*sha-sha-gee*: Blue Heron), three other sinewy warriors, and a big animosh (*an-eh-moosh*: dog) we called Misko (Red) because of his colour. I sat at the back of the boat, handling the steering and bailing water with a wooden bowl. We had previously clipped a small log jutting out of the waterway, causing a slight tear in the birchbark covering, and until the group stopped I was responsible for removing the water that seeped in from the river through the small tear.

My companions in the canoe included Makadewigwan (*mak-a-day-eh-we-gwan*: Black Feather) situated in the front. Directly behind him was Ininishib (*eh-nay-nish-hip*: Mallard). My older brother, Omashkooz (*oh-mush-goes*: Elk), sat directly in front of me. Whenever I changed sides with my paddle, I occasionally splattered his back with water. Each time this happened Omashkooz growled that this action irritated him, telling me that once we got to shore I would suffer his revenge.

We were making our way from our friends, the Omashkiigoo (*oh-mush-key-go*: Cree). Gone more than forty suns from our village, we anxiously looked forward to our return with the results of this trading trip. To visit our Omashkiigoo friends we had travelled the lakes and rivers to the northwest of our villages. The warriors who travelled on the trip came from three villages within Anishinaabe lands.

To avoid the big waters of Anishinaabewi-gichigami (Lake Superior) we worked our way down from Kababikodaawangag Saaga'igan (Lake of Sand Dunes — Lake of the Woods) along the connecting rivers that drained into the Gichi-ziibi (*gich-e-zee-bee*: Mississippi River). Our villages were in the Mitaawangaagamaa (Big Sandy Lake) area.

The canoes heading for home were loaded with dried adik (*a-dick*: caribou) meat and skins from the large animal. We were also able to trade with the Omashkiigoo for mashkode-bizhiki (*mush-ko-de-bish-eh-ka*: buffalo) robes and, of course, there was always frenzied trading among the warriors for a good animosh. The Omashkiigoo in return for their trade goods were always looking for fish, rice, clamshells, squash, and rolled-up birchbark for making canoes. The two or three days spent trading always became a spirited affair with laughter, yelling, games of chance, and a weapons competition.

Our canoe was among eleven other boats, thirty-eight warriors, four boys, two women, and a dozen dogs. Most of the men had removed their deer and moose skin shirts, and their bodies glistened with beads of sweat as they kept up the rhythm of the paddle strokes. With each warrior's stroke the canoes lunged forward, parting the stillness of the waters, scattering the busy pods of water bugs, and rippling the water toward the shore. The boys and women spent their time fishing from the moving canoes.

In keeping with tradition, the day before we left, there was a wild game of baaga'adowewin (lacrosse). The night before the contest the players danced, feasted, and told stories. The day of the game they painted themselves as if they were going to war and made their wagers, placing the items they had bet with on racks that the winners of the gambling could collect from once the match was over. The game was always a high-spirited affair with lots of cuts and bruises to heal from once it was over.

Many years before my brother and I had entered this realm of Turtle Island birthed from our mother, the Anishinaabe people had travelled here from a big sea in the east. The Prophet of the First Fire had told the Anishinaabe to move or be destroyed. Then the Seven Prophets of the Seven Fires told our people where to go and what to look for in the seven major stopping places. With the help of their friends, the Mi'kmaq and the Abenaki, we were able to journey through Haudenosaunee territory without much loss of life, finally arriving at Mooningwanekaaing (Madeline Island) in Anishinaabewi-gichigami. During this movement, we met and made allies with the Odishkwaagamii (Algonquin and/or Nipissing) and the Naadawe (Huron/Ouendat).While travelling, my people left accounts of their trek on rock faces along their route.

Our allies kept us strong in times of want and hardship, enabling us to trade for items we desperately needed. They also strengthened our numbers in times of war.

Although the Anishinaabe had forged strong alliances, they had also made a very powerful and violent enemy. The Nadowessioux (Lakȟóta) became our most feared foe because of two incidents after the Anishinaabe arrival on the shores of Anishinaabewi-gichigami years ago. These confrontations had continually occurred for years in revenge and mourning raids, driven by both the Nadowessioux and the Anishinaabe Nations.

"Zhashagi," Omashkooz yelled at me, "wake up! The others are going to shore for relief and food. Steer us to that opening in the forest on shore."

His sudden shout startled me out of my deep thoughts, sending a shiver down my neck, and I immediately turned the canoe. The other two men laughed, and I joined in with them once I realized how much off course I had taken our boat from the rest of the group in the short time I was inattentive. We were able to quickly regain course and arrive along with the others. The group was headed to a huge bare rock looming up from the river that after a quick glance seemed to be pushing the forest back into itself as the huge granite stone jutted from the river.

As the boat neared the rocky shoreline, Makadewigwan swiftly jumped from the front and pulled it ashore. The other two and Misko hastily made their exit, and just as I stood, my brother rocked the canoe and sent me backward into the water. Ininishib and Makadewigwan had big grins on their faces as both of them waded in, took my arms, and carried me to the shore.

Coming up from the warm water sputtering and spitting, I gasped, "What was that for?"

"To wake you up from your daze," Omashkooz replied. "And, remember, I did tell you of my desire for retribution for your carelessness when switching paddling sides and splashing me."

"Don't worry, friend, we'll look after you," Makadewigwan said. "When we finish our meal, one of us will steer and you can sleep on the furs we have in the canoe to get your rest."

I pulled my arms away from them and kicked and splashed water at them, driving both to shore laughing and still teasing me.

My brother approached and handed me a leather bag containing dried caribou. "You can make tea and prepare the meal. The fire will dry you out." He then chuckled and continued to a clearing where everyone was gathering, wading into the crowd of boisterous people and barking dogs.

I gathered a couple of armfuls of dry wood and kindling, dug a firepit, and threw both round and flat rocks into the hole. In a very short time, I had a good blaze going.

When we were out in open water, the biting insects had kept their distance, but while foraging for wood I had stirred them up in an angry mass. They were now benefiting by feasting on my exposed skin. Unfastening my medicine bag, I tossed two or three handfuls of sage on the fire, creating a smudge and deterrent to the blood-thirsty predators of the air.

Now that the flames were jumping and crackling, I laid the rest of the wood in a tight circle around the fire, butt ends facing in. This enabled me to push the wood into the flames a bit at a time without wasting it by piling it on and burning it quickly.

Next, I needed to make tea. Walking to the canoe for the birchbark container we made tea in, I encountered Ininishib and Makadewigwan hunched over a fire, warming pine resin on a rock they had heated in the fire. The resin would be smeared on the small tear in our canoe. They would put the heated pine gum on the rip with a stick, wet their thumbs, and spread it. Once the resin cooled, the damage would be repaired.

Gathering up my tea bucket and another container, I filled them both with water and returned to my fire. I took the forked stick, stuck it in the fire, and retrieved my red-hot round rocks. Then I dropped the stones into the container to bring the water to a boil. Next, I filled the tea container to the brim with pine needles. Once the water was heated, I skimmed the scum off the top and what was left was hot tea. To drink hot or cold liquids, each warrior and village resident carried a small clay cup for tea, water, and soup.

Taking a chunk of meat, I cut it into thin slices with a clamshell, then approached the fire again and pulled out the flat stones I had put in the pit. After setting these hot rocks on a bed of shore stones to prevent heat loss, I lined up the thin slices of meat on them to fry. Taking the larger container of water, I pulled some more heated stones from the fire and dropped them in. While the water boiled it was time to prepare my last meal item. Not having a corn grinder like the ones women in our village used, I made do with what my environment offered. Finding a large flat rock, I set the corn on it and made cornmeal by pounding a fist-sized stone onto the kernels. In no time at all and after seven or eight handfuls of corn, there was a good supply of meal. Tossing this into the large container of water along with the thin slices of meat that had been fried, some chunks of fish that had been given to me by one of the young boys, and some leeks I had foraged from the forest, I now had a very tasty corn mush soup.

While I prepared our meal, I watched as the others in our group laughed, told stories, and collected wood and roots from the forest. The four young boys were kept busy by running back and forth from the wooded area with armloads of dry firewood. Since wood was needed for the individual fires, people helped themselves from the communal pile the youngsters made. Ours was a culture of sharing. No one went hungry, cold, or in need of aid for anything. The community at large was there for all of us and to help everyone survive in times of need.

During the meal, warriors went from one cooking fire to another to sample what their friends were eating. The two women by far had a larger gathering around their fire than the ones where a warrior was the cook.

In my search for wood, I had found a forked tree branch the length of my arm and the size of my wrist around. This I had put aside. Now, taking three pieces of green sapling, I notched the ends of two of them and forced them into the ground on each side of the fire. Then I placed the third piece lengthwise into the notches. Picking up some good chunks of adiko-wiiyaas (*a-day-ko-we-as:* caribou meat), I hung them from the spit to cook.

The dripping fat juices from the meat on the spit caused the fire to sizzle and the flames to jump higher. The mingled aroma of woodsmoke and cooking meat was overpowering as it flooded my sense of smell and clung to my hair and clothes. Glancing away from the flames, I realized that a very attentive crowd of five drooling dogs had been attracted to the scent wafting from the fire. I stood and whistled loudly, bringing my brother and our two canoe companions to the fire along with a couple of cousins. No worries: there was lots of tea, mush soup, and meat for all. The dogs would have to settle for the putrid fish heads tossed to them by the young boy who had been given the task of cleaning the day's catch.

Everyone now cut off a piece of bark from an oak or elm tree to hold the hot meat they sliced from the spit. Each warrior also dipped his drinking vessel into the tea container and gulped down the hot liquid.

With meat juice spilling out of the corners of his mouth, my brother grinned and said, "Zhashagi, you cook as good as any woman."

They quickly finished the tea, and I again filled the container, adding more heated stones. This time I used the foliage of a cedar tree to flavour the water.

While they waited for the tea to boil, they dipped their drinking vessels into the heated corn mush and scooped it out of the cup with their fingers. After finishing their mush, some wiped their hands on the grass, on their pants, or on the nearest dog within reach. Then they finished the new batch of tea. Very few words were spoken; eating was a serious undertaking, completed with a few rounds of belching, farting, and a sudden rush to the nearest tree.

I left the fire to find my tree and then upon returning doused the flames with water. We didn't need a forest fire following us down this small river.

Once all the fires were completely put out, dogs and people were quick to step into their respective canoes and continue the journey. The river we were on was a connecting stream to a system of lakes that would take us to our villages another day or two away. There would be one small portage on this river, but it was steep going up and then coming down the other side. The river at this time of year of the aabita-niibino-giizis (*a-bi-ta-knee-bino-gee-sus:* Berry Moon — July) was deep enough to paddle in most spots, but there were two areas where we would have to get out — the portage being the second. The first place we would have to get out was a short stretch of white water that wasn't deep enough to shoot through. We would have to walk in the water and guide our jiimaan (*g-mawn:* canoe) through the rocks.

Paddling under the hot mid-afternoon sun, I faintly heard the sound of water rushing over rocks, telling us we were close to where we would have to get into the river and pull the boats. As the other three paddled, I steered the canoe toward the shore where all of us could easily exit and wade the river past this rocky hindrance. Misko swiftly stood on his haunches as we neared the shore, emitting a low, throaty growl and perking his ears. There was probably some sort of wild animal nearby that he had caught the scent of and was trying to identify.

This part of the waterway wound through a thick forest that not even the sun's strong rays could penetrate. The warriors who had left their canoes for the shore to scout ahead and to guard the rest of us from any trouble were soon swallowed up by the darkness as they ventured in.

Forgetting the dog's agitation, I stepped into the water to guide the boat through the shallow rapids. The river rocks were slippery, and I watched as a few men lost their footing and fell into the bubbling froth. The two women and the youngest boy stayed in their respective canoes. Most of the dogs leaped into the river to follow their human companions. Misko stayed in the canoe, still growling.

As I skirted the shoreline, the flies left the cover of the woods and feasted on my bare skin. Skittering fish swam between my legs, with the odd one nibbling at my toes.

Warriors were strung out along the shores of the river. They waded to the spot in the stream where the water deepened enough to get back into the canoes. Here they all grouped together and waited for the boats as they came down single file.

The forest seemed too quiet to me. All the birds and insects had stopped their racket. Then the shrill scream of a solitary diindiisi (*tchin-dees*: blue jay) alerted the forest, setting off the other birds and creating a deafening chorus. One of our warriors who had been scouting ahead slid down the embankment into the stream, reddening the water around him and the gathering canoes.

At that same moment as another boat reached the closely knit cluster at the end of the rapids, I took my eye off where I was walking to watch as the body slid into the water among our canoes. In that instant I slipped, Misko let out a fierce bark, and I fell into the river, grasping the boat and simultaneously hearing what I thought were several whirring sounds. Then there was an intense burning in the centre of my left hand.

An arrow had pinned my left hand to the canoe hull. I couldn't feel any pain, but neither could I remove my hand. Misko was now barking continually because of the screams of the women and the dead and dying warriors. I gazed up at the opposite shore and caught sight of a Nadowessioux warrior with two black lines painted across his face and a red streak on his forehead. I knew this man. He was a sworn enemy of the Anishinaabe and as ruthless as they came. Óta Heȟáka (*oh'-tay he-ha-ka*: Many Elk) was his Nadowessioux name, a warrior who wore many eagle feathers because of the Anishinaabe scalps he had taken.

The Nadowessioux were wading into the river, swinging their war axes, and meeting our warriors who had survived the initial onslaught of arrows in a brutal hand-to-hand struggle.

"Misko, stop your noise!" I cried. "Lie down!"

The dog, startled by my raised voice, immediately obeyed and lay down in the boat with a thump. Turning my eyes to the opposite shore, I spotted where I could get to a landing, remove the arrow, and return to help my people. As I approached the shore, a large rabbit was sitting there on his haunches and seemed to wave at me to come to him. I was starting to feel the effect of the arrow now, and I was wracked with chills. Blood coursed down the side of the canoe, colouring both it and the water red. When I clambered onto the shore, I looked up into the eyes of a tall warrior. He reached down and grabbed me, pulling the canoe and myself to shore. Then he broke the arrow, releasing my hand.

I gazed up again and asked, "Who are you?"

"Nanabozho!"

Then I blacked out.

8

TȞATȞÁŊKA(BUFFALO)

CHAŊKU WAŠTE

"Tell me about the tȟatȟáŋka (*tah-tohn'kah:* buffalo), Chaŋku Wašte (*chan-koo wash-tay:* Good Path)," said my nephew, Tȟáȟča Čiŋčá (*tah-ka shin-sha:* Deer Child).

"It's the smell, the sound, the dust, the shaking of the earth by the huge beast that creates such an excitement among us," I told him. "The following of the herd by the šuŋgmánitu tȟáŋka (*shoon-gur'mah-nee-tee tanka:* wolf) who is always there preying on the old, the young, and the sick, keeping the herd strong by culling the weak. Then there is the *pteyáȟpaya* (*pa-tay-pay-ah:* cowbird) that's so busy following the beast and eating the insects the herd stirs up. It won't take time to make a nest. It lays its eggs in the nests of other birds along the way. It's all these things and many more that create the mystery of this creature."

In the background of the herd, the sun sparkled off the Mnišá Wakpá (*mnee-shah wah-koh'-pah:* Red River, also called Wine River by the Lakȟóta) as it streamed through the tall prairie grass.

"The Wakȟáŋ Tȟáŋka (*wakhan thanka:* Great Mystery) created this animal for all the animals, our people, and other tribes to make use of for survival," I continued. "It supplies us with everything we need, from food, to weapons, to eating utensils, clothing, the making of our lodges, and even the dung we use for our fires."

"Uncle, how can our people kill such a large and powerful animal?"

"He's difficult to slay," I replied. "We have to use all our trickery and skill to bring this animal down."

We were lying on a bluff downwind from the huge herd, watching as they grazed on the prairie grass that came up to the large beasts' shoulders. The sun's warmth made me drowsy. Around us other warriors and young boys from our village observed the same amazing spectacle as we did. The herd was huge, and we could see neither the end nor the beginning. We had been waiting many days for this herd to come near our lands and had travelled from our forest homes (west of present-day Leech Lake, Minnesota) to the prairie's edge.

As we lay there, we witnessed a pack of a dozen wolves harass an old and feeble cow. The pack had separated the animal away from the herd to an area where the grass was sparser. There the wolves took turns attacking her from behind. She managed to kick free a couple of times and attempted to return to the safety of the herd, using her horns to defend herself. The yelping of the wolves as she struck them with her head made them realize she still had some fight in her.

The grunts of the cow and the snarls of the wolves carried to our ears but seemingly went unnoticed by the rest of the herd. This was a death struggle that had only one ending. The outcome came swiftly as the aged cow's strength finally gave out. Two of the wolves desperately held on as they tore at her legs, collapsing her rear quarters into the swirling mass of the pack. There the beast's life ended and the Great Mystery made a gift to the wolf pack.

If the wolves had attacked a calf, the outcome might have been different; calves were always protected. The old cow had lived her life and the herd wouldn't risk defending her. She was sacrificed because of her age.

Tȟáȟča Čiŋčá never said a word while the kill went on. He just watched. Then he turned to me and asked, "Is that how our people kill the buffalo?"

"No, we use our weapons instead of our teeth!" I replied.

He looked at me and started to giggle, and soon we were both laughing as we lay back in the warm grass and gazed at the sky. Then the other men and boys who had been watching the herd came over to where we were to talk about how we should go about our hunt for these huge beasts.

"Chaŋku Wašte," said SnázA (*snee'-zhay:* Scar), "there are no cliffs or rock faces near enough for us to stampede them toward. We'll have to either hunt them on foot in the open or make a čhaŋkáškapi (*chon-kos'kay:* fence)."

"We'll make the fence," I said. "SnázA, you and a few of the younger boys stay here. If anything happens that disturbs the herd or if the end of the animals comes in sight, send one of the boys back with the news. As of yet, there's no end in sight on the horizon and the trailing wolves aren't going to stampede them. If the end does come to pass before we're back, follow the herd, making sure we know where you're going by leaving a sign. I don't think they'll leave this area for several suns. The grass is too plentiful and there's ample fresh water nearby."

Then I motioned to the others and we took off at a run, heading for the village we had previously set up. We had left our winter encampment at Leech Lake less than a moon ago. Now I would have to ask the women to move the camp again, closer to the herd. Arriving at the encampment, I noticed that many of our younger warriors were absent. I approached my friend, Ógleiglúzašá (*oga-lee-sha*: Wears a Red Shirt), and asked him where the young warriors were.

He answered that Óta Heȟáka (*oh'-tay he-ha-ka*: Many Elk), my son, had sent the camp éyapaha (*eh-a-pa-ha*: crier) through the village asking for Dream Warriors. Óta Heȟáka had dreamed of a battle with the Ȟaȟátȟuŋwaŋ (*ha-ha-ton-wan*: Anishinaabe) on a distant river he knew about. That morning, after the dream, he had sent the crier to ask for warriors who had experienced the same dream.

"How many left with him?" I asked.

"Around twenty, plus six dogs," Ógleiglúzašá replied.

"Why now?" I exclaimed. "That's a lot of Dream Warriors who have had the same dream about a battle!"

"You know Óta Heȟáka. When there's a war to make on the Ȟaȟátȟuŋwaŋ, he doesn't sit idly. He goes in headfirst!"

"Yes, I do know, but it doesn't change anything," I said. "We need warriors for this hunt. The food and the robes that the great beast will supply us with will feed and provide shelter and warmth for our entire village for many moons. Even the loss of those six dogs Óta Heȟáka took with him will be felt on this hunt. If we fail because he decided war was more of a deterrent to starvation than a successful hunt for buffalo, how then can he ever expect to be a leader? A dream is powerful, but so is starvation!"

I turned to SnázA. "Have our people take down the lodges. They have to travel to the hunt site and start building the stone and brush piles for the fence before the main part of the herd passes. An enclosure for the kill also has to be constructed. With a village of four hundred, we only have seventy warriors. Now we're down to fifty. This hunt needs every man, woman, child, and dog to be successful. So, SnázA, do what's necessary. I'll go to our brothers who are camped on the Kȟaŋǧí Ȟupáhu Wakpá (*kohn'-gay hoo'-pah wah-koh'-pah:* Crow Wing River) to ask for their help. I should be back to the herd in six or seven suns. Start the fence and corral once you get there."

The people I was going to ask for help with the hunt would be near the Kȟaŋǧí Ȟupáhu Wakpá this time of year. They were a group of only a hundred and fifty, with fewer than thirty warriors. They hunted deer and elk, gathered nuts and berries, and fished. The little band was able to survive because of the abundance of small game in its area, and its needs weren't as great as our group of more than four hundred.

The leader of these people was called SápA Ziŋtkála (*sah'-pah zint'-kah-lah*: Black Bird) and had been a friend for many years.

"Ťháȟča Čiŋčá, pick two dogs," I said. "We're going on a trip!"

Leaving during the early dawn, Ťháȟča Čiŋčá and I kept up a steady running pace. With the two dogs leading the way, we had no fear of being surprised by bears or men. For three days we ran until dark and our eyes couldn't find the way anymore. Each night we made a fire and ate the dried meat we had brought with us. Berries and roots we found were added to our meal and also used to make tea. The dogs looked after themselves; one day they chased down a rabbit, other days they survived on small rodents they discovered rustling in the grass. Each night we slept by the fire with the dogs. The night air was warm now, since it was the wípazukȟa-wašté-wí (*wi-pa-zoo-ka-wash-tay-wi*: Moon When the Berries Are Good — June). It took us most of the first day to leave the prairie and enter the forest. Once into the woodlands, we came across a warrior trail that would take us to SápA Ziŋtkála's camp.

The morning of the third day we were hit with a thunderstorm. We watched through the tree canopy as lightning lit up the sky and the two dogs whimpered with fear each time thunder boomed. Rain leaked through the canopy of the forest, drenching Ťháȟča Čiŋčá and me and producing a glistening sheen on the dogs' coats.

By the time we arrived at the village of SápA Ziŋtkála, the rain had stopped and we were starting to dry out. I gave Ťháȟča Čiŋčá two rawhide ropes usually used to secure enemy prisoners on the trail and asked him to tie up the dogs for the time being and stay with them at the edge of the camp. I was in no mood to separate a bunch of fighting dogs at this time. Once the camp dogs realized there was no danger from these two, we could let them loose.

Members of the akíčita (*ah-kee-chee-tah*: camp guards and/or warrior society responsible for hunting and war parties) took me to the lodge of SápA Ziŋtkála. Once there, we smoked and talked of past battles and hunts. After we ate, I told him about my problem and the opportunity that could benefit both of our peoples.

"Chaŋku Wašte," he said to me, "my warriors will welcome a chance to hunt buffalo and our wives and daughters will be delighted to obtain hides and everything else the great beasts have to offer. It will be an appreciated change from the deer and fish we're accustomed to. Tonight you and your nephew will eat with us and we'll strike the lodges first thing in the morning. I'll send half of my warriors and young boys with you to arrive before the main camp to help your people with the preparations for the hunt. The rest of us should get there just in time for the beginning of the hunt. With so much to move, the group will be two to three suns behind. We'll bury all our extra firewood, winter robes, and other items we don't need until we return in the fall. There's no need to take the extra weight. Tonight you and your nephew must share my lodge."

I left the home of SápA Ziŋtkála and took some food to Tȟáȟča Čiŋčá and the dogs. Once we untied them, there was some serious sniffing, growling, and posturing between them and the alpha camp dog. Our two animals showed submission and were allowed to enter. Ťháȟča Čiŋčá and I left the dogs to their night's fate and entered the lodge of my friend where we quickly went to our dream worlds.

The morning brought brilliant sunshine and the buzz of a busy encampment. There was a constant clamour of people talking and the rattling of lodgepoles as the wakhéya (*wa-kay'ah*: lodges, teepees, dwellings) were taken down. Some of SápA Ziŋtkála's people lived in sod huts, which years ago were more common, but lately they had more access to buffalo and other animal hides, enabling them to replace most of their sod shelters with hide teepees.

Catching the aroma of the early-morning meals being prepared from the surrounding firepits, I felt my stomach contract, telling me it was time to eat. SápA Ziŋtkála's wife, Ťhawíŋyela (*tah-win-yela:* Doe), handed us some thíŋpsiŋla (*timp-sila:* turnip) when we exited the lodge — one of my favourite foods and very popular among my people. It was filling and sustaining, and I made sure I stuffed some extra chunks into my pouch for later in the day. Looking at Ťháȟča Čiŋčá, I saw that he had his cheeks stuffed like a chipmunk and was still trying to cram more into his mouth. I had an intense desire to slap both sides of his cheeks, but I knew if I did that most of what was in his mouth would end up on my chest.

"Ťháȟča Čiŋčá," I said, "make sure you take some of the turnip destined for your mouth and put it in your pouch for a midday meal."

107

With a full mouth all he could do was stare at me and smile. I then left him to his meal and entered the nearby forest to rid myself of my night's body collections.

The village soon disappeared before my eyes. The Lakȟóta women were experts when it came to moving camp. By the time the sun was barely above the horizon, the encampment was in motion. The people moved like a meandering river flowing as one. The women, children, and dogs were strung out in a long line. There were close to four hundred dogs, and each of these animals carted more than their body weight on a hupák'iŋ (*hoo-pock-een:* travois or pole sled). Some of the dogs had to be led on a leather rope by a child, but on the whole, they followed the dog ahead of them. A few of the dogs' travois carried cradled children.

The hokšíčala (*oke-shee-chah'-lah:* baby) was always wrapped on a cradleboard. The board extended above the infant's head to protect against sudden jolts or falls. The bunting was made from animal hide, and the mother decorated it with shells or feathers. Small articles for the baby to play with hung from the bowed wood strip shaped around the child's head. Moss was stuffed into the cradle to absorb the young one's fluids. The plank was carried on the mother's back, fastened to a travois, or hung or propped against trees. Until children could walk this was their home.

SápA Ziŋtkála and his men guarded the procession front, back, and sides. With them were their war dogs, who acted as sentinels, ranging farther afield than the men. The war dogs were bred and trained for battle and hunting, whereas the other dogs were kept as beasts of burden and for food when there was a shortage of game.

Tȟáȟča Čiŋčá and I left camp at the same time as the column. With us were ten warriors and fifteen young boys around Tȟáȟča Čiŋčá's age. Our group kept up a steady running pace for the whole day. For the next few suns we would keep a constant tempo from dawn to dusk. At night the young boys gathered firewood when we were in the forest and aged buffalo dung once we were on the prairie. Both items were used for warmth and cooking, although the wood tended to have a better smell than the dung.

When we reached the tall grass of the prairie, we found a well-used game trail that helped speed our journey. As we hurried through the tall grass that came up to our heads, something to my left caught my eye. It was a curious tȟáȟčasaŋla (*tah-kchah-sohn-lah:* antelope). He bounded beside our group, jumping and looking inquisitively at us. A warrior ahead of us timed the animal's leaping perfectly, and that night we feasted on fresh meat.

During the days with our new companions, we enjoyed a faster pace than we had done coming to their village. My two dogs stayed by our sides, but the four dogs brought by SápA Ziŋtkála and his people raced ahead alongside two sinewy warriors.

"Uncle, why are those men and dogs running so far ahead?" Tȟáȟča Čiŋčá asked on the evening of the second day.

"Because of our enemies, we have to be cautious they don't surprise us," I replied.

"Who are our enemies?"

"The Ȟaȟáthuŋwaŋ," I said.

"Why are they our enemies?"

"It's a long story."

"Uncle, we still have a long way to go and I'm a good listener."

"Well, in that case, if you can keep up with me as we run, I'll tell you the story of why the Ȟaȟáthuŋwaŋ and Lakȟóta are enemies."

9

KȞAŊǦI WAKPÁ (CROW CREEK)

CHAŊKU WAŠTE

"In the time of my grandfather," I told Tȟáȟča Čiŋčá, "our people came from the southern part of this great land on the lower Wakpá Atkúku (*wak-pa' at-ku-ku*: Mississippi River). Forty winters ago the Lakȟóta made the decision to leave the region because of constant intertribal warfare, starvation from crop failures, and the lack of game due to the infringement of other tribes into our hunting grounds.

"That spring scouts were sent to the north, west, and east to find new lands to live on. They were told to go twenty suns in the direction they were assigned to travel, then on the twentieth day they were to come back. When they returned forty suns later, the four main villages were gathered at one location and the scouts made reports of what they had seen in the directions they had journeyed.

After much talk among the Elders, it was decided to go north where there were many lakes and rivers to fish as well as deer, bear, elk, and small game to hunt.

"They left during the čhaŋpȟásapa wí (*can-pa'-sa-pa wi:* Moon of Cherries Blackening — July). During the move, they suffered greatly, barely living off the land. The Lakȟóta at that time numbered around twenty-five hundred people, with six hundred of them warriors and young men. Each family had thirty to forty dogs to carry their belongings on travois. During these times when food became scarce while travelling, they had to eat some of these dogs. However, for each dog that was eaten, someone had to carry that animal's load or leave it behind on the trail.

"After twenty suns, their scouts said they were still a long way from the destination. One group of Lakȟóta then decided it couldn't travel north any longer. That band had suffered many hardships during the winter and was in a weakened state of body and mind. During the move, these people, among all of the villagers, had lost the most members to starvation on the trail. The scouts who had journeyed to the west had originally told of a river, tall grasses, and herds of antelope and buffalo. Now this exhausted band made the determination to follow those scouts to that spot on the thíŋta (*tin'-ta:* prairie). There would be rivers to cross getting there, but the distance would be shorter than where they were headed now. The scouts were to lead them to the area near the banks of the Mníšoše Wakpá (*mini-so-se wa-pah:* Missouri River) to a small stream called Kȟaŋǧi Wakpá (*kohnȧy wa-pah:* Crow Creek).

"Over three hundred Lakȟóta left the main group that day many years ago. My grandfather's people made it to where we now live and divided themselves into their old villages of past years. Our people thrived over those years and enjoyed relative peace.

"The Lakȟóta who had split off and gone west settled on Kȟaŋǧi Wakpá and prospered in the early years. They planted crops and hunted buffalo when the beasts drew near them.

"The antelope, though, proved to be very fast and difficult in the beginning to chase down. However, the hunters came up with a plan and were able to train their dogs to pursue this swift animal. One group of huntsmen took its dogs to a knoll to watch as the other party and its dogs chased the animal in that direction. Once the pursuit was close to them, the warriors on the knoll sent their dogs to turn the animal back into the other hunters. The dogs then continually chased the animal back and forth between the two groups until in the end the creature collapsed from exhaustion and the warriors made the kill.

"These prairie Lakȟóta soon discovered they had moved into a region that others started to inhabit. Eventually, they had to harvest trees from the area to erect a protective wall and then make a ditch to encircle it to keep their enemies from overrunning them. Life became harsh. The rain stopped coming, the skies were cloudless, the sun baked the earth around them, and their crops withered and died from the drought.

"During this time, a fierce tribe from the land of the rising sun entered the lands east of us. We called them the Ȟaȟátȟuŋwaŋ. It was an uneasy peace. Both nations

came across each other during hunting trips, and warriors on each side died in those encounters. While my
grandfather was alive, there were no outright battles until
one fateful buffalo hunt by the Lakȟóta at Kȟaŋǧi Wakpá.

"The Kȟaŋǧi Wakpá people were near starvation after
a very severe winter. Their crops had been poor the previous summer and the buffalo herds seemed to be avoid-
ing them. Hunting the fleet antelope became difficult
for the warriors because of their feebleness from lack
of nourishment. Food was rationed among the women,
children, and Elders. Death that winter stalked all the
family lodges. It got so bad that they ate their dogs and
anything else they could kill or forage in their weakened state, including snakes, mice, grass, and the hides
they were clothed in. Select warriors who were proven
hunters were given extra rations to keep them strong
for hunting trips.

"On one of those trips in the late spring, four warriors
found a huge herd of buffalo to the east. They were able
to slay one and brought back as much meat as they and
their dogs could carry. The buffalo were grazing near a
cliff (present-day Blue Mounds State Park) the Kȟaŋǧi
Wakpá Lakȟóta had used before as a buffalo jump. The
scouts told their people it would take the hunting band
four to five days to journey to the jump, maybe more
because of their frail state. The buffalo had lots of grass
where they were and there was no fear of them moving
on before the hunters got to them.

"The decision was made among the Elders that thirty
of the strongest warriors would leave immediately along
with some dogs. After they departed, the women who

were able to travel would follow behind with the rest of the healthy warriors and most of the village dogs who had survived the lean times. This group would arrive a day or two after the first party. The children, Elders, and remaining men and women who were too weak stayed behind.

"Unknown, though, to the Lakȟóta, about a hundred Ȟaȟátȟuŋwaŋ had come down from the north and stumbled onto the herd. They were over fifteen suns from their permanent homes where the rice beds, abundance of maple trees for sugar, and the teeming lakes of whitefish, along with ample game, kept them well fed. Starvation didn't drive the Ȟaȟátȟuŋwaŋ to Kȟaŋǧi Wakpá. The search for new lands did. Again, unknown to the Lakȟóta, the Ȟaȟátȟuŋwaŋ had made camp on the cliffs where the Lakȟóta planned to drive the buffalo to their deaths.

"The Lakȟóta had had small skirmishes in the past with the Ȟaȟátȟuŋwaŋ over hunting grounds, but nothing ever major. Our people had always hunted the buffalo where they had lived previously on the lower Mississippi, and when we moved north to Kȟaŋǧi Wakpá, we continued the practice. The Ȟaȟátȟuŋwaŋ came from a place where buffalo rarely travelled and weren't familiar with the beasts, how to hunt them, or how the Lakȟóta pursued them.

"Our warriors arrived near the herd's location on a hot midsummer day. In the distance toward the horizon in the east, they could see the rising dust of the herd as some of the buffalo rolled on their backs to rid themselves of flies and tufts of hair.

"The sun's rays created torrid heat in the plains that rose from the ground like a campfire, baking the hunters' feet and their dogs' paws. It made both the men's and the animals' tongues swell from the sweltering temperature and lack of water. The warriors found a small bubbling spring and drank their fill along with the dogs, then topped up their skin containers with the cool water. Here they applied grease to their bodies to protect their skins from the intense glare of the sun. After travelling for a time until mid-afternoon, they were now upon the herd. The men stood overlooking the animals, their bare brown skins glistening in the bright sunshine. They had brought more than fifty dogs with them, and the animals lay on the ground panting and salivating as they waited for their cue to start the chase.

"The decision was made that twenty of the warriors would turn as much of the herd as they could toward the eastern cliffs by running from the west, waving robes at them, yelling, and setting the dogs loose. The remaining men and dogs would come from the north and south to keep the animals from spinning away. The plan worked to perfection, and the unsuspecting Lakȟóta stampeded more than thirty of the beasts to the cliffs where the Ȟaȟátȟuŋwaŋ were camped.

"That fateful day the Ȟaȟátȟuŋwaŋ had only women, children, Elders, and a few warriors in the camp. The rest of the men and their dogs had trekked to the north of the herd to hunt. Most of the Ȟaȟátȟuŋwaŋ were in their lodges, seeking shelter from the sun's heat, and only a few were outside to witness firsthand the spectacle of these immense animals bearing down and trapping them between the onrush and the cliffs behind. Their screams of warning came too late for the people in the lodges. As they stepped out through the entrance openings, they were trampled and caught up in the charge of the stampeding beasts over the sheer drop behind them. It was a tangle of bellowing animals, crumpling lodges, and shrieking people as they hit the ground below.

"When the Lakȟóta came upon the scene, it took them a few minutes to realize what had happened. The crushed makeshift shelters and bodies of the residents confused the Lakȟóta men. Our people hadn't scouted ahead because they knew the location of the cliff where they wanted to drive the animals and there never was any thought of someone camping on the cliff approach. They stood on the edge, gazed below, and saw an entanglement of human bodies among the dead and dying buffalo. Looking at one another in bewilderment at the sight of the broken bodies below, they knew what had to be done. The Lakȟóta warriors descended the cliff to put human and beast out of their misery and to begin the work of burying the dead. Once that was done, they turned their attention to preparing the animals for the women to cut up for transportation back to their village.

"In the distance, a warrior, a young boy, and their two dogs observed the carnage, turned northward, and ran off to find the Ȟaȟátȟuŋwaŋ hunting party.

"The Lakȟóta women and remaining warriors arrived later the next day. The harvesting of the meat then commenced in earnest. Our people replenished their bodies which up until then had been wasting away from starvation. After the first few days, enough of the meat had been cut up so that they were able to prepare loads for more than a hundred dogs, each pulling a travois to take back to the village for the weakened women, children, and Elders who were there. It only took about a dozen people to handle the dogs on the return trip. Four women and eight warriors left with the procession. All the women pulled a sled along with a few of the men, leaving the remaining warriors free to scout ahead and guard the small party.

"The group had brought more than five hundred dogs to handle the transportation of the meat, and in the next couple of days another band left with more dogs. All this time the Lakȟóta never sent out any scouts to watch for enemies, or bears attracted by the stench of the aging buffalo carcasses. Unknown to them, about fifteen Ȟaȟátȟuŋwaŋ warriors were spying from a distance. It was the hunting party that had been away during the stampede over the cliff. Now the Ȟaȟátȟuŋwaŋ warriors were biding their time for a chance to strike back. They watched as their adversaries below slowly lessened their numbers by sending loaded pole sleds toward the prairie with the meat. Attacking any of the departing groups on the open plain would be dangerous, since our people would see them coming, eliminating the advantage of surprise. A battle in the open was always to be avoided because of the potential for devastating casualties.

"On the sixth day after our people had run the buffalo over the cliffs, they were left with only about a dozen men and women to prepare the final load. The Ȟaȟátȟuŋwaŋ warriors took this opportunity to attack. Two men and three women were cutting up one of the last animals, a beast that had died a couple of hundred steps away from where the rest had perished. The others were loading the pole sleds for transportation home the next day.

"The Lakȟóta dogs started barking and howling when they heard the distinctive war whistle and then the war cry of the charging Ȟaȟátȟuŋwaŋ. The enemy immediately set upon the group separated from the rest of our people, quickly slaying the women with their clubs and scalping the two men alive. The Lakȟóta warriors quickly shot as many arrows as they could in rapid succession and at the same time our enemies returned fire. The distance between the two groups of warriors was at the range limit for their arrows. The attack ended as rapidly as it began, with the Ȟaȟátȟuŋwaŋ retreating from the barrage of projectiles.

"Our people suffered the loss of three women and a dog. The Ȟaȟátȟuŋwaŋ were seen carrying two of their wounded warriors from the battlefield. The two Lakȟóta men who had been scalped would live, but the women had to work fast to apply maggots from some rotting buffalo meat onto their heads to ease the wounds. After the maggots cleaned the men's scalps, the women smeared on the juice of the húčhiŋška (hue-chin-ska: milkweed) to stop the bleeding. Then they used yapízapi iyéčheča (ya-pee-zapi eye-che-ca: dandelion) juice to help with the healing. If done quickly, the men would be scarred but alive.

"Our people didn't pursue the attackers. A battle in the open would amount to more casualties than they wanted, and they hadn't yet regained all their strength from the lack of food those past few moons. Instead they buried their dead women. The dog they ate that night.

Then they posted guards and quickly finished their work. They would leave at first light and be gone from this place of death."

"So, Uncle, that's how the bad blood was started?" asked Tȟáȟča Čiŋčá.

"It was the beginning, Nephew, but what happened the next summer sealed the hatred between the Lakȟóta and Hahatonwan," I said.

"What took place that caused this to continue to our own day?" asked Tȟáȟča Čiŋčá.

"A terrible massacre at Kȟaŋǧi Wakpá," I replied. "Even though what had happened to the Ȟaȟátȟuŋwaŋ during the buffalo hunt was an accident because of the lack of scouting ahead by the Lakȟóta, what the Ȟaȟátȟuŋwaŋ did at Kȟaŋǧi Wakpá was planned and carried out as an act of all-out war against the Lakȟóta.

"That fatal late summer day twenty-five summers ago was stifling hot in the village of the Kȟaŋǧi Wakpá Lakȟóta. The people were once more hungry because the buffalo weren't coming near their hunting grounds, the rains had stopped, and the crops were again dying. Our people had built an enclosure of upright logs that they lived behind for protection from their enemies. The two men who had been scalped by the Ȟaȟátȟuŋwaŋ the previous summer had lived but carried the scars of the battle, along with others of their community who had fought many small battles with our enemies. Warriors had been lost in these battles and others were slowly healing from the wounds obtained in the skirmishes. That day, for added protection, they were digging a ditch around their enclosure that they planned to flood with water from the nearby creek. Except for a few Elders and some sentries, everyone was either in the trench or pulling soil up in rawhide bags and then dumping it.

"At around midday they heard the shriek of a war whistle, then the war cries of the attacking Ȟaȟáthuŋwaŋ. Catching the sentries off guard, the Ȟaȟáthuŋwaŋ bowled through them on the run, slashing with knives and swinging war clubs at our people's heads. Once they neared the ditch, they fired arrows in volleys and sent some of the villagers on the sides tumbling backward into the pit and onto the people below. Next, the Ȟaȟáthuŋwaŋ made it a bloodbath by standing on the edges and throwing spears and rocks and shooting arrows down on the defenceless below. The attack was so sudden and ruthless that the Lakȟóta had no time to reach for their weapons. The invaders then jumped into the trench and hacked and chopped our people, rendering them unrecognizable. When they were finished, they got out of the ditch and threw any corpses that remained above on top of the dismembered remains below. Then they turned their attention to the village dogs, killing and tossing them onto the animals' vanquished masters.

"The Ȟaȟáthuŋwaŋ attackers only took two captives: a fifteen-year-old boy and his father, who had valiantly tried to defend the village. That night the Ȟaȟáthuŋwaŋ shared a meal of dog with their prisoners. The next morning they gave each a quiver of arrows, a knife, and a bow, then sent them east to tell their Lakȟóta cousins what had happened. The man and boy were also told to let their people know that the Ȟaȟáthuŋwaŋ would never forget what the Lakȟóta had done to the women, children, and Elders at the buffalo jump. From that day forward our people would be known to the Ȟaȟátȟuŋwaŋ as the Nadowessioux and our enemies would kill any of us on sight."

"Uncle, who was the boy and his father they sent back?" asked Tȟáȟča Čiŋčá.

"The father's name was Sutá Wičháša (*soo-tah wee-chah'-shah:* Strong Man), your grandfather," I replied. "The boy was me."

"So that's why we hate the Ȟaȟátȟuŋwaŋ so much," Tȟáȟča Čiŋčá muttered.

As I ended the story, we exited the heat and dust of the tall grass and came out onto a small hillock overlooking the prairie. "Nephew, look!"

There, ahead of us, as far as our eyes could see, where the earth met the sky, was a solid mass of buffalo.

10

RETURN TO THE RIVER

ZHASHAGI

I dreamed I was stumbling toward the far shore, my mind going in and out of blackness, my legs not doing what I asked them to do, water over my knees. My left hand was pinned to the canoe with an arrow, and my blood reddened the boat and the surrounding water. The sounds of the battle my dog, Misko, and I were leaving behind seemed to fade in the distance, but during the moments that my mind cleared, the noise grew closer again.

It was when I approached the shore that the hand of the warrior reached out for me. I also recalled asking his name and his reply: "Nanabozho."

Now I was being awakened by the rough tongue and whimpering of Misko. Upon opening my eyes, I found myself lying on my back in a pile of cedar branches beside a small fire with the smell of cedar tea boiling in a vessel over the fire. The dream I had experienced before being awakened was one of remembrance.

My hand had a slight prickle in it as if I had come into contact with a thistle. It was completely covered with moss and wrapped with leather to hold in the healing medicine. Beside me was a spear, but there was no sign of my rescuer.

I had no idea where I was in the forest and hoped Misko could lead the two of us back to the river. Sitting beside the fire, I gathered my thoughts and drank the hot tea. By sharing my meagre supply of corn and dried meat with the dog, he gave me his full attention and hopefully his co-operation in what was to come.

Even though my hand tingled, there was no pain. The warrior Nanabozho must be a *nenaandawi'iwed* (*ni-na-na-da-we-e-wed*: healer) to take the pain away from a wound such as I had.

I had no idea how long I was in the dream world; time was elusive at the moment. My best guess was that I had only slept the remainder of the day and had awakened the morning after the battle. Looking at the sky, I searched for the sun through the dense overhead forest cover. The movement of the branches from the wind enabled the sun's rays to enter through the sheltering limbs like droplets of rain. Spots of sunlight danced on the forest floor like embers in a fire. When the winds died down, the sun filtered through as soft beams of light, with specks of dust and insects inside the lighted areas.

Still, I was unable to determine the time of day because the woodland's branch limbs hid the sun's place in the sky from me. "Misko?" I asked. "Can you lead the two of us from this place of safety back to where we left our people at the river?"

He cocked his head as if to listen and stared at me with unblinking eyes. I turned to the fire, reaching into my medicine bag for some tobacco and tossed it into the flames, saying a short prayer of thanks to Gichi-Manidoo (Great Spirit) and asking him to guide us back to our village.

Grabbing the spear, I walked around the camp area until Misko caught his own scent from our back trail. By following his scent back, a dog could always be depended on to return to where he started from if he got lost on a hunt. This was my only hope to find the river again. I was puzzled, however, as to why my rescuer had left me alone after bringing me here.

When Nanabozho was seen as the Great Rabbit, he was known as Mishaabooz, which was my first sighting of him that day when he pulled me from the river. Known as a powerful shape-shifter and a co-creator of the world, he was born of a human mother, Wiininwaa (Nourishment), and E-bangishimog, the Spirit of the West Wind. Nanabozho was sent to earth by Gichi-Manidoo to teach the Anishinaabe. Once here, he gave us our religion known as Midewiwin (Grand Medicine Society) and named all the plants and animals. His actions had saved my life this past day, and for that I owed my life in return.

Misko quickly discovered the trail back to the battle site and led me through the forest at a fast pace. The game trail we travelled on was old and overgrown, but no problem for a low-to-the-ground four-legged creature.

An erect follower like me, though, received a fair share of thorn scrapes and lashes to the face from branches. Blood trickled down my arms and face from the abrasions, and Misko's scurrying stirred up an infestation of winged forest biters that congregated around my nostrils, ears, and eyes, entering my mouth as I gasped for air.

Our path led us to a small spring exiting a rocky area. Misko and I stopped and slaked our thirst from a tiny pool of clear water kept fresh by the liquid exiting from the rocks on the opposite end, running out onto the forest floor, and disappearing into a crack in a large, flat rock below.

When the water left the pool, it streamed for a short distance on the bare ground. Scooping handfuls of mud from the little rivulet bed, I covered my exposed skin with the soothing coolness of the muck, giving my body immediate protection against the swarms of bugs. Misko gazed up at me, shaking his head and snorting to rid himself of the flying menaces that were now attacking his nose and eyes. Grasping the dog by the neck, I smeared mud on the areas where the insects were bothering him. This seemed to please the suffering animal, and then with a quick nod from me, we took off again, pushing our way through the hordes eager for quick nourishment from any warm-blooded creature that crossed their path. The mud I had applied now protected me from their bites, and as we loped through the forest, the only bothersome problem was the return of the thorns and branches.

Misko and I came upon the river as the huge ball of the disappearing sun reddened the dusk sky, streaking the river with bloody smears and providing me with a stark reminder that many Anishinaabe had lost their lives here.

The carnage of the battle lay on the opposite shore, and our sudden emergence from the dark woods scared off the crows, ravens, and ozaawaa-memengwaa (*o-zaa-wah me-mean-gwa:* yellow swallowtail). The ravens and crows had already removed the eyes from the dead and were now competing for the flesh of the lifeless bodies in and around the river. The wolves, however, weren't in any hurry to leave their newfound bounty. Whereas the birds and butterflies swiftly departed in a flurry of activity, the canines stood over their corpses and were prepared to defend the meals their keen sense of smell had led them to.

I recognized the faces of friends that for many days I had travelled with to and from the land of the Omashkiigoo. There were no women or children among the dead, leaving only two questions about their destiny. Were they captured, or did they escape?

Three Lakȟóta warriors had perished, each propped against a tree facing west, the direction they would travel to their Spirit World. There they sat with dried blood on their faces and flies buzzing around, preparing to lay eggs on the decaying bodies. The wolves, birds, and butterflies had yet to turn their attentions to these solitary corpses.

Nowhere could I see Omashkooz, my brother. This gave me hope, since there were many other unaccounted-for bodies, giving rise to the realization that several of the warriors had escaped death.

The sound of the river rushing over rocks and shallows and the sigh of the wind rustling through the leaves couldn't drown out the throaty growls and snaps of the wolves as they jostled and fought over their meals. Reaching down at my feet, I picked up some fist-sized river rocks, turned toward the wolves, and fired several stones in their direction, watching as many of my throws hit with resounding thumps followed by sharp yelps. My rock throwing and Misko's throaty growling and barking took the wolves by surprise, causing them to slink back into the nearby forest and disappear. I hoped they wouldn't return during the night to finish their gruesome meals before I could bury the bodies tomorrow.

My hand ached, but the wound wasn't causing me any fever or light-headedness. Whatever Nanabozho had done to repair my wound seemed to be working.

It was crucial that I find food. Entangled in some reeds along the riverbank, I discovered a container to make tea that must have fallen from one of our canoes and ended up here.

Walking along the shoreline, I came across a discarded bow and some arrows. I also located my canoe where I had left it, the sides still red with my blood. Pulling it out of the water, I dragged it into the undergrowth of the treeline and flipped it upside down to create a shelter for the evening. Then, taking my spear, I waded into the river. There I stood motionless with my weapon at the ready as Misko lay on the bank considering me with curiosity. Once the sun sank below the trees, I left the darkening and cooling water with three fish and seven clams. Removing the heads, skin, and guts, I tossed them to Misko, who made quick work of the scraps.

Soon I had a fire going with three fillets of fish hanging on a spit, which would satisfy my cravings for the time being. Spotting some violets, I picked, crushed, and sprinkled them into the boiling water to make a sweet tea. When I finished my tea, I refilled the container with river water, threw some more hot rocks from the fire in to bring the water to a boil, and dropped the clams in to cook. These I would eat in the morning before leaving.

After finishing my meal and daubing mud on my bare skin to keep the insects at bay, I crawled under the canoe to sleep, but not before fashioning a birchbark snake to hang on the canoe. This symbol would tell the wandering spirits of the dead Anishinaabe warriors that they were to journey to the Spirit World alone, leaving me here. The living never refused the dead supplies for their journey, so I left some corn I had and a few pieces of fish near the canoe for them.

I had a big job ahead of me to bury the fallen warriors' remains. I needed to wrap the bodies in birchbark, along with food and water to help them on their travels to the next world. Ceremonial drums should be played to contact the afterlife and tobacco offered to the long-departed spirits to guide the recent fallen warriors on their way. But with no drum and very little tobacco and food, I would have to make do with what I had and hope the spirits understood my dilemma.

Children were always kept away from funerals when possible. Because of their age, they could easily be tricked into falling into the grasp of spirits to accompany the dead on their journey. If children did attend, their foreheads were blackened to signal to the deceased that the young ones wouldn't be going to the afterlife with them. Children were also told to avoid eye contact with others in case the spirits tried to speak to them through another person.

I sat there for a while as the last rays of the sun caused the river to shift from red to gold. At the moment the river's colour changed, a mother duck swam by with twelve little ones behind, two of which disappeared below the water without a sound. The ginoozhe (*kin-nose-hay*: pike) ended up with the final say to this river of death's day. The beauty of this land held many dark secrets.

The last things I remembered before nodding off were the moonlight caressing the river's surface with its soft light, the soothing sound of gentle waves lapping the shore where Misko noisily slurped water, and then his grunt as he flopped beside me to rest.

The next morning I awoke to the smell of the decaying bodies nearby and the racket of a baapaase (*baa-pa-say*: woodpecker) pounding on a tree for its early meal. Then the woodpecker suddenly stopped, and glancing across the river, I noticed a jooweshk (killdeer) running around faking a broken wing to draw something away from its nest. Silently grabbing my weapons, I patted Misko on his head to quiet him as he emitted a deep growl. There was something or someone nearby. The woodpecker's sudden halt in tapping the tree for insects and the killdeer pulling off its diversionary ploy were all the warning I needed.

11

THE ANISHINAABE

ZHASHAGI

Misko and I lay hidden in the underbrush beneath the canoe, from where we could see the opposite bank. We watched as three large figures dressed in animal hides exited the dark confines of the forest. One was wearing a bearskin, another was draped in a cougar pelt, and the last sported the horns and hide of a deer. All carried weapons and their faces were painted. These men would strike fear in anyone who came upon them.

Crawling from the shelter of the canoe, I stood but stayed hidden behind a large oak tree. I peered around the massive trunk and took a deep breath. "Apiitendang Makwa (*a-pete-tan-den ma-kwa:* Proud Bear)!" I yelled.

The bearskinned warrior glanced at me, growled, and ran across the shallow part of the river where the attack had taken place. Once he arrived on the shore followed closely by the other two, he grabbed and nearly crushed me in a huge embrace. "You're alive, Zhashagi!"

"Yes!" I answered. "I'm so happy to see you and your two cousins!"

Apiitendang Makwa was strong and powerful in battle. Gichi Bizhiins (*gich-e be-zeans:* Big Cat), who wore the pelt of a cougar he had slain, struck quick and deadly and was an excellent hunter who never came back without a kill. Gizhiibatoo Inini (*giz-e-baa-too in-in-e:* Run Fast Man), who was clad in the skin of a deer, had no equal in running speed and struck like lightning in a fight. Together they were a formidable trio who had had many encounters with the Nadowessioux over the years.

They all wanted to know how I had survived the ambush, and I told them about Nanabozho. Taking off my wrappings, I showed them my wound.

All three looked at me in amazement. The wound was completely healed, and in its place was a scar about the size of a pebble on both sides of my hand where the arrow had entered and exited. Opening and closing the hand, I felt stiffness but no pain. My hand had completely healed in two days. I was stunned!

Apiitendang Makwa then spoke. "We're the scouts for about thirty warriors. Your brother suffered an arrow wound and survived along with twenty-five others. We were told the battle was fierce and the Nadowessioux drove many of our warriors away from the river. The ones in the canoes paddled downstream to save the trade goods they received from the Cree and then, after hiding the canoes, came back upstream and counterattacked. Most of our casualties were the ones the enemy had caught in the water on foot helping the canoes through the shallow rapids. The young boys were quick thinkers and escaped capture, while the two women who did suffer that fate were Nadowessioux captives from many years ago. They leave grieving families behind in our village. About five canoes of items obtained in trade during the past journey were lost, but the deaths of the warriors are far worse since they can't be replaced. Your brother said the leader of the enemy was someone the Nadowessioux call Óta Heȟáka."

"Yes," I said. "I also saw Óta Heȟáka. I'm sure it was his arrow that went through my hand."

Gichi Bizhiins then spoke. "Óta Heȟáka has attacked us several times. The Elders have given permission to gather warriors for a mourning revenge raid and to attack the enemy in its lair. When we left the village, the belts for wampum were being made to take to our allies, the Odishkwaagamii and Naadawe, to ask them to join us in war. Other Anishinaabe communities will be sent the red-ochre-painted belts to summon them to war also."

Apiitendang Makwa, Gichi Bizhiins, and Gizhiibatoo Inini) were lifelong friends and cousins. Each warrior wore the skin of the first animal he had killed. It was their belief that by wearing them, they took on the powers of the creatures when the beasts had been alive.

Once the other warriors reached the river, our fallen friends and families remains were rescued from the scavengers and wrapped in birchbark, then the funeral ceremony was performed. Rocks were piled on their graves to keep wolf packs from digging them up to devour.

That night was a solemn gathering around the fires before our trip back to my village. Everyone had revenge in their hearts for the losses that had occurred at this river. It was decided that our warriors would go to the Gaagaagiwigwani-ziibi (*gaa-gaa-gi-wig-wani-zee-bee*: Raven Feather River, also known as the Crow River to the Lakȟóta). There we would look for the camps of the Nadowessioux and take our bloody vengeance. But first we had to contact our allies for help. The loss of the warriors here had weakened us, thus the reason to call on our friends to the south for their aid in this coming encounter.

We reached my village early the next morning. At the river's edge we came upon children playing on the shore, catching frogs and fishing. A few of the older boys had a birchbark pot of hot resin to repair two canoes. One boy glanced up and asked, "Did you bring my father back?"

I avoided his question and strode up the embankment with my companions to the encampment. The first thing I sensed was the lack of smells. There was no distinct odour of food being cooked, and the aroma of wood from campfires was non-existent. All of the wanage-kogamigoon (*wan-a-gay-ko-ga-may-goon*: lodges) that had suffered losses from the river battle had birchbark snakes hanging by the front door. The female relatives wailed for their dead and would mourn the passing of their men for the next year. Some would give away all the deceased's possessions or burn them. At this moment they had no time for the living, not for cooking their meals or tending their fires. The sadness of death had overtaken many of the women in our village. That night a drum ceremony was held, and for the next four moons the camp lamented the departed and prayed they would be able to attain the afterlife.

After the fourth day, the council met and decided that early the next spring, once the ice left the Big Lake we called Anishinaabewi Gichigami, one group would be sent to our allies to the south with the red wampum belts to summon them to war. Another group would be dispatched to our Anishinaabe brethren for their assistance. Hopefully, the call to arms would produce a couple hundred warriors.

The speaker at the council, Ogichidaa-nagamon (*oh-each-e-da na-ga-mon:* Warrior Song) stood and asked, "Zhashagi, will you and your brother, Omashkooz, lead a small band to the south with a belt for a call to war?"

My brother had suffered an arrow in his shoulder, and his wife was using the healing powers of ozhaashigob (*ooh-sosh-eh-go-a:* slippery elm) on his wound. Until he healed I would have to hunt for my brother's family and hoped by the spring that he would be strong enough to paddle. Of course, he could take my place in the back and steer!

Standing to answer, I replied, "I will, and I ask if I might take the three cousins who wear animal skins with us."

"It is done," the speaker replied.

Smiling, I left the council lodge. My eyes followed the light of the full moon toward the edge of the forest. There, standing in the brightness of the moon's beams, sat a large rabbit on its haunches.

12

ONE DIES SO
ANOTHER CAN LIVE

CHAŊKU WAŠTE

As my nephew, Tȟáȟča Čiŋčá, and I cleared the hill, we came upon a Lakȟóta woman giving birth in a small grove of trees on the hillside. She was just cutting the umbilical cord when we saw her. The woman then took the cord and put it in a decorated case in the cradle-board beside her.

We sat and watched the woman from a distance while the other warriors and dogs made their way down to the encampment. I wanted to make sure the woman was well before we continued on. We hadn't been there for the actual birth, which was something men weren't allowed to see.

Taking her baby in her arms, the mother wrapped the child in a soft fawn skin and put the infant on the cradle-board where it would spend most of its days and nights until it could sit unsupported. The board protected the child while its mother performed her daily tasks. Until the child could walk, he or she would be bound to the board most of the time.

Once she had secured her child, the mother removed her clothes and wrapped the tȟamní (placenta) along with the last bit of umbilical cord in them. She then placed the wrapped bundle high in a tree away from animals. This would ensure that the child would grow straight and smart. After donning a new robe that she had with her, she and the child left for the river, where she bathed the newborn.

The Lakȟóta called their children wakȟáŋheža (*wak-han-hay-za:* sacred ones) and cuddled and encouraged them to play. There was never a need to scold children, or to ridicule them, or to strike them. It was the way Lakȟóta children were raised. It was the Lakȟóta tradition to be kind and compassionate to one's children.

A baby was never allowed to cry and was taught by its parents to withhold the sound of weeping. In its early years, if a child cried, the mother pinched its nose and put her hand over the infant's mouth. In this way, a child learned not to cry and give away the hiding place of its people in time of peril.

"Uncle," asked Tȟáȟča Čiŋčá, stirring me from my thoughts, "is that what my mother did when I was born, what this woman is doing now?"

"Yes," I replied.

"Uncle, is it true the cradleboard saved my life?"

"Yes, young one, it did, and along with the love of your mother and father it is the reason you're here today."

Tȟáȟča Čiŋčá's question brought back memories of the boy's parents. Eleven summers ago, just after Tȟáȟča Čiŋčá was born, his father and my brother, Oȟ'áŋkȟo Napé (*oh-hoŋ'-koh nah'-pah*: Swift Hand), and his mother, Wičháȟpi (*wee-chalk-pee*: Star), had left the village to go hunting, taking their newborn son with them. Oȟ'áŋkȟo Napé had slain a deer, and they were butchering it to take back to the village. Wičháȟpi had hung her son's cradleboard in a nearby tree.

The matȟóȟota (*mah'-tah-ho-ta*: grizzly bear) has a sense of smell that can pick up the scent of a carcass from a great distance, and, unknown to Oȟ'áŋkȟo Napé and Wičháȟpi, one of these huge beasts had caught the distant aroma of this deer's death.

The two dogs with the couple probably barked a warning too late for the parents to reach their weapons. The swiftness of the huge beast once he neared his prey would have taken them by surprise.

Two days after the couple had left the village with their child, one of the dogs made his way back to the camp in terrible shape. A few warriors and I tracked the dog's blood trail back to the scene, where we discovered the boy fast asleep in a tree. The big bear, after his battle, had eaten his fill, and the faint smell of a baby wouldn't have interested him at all by then.

Two summers after the deaths a hunting party of our village slew a huge grizzly. Embedded in his neck was a broken blade of a bone knife. Oȟ'áŋkȟo Napé had battled to the end to protect his family.

My wife, Wawát'ečala Iȟá (*wah-wah'-tay-chah ee-'hah*: Gentle Smile), and I took in the boy to nurture as our own. He turned into a thoughtful and resourceful young man full of questions, who learned very quickly anything that was taught him.

His skill with the weapons of a Lakȟóta warrior surpassed that of all his friends. My son, Óta Heȟáka, told Tȟáȟča Čiŋčá that once he slew his first hoofed animal he could come along on a strike against the Ȟaȟátȟuŋwaŋ. Our young boys had to grow up fast to replace the fallen warriors of past battles. Strong numbers of warriors were necessary for our survival.

After watching the baby being tended and having his questions answered, Tȟáȟča Čiŋčá remained silent for the rest of the short journey down the hill.

Before we descended, we stood at the crest and admired the scene: more than seventy lodges, all facing east to the rising sun with their backs to the prevailing western winds, wisps of smoke exiting the top of the lodgepoles against the brilliant blue sky, leaving dark smudges on the exit areas of the skin coverings. I could smell the pleasant aroma of wood burning from our vantage point, and the warmth of this day's sun tempted me to lie down in the long grass to enjoy the seeming tranquility. As we entered the village, children ran around and greeted us with laughter as dogs barked their welcome. The women were making meals, and the men and young boys sat and took stock of their lances and arrows for the hunt.

Each male hunter had an identifying colour design on his weapons so that his wife and mother knew what animal was his to butcher. There were many more women than men in the community, the consequence of warriors dying in battle and during dangerous hunts. Because of this, it wasn't uncommon for a man to take more than one wife. Usually, he married a sister, which resulted in a much more harmonious relationship between wives and meant less competition than if they were unrelated. A man had to be a good hunter and provider to support more than one wife, and the more wives he had, the better off he and the whole family were. By being an expert hunter, he could supply his wives with more skins to make the family a bigger teepee, because it was the women who tanned the hides, butchered the meat, and cared for the children. With more skins being prepared, the family would be well off because the man would then be able to trade for dogs and other valuable possessions with the newfound wealth supplied by his hard-working wives.

I turned to Tȟáȟča Čiŋčá outside our lodge and said, "Go inside and prepare your extra weapons for the hunt. You're old enough now to join the men. I also need you to go out beyond the village to find some gooseberry or Juneberry shoots for arrow shafts."

"All right, Uncle, and while I'm gone perhaps I'll bring home something to eat for tonight!"

The akíčita, the society responsible for the hunt, would be gathering the hunters together now that we had arrived with the advance warriors from SápA Ziŋtkála's village. Here the rules would be laid down for the protection, safety, and success of the hunt. Any deviation from their laws would be dealt with by the akíčita. Punishments could be anything from a whipping, destroying personal property, banishment, or in severe cases, death.

It was also the akíčita's duty to control the movement of the camp, to organize war parties, and to enforce the customs of war. Its leadership was an important aspect of Lakȟóta life and was needed to ensure the success of the community as a whole.

An akíčita leader was recognizable by his facial markings: a black line of paint starting at the forehead above the right eyebrow that continued downward on the outer right edge of the right cheekbone to beside the mouth. This marking signified that he had control of the camp. A war party head had two of these marks, and his word was the law!

The rules of the hunt were few but important. No one was to branch off, fall behind, or go in front without permission. Absolutely no one could run the buffalo before the general order to do so. Group leaders were to take turns patrolling the camp and keeping guard to guarantee no one left before the hunt began.

Nážiŋ Išnála (*nah-zhee is-na-la*: Stand Alone), the head of the akíčita, told everyone gathered that the buffalo pound was ready and that the chute constructed of rocks and branches now stretched to the horizon. Warriors had been sent out to watch the herd and plan the attack. The animals were still a good distance away from the čhaŋkáškapi (*chon-kos'kay*: fence), and the thought was that in less than two suns the hunt could begin. He had told his scouts they were to start carefully driving the herd toward the chute and to not stampede it. This would be done by burning buffalo chips to start a controlled grass fire, directing the herd toward the opening of the drive lines.

Chosen warriors then would have to separate about fifty or more animals from the herd without spooking them. A few of these warriors, dressed in wolf robes and on all fours, would follow the herd. Because wolves were always present, this wouldn't scare the great beasts into a run. Once the animals were in position, a caller wearing a buffalo calf robe would make the bleating distress sound of a lost calf to lure the animals into the chute. Then the warriors garbed as wolves would jump up once the animals were in the chute and get them running.

The warriors would drive the animals down the interior of the runway until all of our people would rise from their hidden positions alongside the outer edges of the travel way and wave their robes over their heads to keep the animals on course to the killing area. The dogs would run behind the herd and along the sides to prevent it from turning off and rejoining the main herd. The people along the flanks had to keep their wits about them because if an animal decided to make a turn to escape, it would trample anyone in its way. Deaths like that were common during the hunt.

Our hope was that SápA Ziŋtkála and his people would arrive before the hunt started and that Óta Heȟáka and his raiding party might also be back.

But in the meantime everyone would gather to feast, dance, and pray to Wakhan Thanka for a successful hunt. During the time the village was waiting for the herd to approach, two games of skill would take place to prepare for the hunt.

That night in our lodge Tȟáȟča Čiŋčá and I sat and gathered our arrows. During the day, Tȟáȟča

Čiŋčá had found some shoots of gooseberry and Juneberry to make shafts, enabling us to add to our arrow collection for the hunt. While I prepared the arrow shafts, Tȟáȟča Čiŋčá feathered waglékšuŋ (*wal-gay'-leck-shahn:* turkey) feathers to glue on the end of the shafts with the buffalo hoof glue my wife, Wawát'ečala Iȟá, was preparing.

Wawát'ečala Iȟá was also making a meal for us. She had filled a lining of a buffalo stomach with water and into it she dropped heated stones to warm the water. Once the water heated up, she tossed in turnips, wild onions, and the meat of a pispíza (*peace-piza:* prairie dog) that Tȟáȟča Čiŋčá had shot today during his roaming.

Looking up from her tasks, Wawát'ečala Iȟá advised us, "Don't forget to mark your arrows so I know what buffalo to butcher. Also tonight we'll have a special treat. This stomach lining I've been cooking with is becoming too soft to use anymore, so it will also become part of our meal."

Continuing with my arrow preparation, I measured the shaft from the length of my elbow to the end of my little finger and then again the same length. Then I took two pieces of grooved sandstone and pulled the shaft through them to smooth it out. Once this was finished, I added a flint arrowhead to the end and wrapped it with leather to hold it in place. To three of the arrows I attached sharp, coloured stones I had obtained from the wóphiye (medicine bag) of a deceased Psáloka (*sa-ah-loo-ka:* Crow) warrior I had slain in a battle many years earlier. The stones were very magical, and I only used them for special hunts when I knew I could retrieve them. I had never employed them in a battle because I couldn't guarantee getting the arrow back if I missed or only wounded a foe.

When I was done with the arrowheads, I turned the shafts over to my nephew and he glued the feathers on and wrapped leather around the shafts where the feathers were affixed. Once he was finished, I added the lightning marks to make our arrows fly true and coloured each arrow with a dye marking so that Wawát'ečala Iȟá could pick out the buffalo we had slain. When we were done, each of us had added another seven arrows to his quiver.

Right after the sun rose to lighten our lodge, I stepped out into the early-morning chill and dew. There I caught the faint smell of cooking fires cutting through the morning freshness. Then my ears were awakened by the crier announcing that the tȟahúka čhaŋgléška na wahúkheza (*tah-ha-uka chan-glay-sh-ka na wa-hu-keza:* hoop and spear game) would commence soon. The call to the contest area would be made by the beating of a drum.

After the crier made his way through the camp, everyone suddenly came alive. Meals were eaten in haste, and when the drum beat started, all the males who were old enough for the hunt made their way to the competition area with their spears.

Tȟáȟča Čiŋčá turned to me. "Uncle, do you think we'll be on the same team?"

"Yes," I replied. "Friends and families usually play together."

The whole village gathered in an open field where the grass had been trampled down previously by young children and Elders. The sides were quickly decided on and there was much laughter and betting.

The hoop for the game was made of ash bent into a circle with a web of rawhide woven into the entire hoop. There was a small hole in the middle called the heart. The idea was to throw a spear through this heart while the hoop was in the air, which scored the team a five count. A spear through the heart while it was rolling after it landed earned a three count. Any other spot in the hoop was a one count.

A few chosen Elders were selected as the tossers, and the game began.

The teams stood in line and took turns throwing their spears amid much hollering, hooting, and whistling from spectators and contestants. There were many strikes and rarely did the hoop hit the ground without a spear thrown through the game piece. However, when it did fall to the ground, the hoop throwers were so skilled that it rolled for quite a distance until someone speared it.

When it was my turn, I hit the hoop in the air but only scored one. Tȟáȟča Čiŋčá, though, pierced the heart while it was rolling on the ground for a three count, which inspired much whistling from the spectators and many hoots sent in my direction because my nephew had bested me.

Tȟáȟča Čiŋčá had a huge smile on his face, and I whispered to him, "Well done."

The game went on until the noon sun and then broke up. Our side lost by eleven counts, and as people paid their bets, the crier announced that after the noon meal we would be called back for the ogleče kutepi (*oh-glay-say kue-day-pi:* arrow shooting).

These games honed our skills with the weapons that would be used during the hunt, relieved the tension of waiting, and also helped pass the time until the akíčita told us it was time to start the buffalo chase.

For the noon meal the women contributed to a huge feast, and everyone ate together in the middle of the encampment. As Tȟáȟča Čiŋčá and I sat and ate, warriors came up and congratulated him on bettering me during the spear throw. There was much laughter and teasing as they came and went during the meal, and Tȟáȟča Čiŋčá beamed at the attention from the warriors.

I turned to him and said, "I hope this newfound skill will continue with you once the hunt starts."

"It will," he answered.

Just as the meal was ending, there was a disturbance on the east side of the camp. Some of the men there were yelling a welcome. Everyone rushed to the spot, and we watched as a painted warrior made a zigzag running approach to the village. It was one of the warriors who had left with my son, Óta Heȟáka, on the dream quest war party to the land of the Ȟaȟátȟuŋwaŋ. By running in this zigzag formation, he was announcing that their raid had been successful.

Now that the returning party had everyone's attention, another one of its members came forward and threw a round ball-shaped robe in the air three times, signifying the number of raiders who had lost their lives. Nážiŋ Išnála, the akíčita head, then went out to greet the returning warriors, get the names of the dead, and escort the war party back to the community. The akíčita head then related the bad news to the families of the fallen warriors. Once the news was given to the relatives, they fell to the ground overwhelmed with grief. The women became so distraught that they wailed uncontrollably, cutting their hair and slashing their arms in despair. For the next year these families would mourn and keep places for the departed spirits to eat with them at meals. After a year, they would let the spirits quit this world during a ceremony.

Óta Heȟáka came up to me and nodded. "It was a successful raid, Father. We captured many furs the Ȟaȟátȟuŋwaŋ were bringing back to their village. Also two women who had been taken from us a few years ago have been returned with great happiness to their families. Our warriors killed twelve of their best and we've brought their scalps home to hang in our lodges. It was a good day to be a Lakȟóta!"

"Óta Heȟáka, even though you were successful, you know the Ȟaȟátȟuŋwaŋ won't let this act of war go unheeded. They'll come upon us with a vengeance. A loss of twelve warriors is a defeat and loss of life they will certainly avenge with all their power. The Ȟaȟátȟuŋwaŋ are a strong and powerful enemy. They will lick their wounds and reach out to their allies for aid in a mourning revenge attack."

"Father, we'll be ready. The Lakȟóta are strong!"

"Remember Kȟaŋǧi Wakpá," I said. "The Ȟaȟátȟuŋwaŋ proved their power that day by wiping out my father's village."

"The people of Kȟaŋǧi Wakpá were starving and weak. The Lakȟóta today aren't like our forefathers. We're stronger and better warriors and hunters than they were."

"I hope you're right, my son. Now prepare your warriors for the hunt. We have a game of ogleče kutepi to win! Tonight you and your men can dance and tell the story of how you brought the mighty Ȟaȟátȟuŋwaŋ to their knees."

For the arrow-shooting game, one of the Elders fired an arrow high into the sky at an angle. When it came down, the Elder took a robe and laid it in the area around the shot arrow. Then the teams took turns firing at the target. When each team had its turn, the sky was full of arrows. Then the young boys and a few Elders counted and collected the arrows after each turn. The team with the most arrows stuck in the robe was the winner for that game.

Tȟáȟča Čiŋčá was very accurate with his arrows and showed great promise as a marksman. He turned to Óta Heȟáka after a good shot and said, "I'll get a buffalo tomorrow and then you'll have to take me the next time you go to war."

"That was the deal we made," Óta Heȟáka said. "Shoot a hoofed animal and I'll take you."

The game went on until just before sunset. There was lots of teasing, betting, and flying arrows. In the end, though, the games won between the teams ended up almost even. I was down one eagle bone whistle lost in the betting when we finished. These competitions readied us for the big hunt, which was vital for the long-lasting survival of our people. The buffalo had to give up their existence for our lives to continue. It was all part of the Great Mystery.

As the men made their way back to the village for the evening meal and also to prepare for Óta Heȟáka's warriors to dance and tell their stories of battle, a lone scout rushed into the camp. He approached SápA Maȟpíya (*sah'-pah maii-hoh'-pee-ah:* Black Sky), the akíčita's leader of the hunt, and said something. SápA Maȟpíya then turned to everyone and said, "Tomorrow at first light, be ready: the hunt will begin. As of now, no one leaves the camp until I give the order. All hunt rules and restrictions are on. Tomorrow you all know your places and duties. If you have any questions, come and ask me or one of my fellow akíčita members tonight during the storytelling dance."

That evening the drums beat and the warriors of Óta Heȟáka's party told of their deeds and how they had struck their enemies down. The fires blazed high and the dancers' bodies glistened in the heat from their sweat and the energy they put into their stories. During this time, many warriors also underwent a smudging ceremony to guide and protect them on the next day's hunt.

Just before sunset, SápA Ziŋtkála's people entered the village to enthusiastic cheering. The Great Mystery was lining everything up for a successful hunt.

In the morning, the crier came through the village waking everyone up to start this important day. I left the lodge and ambled down to the river. Facing the sun, I woke my body up with the cool water and asked Wakhan Thanka to watch over me and help my arrows fly true. After I was done, I looked around and watched as all the warriors and young hunters did the same. Óta Heȟáka had Tȟáȟča Čiŋčá at the river and was instructing him in the ceremony.

The Elders gathered the children to amuse them while the hunt ensued. Once the butchering began, they would all come to aid in any way they could.

After the warriors and hunters left the river, they headed back to their lodges to collect their weapons and dogs. The women gave each man a robe to wave over his head when the great beast came his way, and then more than five hundred of our people started on a run to their appointed places, trailed by the village's dogs. The women moved toward the penned-up area where the killing would take place to assume their positions out from the pound. They would be responsible for doing as the men did with their robes, but closer to the great pen. The women would also butcher the animals once the killing was finished.

To keep the buffalo from escaping once they were in the pound, a ramp had been built for them to enter the killing area. It sloped down and away from the entrance, which was the height of a man. Once in, though, if the buffalo turned to break out, they would discover that the ramp was far too high to do so and neither could they jump back onto it to retreat.

Our fastest warriors now went toward the end of the chute to wait at the entrance. In the distance, we could see the dust of the herd and the smoke that was driving the beasts in our direction. The wind was in our favour, gently blowing away from the herd and carrying with it the sharp smells of burning dung and prairie grass. There was no sound except for the people's footsteps on the prairie, the rustling of the women's skirts, and the almost silent breaths everyone was taking.

The men were stripped to breechcloths and moccasins, with one or two spears in their grasp and bows and arrow-laden quivers on their sweat-coated backs. Even the dogs were quiet in their approach, hundreds of them following their masters, their slanted eyes wide open. The only outward sign in these ferocious mongrels that indicated any excitement was the saliva dripping from their mouths.

If the oncoming buffalo herd had any sense of reality, it would see a column of dust made by hunters toward the hunted and recognize that good things weren't coming its way.

Ťȟáȟča Čiŋčá, Óta Heȟáka, and I were lined up along the west side of the fence a short distance from the start. Once the beasts ran by us, our job was to race as fast as we could to occupy an open space farther down the drive line. To our right were some young boys a year or two older than Ťȟáȟča Čiŋčá. They nervously checked their weapons, chattered, and compared their distraction robes. Across from them were their fathers and uncles.

"Uncle, I can hear the scouts yelling and moving the herd," Ťȟáȟča Čiŋčá said.

Turning to our right, I spotted the dust raised by the onrushing animals being pushed toward us by the wind as cowbirds rose in the air and made their distinctive whistles. Suddenly, out of the dust cloud, a huge bull charged, tail raised in agitation, body sprinkled with dust as it snorted loudly.

The warriors raised their robes, flapping the skins and hooting and whistling to keep the animals in the chute running toward the pound. The boys beside us were slow getting their robes in the air because of their inattention, and in their tardiness they created an opening that one frantic young bull saw and made a lunge toward. Reaching the opening just as the boys tried to shut it by raising their skins and twirling them above their heads, the bull caught one of the boys with a horn and tossed him high into the dust-laden air. The young man hit the ground with a thump and a gasping rush of air from his lungs, causing grasshoppers and powdered dirt to rise in unison. Having landed ahead of the rampaging bull, the boy was in danger again when the bull turned its head to toss the youngster again.

While all this was happening, the boy's companions were chasing alongside the bull to divert its attention, opening up an even bigger gap in the line. The fathers and uncles who were directly across from the boys now tried to cover up the breach which, if not soon closed, would allow more buffalo to escape. A couple of roving akíčita members also lent a hand to block the opening.

This whole incident unfolded in so short a time that I could hardly take three breaths and reach for my bow and arrows.

Just as the young bull was about to reach the boy on the ground to toss him again, two arrows whizzed by my head and buried themselves up to their feathers in the area behind the bull's left front leg. The bull stumbled and twisted its head toward me, opening its mouth in a bellow and ejecting a mixture of foam and blood. I could feel the hot breath of the beast on my face and smell the contents of its stomach. As the buffalo dropped to its knees, two of the delinquent boys' relatives drove their spears into the beast to finish it off.

As the bull groaned and rolled onto its side, dead, I heard a high-pitched cry, "Hie, hie, hie," behind me. Turning to look, I saw Óta Heȟáka with his bow and spear raised in the air, yelling and whistling as he danced around Tȟáȟča Čiŋčá, who stood with an arrow in his bow and a huge grin on his face. The other warriors and the fallen boy's relatives also shouted and sang praises. It was Tȟáȟča Čiŋčá who had fired the two rapid arrows that had slain the raging animal, saving the boy's life.

The gap was now closed and the buffalo were contained in the chute. Warriors sprinted past us to fill gaps ahead. The dust from the passing animals entered my mouth and nostrils and changed my exposed skin to a powdery white with streaks of sweat creating lines that crisscrossed my torso.

Tȟáȟča Čiŋčá glanced up at me. "Uncle, you look like a Ghost Warrior!"

SápA Maȟpíya, the akíčita's hunt leader, approached the young boys who had caused the break that allowed the bull to escape, grabbed their weapons, and snapped them in two as punishment for violating the hunt rules. He then told them they would escape the wrath of the akíčita's whips but would have to report to the women once the butchering began and do whatever they asked. Indicating the direction of the pound, SápA Maȟpíya told the boys to run to the front and help close off any holes.

The boy who had been thrown had suffered only a small scrape on his left leg and a bloodied elbow on the same side when he hit the ground. A slice of his cheek was also hanging over his lip where the animal had gored him. SápA Maȟpíya popped some ȟaŋté čhaŋȟlóǧaŋ (yarrow) into his mouth and chewed quickly. When it was a paste, he pushed back the boy's dangling cheek and smeared the substance on it to stop the bleeding and prevent infection. Once the cheek was back in place, he handed the wounded young man some yarrow leaves to hold against the wound. Then, pointing in the direction of the women, the imposing warrior ordered, "Get the healer to sew that back in place and be gone with you!"

The negligent friends took off with the speed of a pack of scared dogs and ran to the forward position, with the bull's victim leading the way. One of the warriors started laughing, breaking the tension of the moment and sending everyone in the vicinity into bouts of mirth that seemed out of place among the yelling and whistling of the pursuing warriors, the barking dogs, and the bellowing beasts. All of this occurred in a billowing cloud of thick dust.

Óta Heȟáka then turned to Tȟáȟča Čiŋčá and me and said, "The scar from the goring will be a badge of honour in years to come for that boy. Not many Lakȟóta have survived a goring and a flip in the air from an irate bull buffalo!"

Chuckling at the thought that the story of the scar would be a future winter storytelling tale, I motioned to Tȟáȟča Čiŋčá and Óta Heȟáka, saying, "Come, we must keep up with the herd!"

Óta Heȟáka turned to his cousin and shouted to him as they sprinted beside me, "You fulfilled the task I asked of you, so you can now join my next war party. You slew a hoofed animal, and now I give you a gift. From this moment forward you won't be known as Ťháȟča Čiŋčá ever again! Your new name given by me, your uncle's son, Óta Heȟáka, will be Ťhatháŋka Kaťá (*tah-ton-kah k'tay*: Buffalo Kill)."

Racing beside my son and nephew, I raised my weapons above my head and cried, "Ťhatháŋka Kaťá, Ťhatháŋka Kaťá, Ťhatháŋka Kaťá, we have a new Lakȟóta warrior, aye, aye!"

The other warriors running with us then raised their weapons and robes into the air and repeated my words, causing my nephew's smile to widen. I then turned to Ťhatháŋka Kaťá and cried above the din, "Your aunt will be mad at you for killing a buffalo so far from the pound, making her and her sisters come all the way out here to prepare the animal!"

"Uncle, I'll gladly help them to repay for my negligence."

We loped ahead of the herd, choking back the stifling prairie heat and smothering dust to gain our place in the line where we waved our skins and kept the stampeding animals on the intended course. Gazing around at the other warriors, I noticed they were also coated in dust with muddied spots where their sweat had seeped through the powdery covering. I now knew what my nephew had meant when he said I looked like a Ghost Warrior. All the pursuers were smiling, hooting, and whistling loudly as they herded the huge beasts to their death and our survival.

Soon the buffalo reached the opening, charging up and over the stoutly built ramp that had been constructed with tightly packed rocks. Once over the ramp, they tumbled into the closed-off area to meet their deaths. Surrounding the corral were warriors sending arrows and spears into the animals' bodies. The noise was deafening, with warriors shouting, dogs barking, women singing, and the buffalo bellowing as they took their last breaths. The rising dust and stench of dying animals as they released urine and emptied their intestines upon their deaths filled my nostrils and made me dizzy from the excitement of the hunt. Ťhatȟáŋka Kaťá, Óta Heȟáka, and I shot all our arrows, keeping our spears for any unseen dangers.

When it was over, the men entered the compound and finished off any of the animals that were still alive. The women then came in after the men had completed their killing and began butchering the meat with their knives. Many of the people, to satisfy their hunger, cut off pieces and ate them raw, while the dogs were thrown guts to fight over along with the crows and ravens.

The women skinned each buffalo down the back in order to get at the tender meat just beneath the surface, the area known as the "hatched area." Once this was removed, the front legs were cut off as well as the shoulder blades. This exposed the hump meat as well as the meat of the ribs and the beast's inner organs. After all this was exposed, the spine was then severed and the pelvis and hind legs removed. Finally, the neck and head were separated as one. This allowed for the tough meat to be dried and made into wasná (*wah-snah:* pemmican).

Once the animals were cut open, the stink became almost unbearable in the late-day heat. The akíčita posted scouts around the kill site to watch for grizzlies, which had an excellence sense of smell for carrion and could detect the scent of death from a great distance.

Everything on this great animal that Wakhan Thanka had given us would be used in our everyday lives. The women took great pride in making wókpȟaŋ (*who-kpah*: parfleche-rawhide bags) from the hide once the hair was removed. They then decorated these bags and used them to carry all of their possessions. The bags were so strong that they could stop an arrow or spear. The hides were also used for clothing, teepees, shields, and drums. The sinew: for thread, bowstrings, and attaching arrowheads. The meat: for sustenance. The bones: for weapons, sled runners, tools, and scrapers. The horns: for spoons, cups, and bowls. The hair: for rope and decoration. The hooves: for rattles and glues. The brain: for softening hides. The fat: for pemmican, hair grease, paint base, and soap. The stomach, intestines, scrotum, and bladder: for bags and water containers. The teeth: for necklaces. The skull: for ceremonies and prayer.

Without the buffalo we wouldn't have survived as a strong nation. For this we offered prayers of thanks always before the final butchering. We thanked the great beast for giving his life so that we could live, and we thanked Wakhan Thanka for creating the beast and giving us the strength to slay him.

As the women continued their bloody, smelly work, the men rotated the great beasts, enabling their wives, aunts, and sisters to cut around the animal and get the skin off. The young boys built fires of buffalo chips and along with some of the Elders started roasting the tongues, which were a great delicacy, and sharing the meat with the women. The warriors who had slain an animal consumed the heart raw with the hope of gaining the buffalo's strength. There was much happiness and excitement among the people because now we all knew that no one would go hungry this coming winter. There would be enough meat to feed everyone.

Each carcass would be cut into eleven pieces for transportation: the four limbs, the two sides of ribs, the two sinews on each side of the backbone, the brisket, the croup, and the backbone. Then, once we got everything back to the village, we would hang the parts on racks and smoke and dry them for storage and to make pemmican, which consisted of the meat, berries, and fat.

Because Ťhaťháŋka Kaťá had slain the buffalo now lying on the prairie away from the main pound, my family was responsible for it. All the meat was shared among the people, but it was the responsibility of whoever had slain an animal to harvest the beast. The extra meat would be given to Elders, warriors who hadn't made a kill, or warriors of the akíčita who were responsible for the oversight of the hunt and who hadn't participated in any of the slaying.

That night fires were built to keep the wolves and bears away and the people went to sleep exhausted. The next morning Ťhaťháŋka Kaťá, Óta Heȟáka, Wawáťečala Iȟá, her younger sister, Pȟáŋžela Napé (*pohn-zhah-lah nah'pay:* Soft Hand), and I left the camp to butcher the buffalo my nephew had slain. Also with us were fifteen dogs hooked up to travois to bring the meat back.

We were busy talking and laughing when Pȟáŋžela Napé stopped and asked, "What's that awful smell?"

Once she pointed it out, my nostrils flared with a horrendous stench, and shivers ran down my spine.

Óta Heȟáka was ahead of everyone else and walked up the small rise in front of us with a couple of dogs. Then he turned to me and cried, "Father!"

The dogs beside him growled as their manes bristled. I knew what it was before even casting my eyes upon it.

13

SEARCHING OUT OUR ALLIES TO STRENGTHEN US

ZHASHAGI

"You can't wait until the spring warmth comes, Zhashagi," my brother, Omashkooz, said, "hoping that I've healed enough to take the red wampum war belts to our friends, the Naadawe and Odishkwaagamii. That's too much of time from when the Nadowessioux ambushed us on the river to when we seek revenge. If you wait until spring to seek out our allies to the east, you'll lose a hundred moons of travel. Going in the next few suns and leaving during the manoominike-giizis (*man-oom-inik-gee-zas:* Ricing Moon — August) will ensure you'll make it back by the iskigamizige-giizis (*is-ki-gamo-azing-a-gee-zas:* Sugar-Bushing Moon — April). By then I should be fully healed and might be able to paddle. If you wait until spring and I'm still not completely healthy at that time, you'll lose all the winter months to visit our allies. The three cousins will be more than enough help for you. They're strong, brave, and great warriors and hunters. No harm will come to you with them as your companions. Misko will also be with you, so you'll be well looked after."

"Brother, you make it sound as if I'm a weakling and need these three men and my dog just to survive," I replied.

"No, Brother, just concerned."

"All right, then, I know your wife, Dagwaagin (*dag-waa-kin:* Autumn), has done well looking after you, but I'm going to ask the Mide healer to come and visit you. If you're to stay here, I want you fully able when I come back in the spring. I'll also ask some of the younger boys to hunt for you this fall and winter until you heal. I'll tell them if they do a good job we'll take them with us in the spring when we go to war. In the meantime, before I leave, I'm going to attend the Midewiwin ceremony for the Wiikwandiwin (*wick-wan-de-win:* seasonal celebration for the summer season). Hopefully, there I'll receive the blessing I need for a good future and for my coming trip."

After leaving Omashkooz, I visited the three cousins in their aunt's lodge, where I found them with some of the children playing a game of makizin ataagewin (*mak-e-zin a-tash-win:* moccasin game) punctuated by a great deal of laughter, shouting, and cheering. The game they were taking part in was played with four moccasins and a round pebble. There were two teams that took turns dropping the pebble or finding the small stone. The team hiding the pebble had one member take it in his hand, wave his hands over the shoes, and drop the stone into one of them. The other team then tried to guess where the pebble was until it was found. Once it was discovered, a certain number of counting sticks according to the number of guesses taken was given to that team.

The cousins' aunt was cooking venison, which added to the pungent atmosphere inside the lodge: smells of cooking meat, body odours, and smoke. Enhancing the aromas was a group of Elders watching from the sidelines, smoking their pipes and farting.

I sat and observed the game, having decided to let it finish before I mentioned to the cousins about going to the Midewiwin ceremony. Among the group of young people participating in the game were two boys who caught my eye. I would ask these boys to help my brother's family get through the winter while he healed. These two youngsters had been with us on the river and had escaped capture and death, which showed me they were at the very least resourceful in keeping themselves alive.

The cousins' aunt, Giizhizekwe Ikwe (*key-zee-zay-kway e-kway*: She Cooks Woman) offered me some venison and steaming tea to enjoy while the game proceeded. After eating the warm meal, the heat of the room, along with the pleasant sounds of laughter, put me to sleep. I had no idea how long I slept, but it must have been the sudden lack of noise that woke me, or the burst of cool night air from the opening of the doorway as the Elders left. Once I readjusted my eyes to the dim and smoky interior of the lodge, I saw the three cousins and the other players quietly devouring Giizhizekwe Ikwe's meal.

I broke the silence by calling one of the cousins' names. "Gichi Bizhiins, I need you and your cousins to come with me to the Midewiwin ceremony to get our blessing for our trip. We'll be leaving in two days before the fall weather to take the red war belt to our allies."

"We'll be there, Zhashagi, on the day you want us," he replied.

I then turned to the two boys, Mayagi-bine (*my-a-gay-bee-neh:* Pheasant) and Bikwak (*be-kwak:* Arrow), and asked them, "Will you hunt for my brother this winter while he heals from his wound? To repay you for your hunting skills this winter, Omashkooz will make each of you arrows and a spear for the spring when we take both of you on the war path against the Lakȟóta."

They looked at each other in amazement. The older one, Bikwak, answered, "To even be considered to go on this upcoming raid with you and your brother is such an honour that supplying a hundred deer this fall and winter will never be enough to repay the two of you for this opportunity. Zhashagi, we'll make you proud! Mayagi-bine and I will bring your brother more meat than he and his wife have ever seen in past winters."

"Boys," I said with a smile, "if I come back in the spring and there's a lack of dogs in the community, you'll have to answer to me for your laziness. This will be your first step to being warriors, so do the job well! Now I would like to take both of you on in a game of makizin ataagewin!"

Two days later the three cousins, Misko, and I pushed our canoe off from the shores of our village into the Gichigami-ziibi (*gich-e-gam-e-zee-bee:* Great Lake River, present-day St. Louis River), which would take us to the big lake called Anishinaabewi-gichigami. From there we would stay close to the shoreline and away from the big lake's perils.

Our canoe was loaded with just enough food to get us all the way if we were careful and didn't eat too much. Our intention, though, was to hunt and fish when the opportunities presented themselves. By leaving now during the start of the manoominike-giizis, we would easily make it to our allies, the Naadawe, before the next moon cast its shadow. If the weather was kind to us and the Midewiwin blessing was a good one, we would be warming our bodies in the Naadawe longhouses before twenty suns passed. There we would spend the winter and leave to come back to our people by the zaagibagaa-giiziz (*zaa-gi-ba-ga-gee-sus:* Budding Moon — May).

Our second day of paddling found us nearing Mooningwanekaaing (Madeline Island) where our ancestors had come during their journey from the east. Here they had found abundant rice beds that helped sustain them that first fall.

"There will be a village on the eastern side of the island where we'll ask for their kindness for one night," I said to my three companions.

As we pulled ashore among a group of barking dogs and chattering children, we were approached by their leader, Misko Zhiishiib (*miss-ko zhe-sheep:* Red Duck). My dog, Misko, jumped from the boat and soon disappeared into the swirling, noisy mass of children and other canines. All I could see was his large red tail sticking up in the air as he wagged it with excitement.

"Welcome, my brothers," Misko Zhiishiib said with his arms outstretched in greeting. "Please accept our food and lodges on your journey and tell us the news from our people to the west of us."

The village was composed of about a hundred and fifty men, women, and children, and that many dogs plus some. That night we enjoyed a meal of mooz (*moans:* moose) with manoomin (*man-oo-men:* rice) sweetened with zhiiwaagamizigan (*zhe-wah-ga-miss-e-gan:* maple syrup).

When we showed Misko Zhiishiib our wampum war belt after we ate, he said, "On your return trip you must stop to dance and feast with us. During the feast, our young men who want to accompany you on your pursuit of the Nadowessioux will strike the war post!"

The next morning we departed at dawn, leaving the smells of the early-morning cooking fires behind. That morning brought heavy dew, which covered our canoe, making it slippery to the touch. The camp soon disappeared from sight as we paddled into a mist. Our presence on the water was greeted by the soulful echo of a maang (*mong-ca:* loon) and the flutter of a flock of ducks rising from the steamy water.

Gizhiibatoo Inini looked around at me and said, "We must try to keep the shoreline in sight as long as this early-morning haze shimmers above the lake."

The first night after leaving the village of our friends we camped along the shore. Here we were able to spear a few fish to accompany our dried meat and tea. The next day found our boat approaching the peninsula of Keewaynan (*kee-wi-wai-non-ing*).

While we were there, we were able to pick up pieces of miskwaabik (*miss-kwa-bic:* copper) to trade with our allies. Our ancestors had taught us how to break up copper into powder by hitting it with other rocks or a stone axe. We dug a pit in the ground and started a fire. Charcoal from our cooking fires was then thrown on top followed by the copper powder. More charcoal was added, the hole was covered, and a channel was left open by making a narrow chute lined with rocks. Then we created airflow into this chute by waving our hands rapidly, blowing, or taking a cedar bough and moving it quickly across the opening to increase the temperature in the hole. After a while, we dug up the pit, picked up the liquid rock with a stick made into a small shovel, and dropped it into the water to cool. The solidified material was then made into arrow and hatchet heads and jewellery we could use for ourselves or trade.

After leaving Keewaynan, we continued along the shoreline. Misko, when not lying in the bottom of the boat sleeping, stood in the bow replicating a lookout. This day started out as a calm, sunny one and stayed that way until the wind rose toward evening. We took that as an omen and came ashore to camp and eat. This was a welcome rest, since we rarely stopped canoeing while it was still light, always eating in the boat during the day and occasionally dropping a fishing line. Relieving ourselves of our liquid intake was handled by standing in the boat.

That night, after we ate, the three cousins mentioned that I should get a tattoo on my hand where I had been wounded. Apiitendang Makwa decided that the tattoo should be an arrowhead over the scar. Gichi Bizhiins had kept some charcoal from the previous night's fire and would use this to make the black tattoo.

I sat by the light of the fire and drank tea as Gizhiibatoo Inini took my hand and etched an arrowhead on my hand with the teeth of a fish he had caught in the past few days. There was little pain, only the punishing of the teeth as they broke the surface of my skin. Gizhiibatoo Inini kept the cuts clean by wiping the blood off with fine moss and water.

Once he was done, he asked, "What do you think of the carving on your hand?"

I shrugged. "It looks fine, but I'll be able to tell better once the colour is added."

Gizhiibatoo Inini then took the charcoal and rubbed it into my skin. "Zhashagi, don't wash your hands until the cuts heal and lock the colour in."

I looked down at my hand and smiled. iI was a wonderful likeness of an arrowhead and a reminder of my close call.

After three more suns of travel, we reached the rapids our people called Baawitigong (Sault Ste. Marie), which connected the two lakes, Anishinaabewi-gichigami (Lake Superior) and Naadowewi-gichigami (Lake Huron). We rode the rapids toward calm water and then went ashore to rest. Once we made camp, the four of us waded into the water below the falls and speared thirty fish, most of which were adikameg (*a-dik-a-meg*: whitefish).

Misko enjoyed a feast of fish guts and eagerly ate whatever we threw his way. As we were washing up after cleaning the fish, I was careful not to get water on my tattooed hand. Then we sighted three canoes coming upstream. It was a group of Anishinaabe families who lived to the southwest in a village on the shores of Naadowewi-gichigami. I recognized the man in the lead boat. He had been with us when we visited the Naadawe the previous year. We had allied with them and the Odishkwaagamii to battle the Onöndowága. His name was Nitaage Niibiwa (*ni-ta-gay knee-be-wa:* Kill Many). He was a strong warrior and a brave fighter who handled himself with ability that bordered on mayhem when he fought.

The fish that our visitors had speared before sunset were cleaned and hung on drying racks that the women had erected immediately after their arrival. Once the cooking fires were lit, we feasted on fresh fish and spruce tea.

Before we made our beds for the night, we lit our pipes, smoked, and told stories of past deeds of warriors we knew. As we emptied our pipes, Nitaage Niibiwa asked if he could travel with us to the land of the Naadawe with my group and then continue on the trail when we made war on the Nadowessioux.

"What about your family?" I asked.

"These are my sisters, their children, and their husbands," Nitaage Niibiwa replied. "My wife died last year giving birth to a son after I came back from the land of the Naadawe. My son passed away the next day after my wife. It is now time for me to move on and take my mind off my losses. What better way to do this than to travel with you and these three Spirit Warriors and help revenge your losses. The excitement of battling death in warfare and living through it makes a man feel like he is invincible. Isn't that what life is about, my friend, Zhashagi?"

"That's a unique way of describing survival, my friend," I said, laughing. You're welcome to leave with us in the morning as long as you don't mind sharing a canoe with a dog, a deer, a bear, and a cougar."

"Zhashagi, what are you among those you've mentioned?" Nitaage Niibiwa asked

"Just a man," I answered. "Just a man."

The next morning, before we left, the women took all the fish off the drying racks and gave them to our group.

"We'll be here for many days to spear and smoke a lot more fish," said one of Nitaage Niibiwa's sisters. "This will sustain you for a couple of days in case the game is sparse."

"Thank you for your generosity," I replied.

After leaving the rapids of Baawitigong, we travelled for two more days. We made exceptional time with the added paddler, and except for a short rainstorm that drove us to shore for a bit of an afternoon, we experienced no problems. As always, we had one or two fishing lines hanging over the sides as we paddled, and this kept us in a continual supply of fish. Our dried meat was almost gone, and we needed a break from fish each and every day. However, the chance would soon come to do something about our diet.

Two suns after leaving our friends, we came upon a waterfall on the Kagawong-ziibi (*kag-a-wong-zee-bee*: Kagawong River) on the northwest side of Manidoowaaling Minisi (*mana-do-wah-ling men-eh-si*: Cave of the Spirit — Manitoulin Island).

That night we camped at the waterfall and agreed that Gichi Bizhiins, Misko, and I would travel along the northeast shore of the island to hunt for game. We agreed to meet in five suns at the southeast end of the island.

The next morning Gichi Bizhiins and I covered ourselves with jimson weed juice to keep the biting bugs away. We had to be careful, though. If ingested, this plant caused hallucinations and sometimes death. There was not much of a choice between being driven to hysterics by insects or by the juice of a plant.

The first day we kept along the shoreline, searching for fresh activity on the game trails. The second day we located a game trail with fresh deer scat that led to a meadow. Once there we sat in silence and hoped for a deer looking for fresh grazing grass.

Sitting under a huge pine that allowed us to view the whole meadow, we became very comfortable. I started to doze off from the warmth of the day and the buzz of the bugs trying to take a piece of me. I nearly nodded off, but was awakened by the sudden stiffening of Misko's body beside me. Opening my eyes, I saw the dog's ears perk up and the hair on the back of his neck bristle. Misko emitted a throaty growl and hunched in readiness to spring into action.

Gichi Bizhiins touched my shoulder and pointed. Being downwind, I then picked up the odour the dog had sensed. It was a mixture of berries and carrion that an advancing animal had eaten — pungent and thick to our nostrils. Then, as my eyes adjusted to the dull light under the tree, I spied what my two companions had seen: a male black bear, fat from summer berries and anything else he could devour.

I held the dog back. We needed the bear to enter the meadow at least halfway so that we could get a good shot at him. The dog, when released, would try to get the bear to stand on its rear haunches so that Gichi Bizhiins and I could fire at its exposed organs. The dog would also need to keep the animal from turning and running back to where it had entered the meadow. The bear then would have to make a decision to stand and fight or to run toward us. Either way, whatever choice the animal made would benefit us in our quest to bring him down.

The bear took his time, oblivious to us in our hiding spot. He sauntered through the grassy field, stopping and shoving ground-covering berries into his mouth every few steps. At times he sat on the ground and used both paws to fill his mouth. At this distance we could see the saliva coloured by red berries dripping from his mouth. It plastered the front of his furry stomach, changing it from black to a muddier hue.

Misko sat calmly and waited for my signal, while Gichi Bizhiins chuckled at the actions of the insatiable bear. My dog loved baiting bears and was an expert at getting the animals to rear up, enabling a kill shot. He and I had slain many bears using that method.

"Get," I whispered to him, and Misko was off like a shot arrow. His ears were flattened against his head and his legs barely touched the ground as he charged at the rooting bear. Misko didn't bark until he was within spitting distance of the beast. The bear roared mightily, upset that his carefree meal had been disturbed. Standing on his haunches, the brute swiped a huge paw at Misko. The dog dodged the swing, backed up, then stood his ground. The bear swerved his head and bellowed. In the sunlight, we saw saliva spray from his huge mouth.

Gichi Bizhiins and I darted across the meadow to close the distance between us and the bear. Once we were in range, we stopped long enough to gain our breath and slow our heartbeats down. Then, rapidly, we fired three arrows each. The arrows found their mark around the bear's heart and lungs. The animal roared, then coughed up a spew of berries and phlegm, showering Misko in the process. The dog, insulted by this turn of events, loped a short distance away and rolled on the ground to remove the smell and wetness from his fur. All Misko accomplished with this action was to coat himself with dirt, grass, and ground-in berry juice. Gichi Bizhiins and I laughed at the dog's antics and his new appearance.

The bear sat down and started pawing at the arrows embedded in his chest, breaking off the shafts. He then fell forward, coughing, sneezing, and spewing blood, berries, and mucus from his nostrils on the grass in front of him. Sitting up on his haunches, he stared at Gichi Bizhiins and me and released a noise like thunder that sent shivers up my back and produced goosebumps on my arms and neck. Reacting to the roar, Gichi Bizhiins drove his spear into the animal's heart. Even with that, the bear had enough strength left to snap the spear shaft.

Misko took time out from rolling to return to the bloody site and bark at the bear, distracting him long enough for me to walk behind the beast and crush his skull with a tremendous blow to the head with my war axe. As the animal dropped dead at our feet, I released an earsplitting victory scream that echoed to the treeline and back, sending into flight hundreds of birds. Gichi Bizhiins and Misko stopped and stared, surprised at my outburst.

I stood there clutching my axe limply at my side, completely drained from the adrenaline that had previously driven my body to slay this animal.

"Gichi-Manidoo made sure the spirit of this bear didn't die easily," Gichi Bizhiins said. "However, I've slain bears before and they always charge or attempt to charge the hunter. Why didn't this one? Was it because we had shot so many arrows into him?"

I was about to answer him when something caught my eye on the western edge of the meadow at the treeline. It looked like a warrior, but then it turned into a big hare and vanished into the forest. "Nanabozho," I murmured.

Gichi Bizhiins turned to me. "What?"

"Oh, nothing, my friend, just my eyes playing tricks on me."

Gichi Bizhiins reached into his medicine bag and took out some tobacco as a gift to the fallen animal's spirit. He thanked the bear for giving such a fight to remain in the land of the living. Gichi Bizhiins also thanked him for offering himself to us so that we could live on by his death. We then sat down and cut out the heart of the bear, dividing it among the two of us and Misko. Now the three of us would gain the strength and bravery of this animal.

It took the better part of the remainder of the day to butcher the animal. We cut off the claws to make a necklace and saved the bladder to hold water. We also made sure to remove our arrowheads and spearhead from the carcass.

While I finished cutting up the animal, Gichi Bizhiins made an odaabaan (*ou-da-bah:* pole sled) from small saplings intercrossed with vines to hold the meat on for Misko and an extra one for us to take turns pulling. Ours would have the added weight of the bearskin. We had decided to have only one of us at a time pull the sled, keeping the other man free to guard us in case of any surprises.

As we butchered the animal, taking the choicest parts to bring to the meeting point, Gichi Bizhiins glanced up and cried, "Ravens!"

We both knew what they would bring — wolves. I was in no mood to try to defend a bear's carcass from a pack of hungry wolves. Quickly, we grabbed what we could carry and left the area. This fresh kill would prevent the resident pack from trailing us and taking what it wanted. Many a lone warrior had lost his life to a pack of hungry wolves when he didn't leave it part of the kill. The residents of the forest expected their due, and woe to the visiting hunters who didn't understand that. I had seen hungry wolves trail a party of hunters for days, waiting for a chance to snatch the meat being carried out. Hunters always had to know not to be selfish and to share. If not, they would suffer the consequences.

We decided to travel away from the area as far as we could before we prepared the hide and ate. Hiking until just before sunset, we came upon a cliff that overlooked the channel situated between the island and the mainland. Here we camped and enjoyed the view. We watched as huge flocks of geese landed in the water to spend the evening, sharing the water with thousands of ducks. I took Misko down to the edge of the water to follow a game trail. There, to his disgruntled surprise, I tossed him into the water, then used handfuls of sand to rub the bear smell and grass from his fur. He wasn't happy with my actions, and when I released him, he shook vigorously to expel the water from his fur and rolled on the grassy shoreline.

When we reached the top of the outlook, Gichi Bizhiins had a fire going, tea brewing, and the bear's stomach boiling in a bark container heated by hot rocks. The smells wafted through the air and mingled with the pine and cedar scents of the surrounding forest. The stomach was full of grass, berries, and pieces of carrion the animal had eaten that day. It was a delicacy the two of us soon gobbled up. After tossing a well-earned piece of bear meat to Misko, Gichi Bizhiins and I sat in the darkness and gazed at the starry night, smoke from the fire keeping the bugs away from us.

By the light of the fire, I attached the spearhead retrieved from the bear's body to a new shaft, which I had cut when down by the water with Misko. Gichi Bizhiins was able to make some pine arrow shafts, and we fashioned new arrows from the ones the bear had broken. Of the six arrows in the bear's body, we had retrieved three of the flint points. The others had their tips broken and were too fragile to repoint. I had some turtle spike claws in my shoulder bag that we used as replacement heads. Turtle claws were employed as arrows in times of battle; the claws carried with them the spirit of the turtle as a good omen. For now they would do until we could locate some flint.

With full stomachs we went to sleep with visions of the successful day of hunting still in our memories. Alive and well for another day!

At sunrise we rose and packed the sleds for Misko and ourselves. I took the first turn pulling the pole sled and did so until the noon sun. Gichi Bizhiins had his turn then and we continued on in a heavy rain. There wasn't time to stop and wait out the storm. Removing all our clothes, we bundled them up and strode naked in the downpour. The rain was warm, and it was a wonderful feeling to have it beat off our bare bodies, plus the insects seemed to dislike the shower so we suffered no bites from their usual constant attacks. It gave us a real sense of freedom in the elements.

The other three would be waiting at the designated point to pick us up, so we had to maintain a quick pace. I glanced down at Misko as he trotted in the rain. His demeanour never changed; he was a wet dog and smelled like one, but exuded a sense of enjoyment, pulling his load and keeping up with us. Misko was repaid in kind with bear meat, which was much more of a meal than he got when he was in camp. There, all he could expect were entrails, bones, and small scraps of meat.

After walking for two suns, we neared the meeting place fully clothed. We could see the lake in the distance and smell the faint aroma of a campfire. The three of us picked up the pace with a spring in our steps, knowing we would soon be relieved of our heavy burdens.

We reached an embankment and looked down upon Nitaage Niibiwa, Apiitendang Makwa, and Gizhiibatoo Inini beside a fire. They were making tea and roasting a duck on a spit.

I gave the whistle of a bull elk to get their attention, and when they glanced up, I yelled, "How about a little help here, you lazy dogs!"

They quickly rose and hurried up to our position, laughing as they came. Gizhiibatoo Inini said as they neared us, "You're lucky. We decided that once we ate the duck and drank our tea we were leaving without you. Being over half a day late, we figured the spirit that lives in the underwater cave came out onto the island, caught you, and ate you. Not wanting to suffer the same fate with such an important war belt to deliver, we were going to depart."

I studied the three of them. "If you had left us here, the cave spirit would have been the least of your worries in the coming future."

That started everyone laughing, teasing, and shoving good-naturedly.

Gichi Bizhiins undid Misko from his pole sled, and the big dog rolled on the ground to show his delight in being freed. Even though the dog excelled at his job, he took great delight in being relieved from his duties.

The trio eagerly helped us with our loads and took everything down to the campsite. It was a happy time for these three: having fresh bear meat and knowing there would be a good story told that night around the fire about the success of the hunt.

We agreed to take another day to rest ourselves and smoke the meat so that it wouldn't spoil. The sled poles would now be put to use again as drying racks. Our culture didn't squander or throw away anything. Ashkaakamigokwe (Mother Earth) supplied us with the materials, and we showed her that we wouldn't waste anything she gave us.

While the meat was being smoked the next day, we used the brain of the bear to tan the leather and prepare it. It was staked out to dry, and when we got to the Naadawe village, it would make an excellent gift.

On the day we left, the water was calm and a slight breeze from the south brushed our faces. Misko slept on the bottom of the boat, and with five paddlers we made good time. We had a couple of lines strung over the side of the boat with frogs attached to the bone hooks. Even when we had an abundance of food, as with the bear meat, we always had an eye to the future to ensure we didn't go hungry. By the time we could see the shoreline of our destination, a large peninsula jutting into the lake the Ouendat called Attigouatan (Georgian Bay), we had seven fish flopping in the bottom of the canoe, much to the irritation of Misko, who was trying to sleep. Every once in a while a fish wriggled near Misko, waking him, only to be dispatched by a swat of the dog's paw. The antics of the fish and the dog gave us some much-needed entertainment from the monotony of paddling from the island and across the watery expanse.

Covering our canoe with brush, we loaded the bear meat, fish, copper, and bear pelt on our backs and started for the Ouendat village of Ossossanè. That night we camped at the foot of the peninsula and feasted on our bear meat and fish. Stomachs full, we slept soundly until wakened in the early morning by Misko's growling. Upon opening my eyes, I was momentarily blinded by the rising sun, and when my vision readjusted to the sudden light, I caught sight of a dozen fierce-looking warriors surrounding our campsite, made almost invisible by the bright sunlight.

14

A WARNING
FROM A LEGEND

CHAŊKU WAŠTE

Ťhaťháŋka Kaťá, Wawát'ečala Iȟá, her sister, Pȟáŋžela
Napé, and I approached the rise where Ťhaťháŋka Kaťá
had slain the buffalo during the running of the beasts to
the killing pen. Óta Heȟáka was already there and had
asked me to come forward after Pȟáŋžela Napé had told
us she smelled something awful. Now Pȟáŋžela Napé
asked, "Has that buffalo rotted so much in a day that it
smells like this?"

As soon as she said that, the dogs immediately stopped,
lay down, and started to whimper. "Ťhaťháŋka Kaťá," I
whispered, "come with me. You're going to feast your eyes
on a magnificent sight." I motioned to the two women
to follow, and we made our way to where Óta Heȟáka
was standing. At the top we looked on in amazement at
the Čhiyé Ťháŋka (*chee-'ay ton-'kah*: Big Elder Brothers).

There were two males and a female tearing strips of meat from the dead buffalo and gorging themselves. The Čhiyé Tȟáŋka had never been known to harm a Lakȟóta. We perceived them as our Elder Brothers. They lived in another dimension and only appeared whenever they had a reason to tell us something or to eat. When a Lakȟóta died, he moved into another dimension, but the Čhiyé Tȟáŋka had the ability to shift between dimensions. They were messengers from the Great Mystery. The man beasts had only one foe and that was the grizzly bear. The great bears kept their distance from these huge denizens of the two worlds. The Čhiyé Tȟáŋka stood over seven feet and when provoked were powerful beyond compare, enough to gain the respect of a grizzly.

My father once told me a story of watching a Čhiyé Tȟáŋka and a grizzly fighting over an antelope carcass. He was amazed as the Čhiyé Tȟáŋka picked up and threw the grizzly over twenty feet in the air. When the bear hit the ground, he gasped, roared deafeningly, and charged right back at his foe, only to be met by a huge hand catching him flush in the face and sending him tumbling backward head over heels another ten or fifteen feet. My father said the bear sat up, shook his head as if to clear it, and took one more look at the hairy beast that had twice sent him hurtling through the air. He then turned and sauntered away, glancing over his shoulder once or twice as if to see whether what had just happened was real. There was nothing in the Lakȟóta lands that could fling a grizzly around like that, and my father was certain the bear had been as shocked as he was at the power of this being.

As I gazed past the three smelly creatures toward the prairie, I spied a grizzly in the prairie grass waiting for his chance at the buffalo carcass. Very wisely, he had chosen to keep his distance for the time being.

When a Čhiyé Tȟáŋka wanted to talk with us, he used sign language, and today the oldest of the three, one of the males, beckoned me to come and sit. After I did so, the Čhiyé Tȟáŋka came to my side and handed me a chunk of bloody meat. His smell was stifling, but he had a kind face completely covered with hair, with a smile peeking through. The bodies of Čhiyé Tȟáŋka were hairy except for the palms of their hands and bottoms of their feet. When this one grinned, I saw that his teeth were yellow and his breath outdid his body odour for rankness. His fur was the colour of my hair, black with grey streaks. Peering closely, I noticed twigs and grass caught in the matting of his fur.

We sat there for quite a while signing back and forth. My family waited with the other two Čhiyé Tȟáŋka, who continued their eating. The dogs kept their distance, lying on the ground, not knowing what to think about these huge beasts. As long as we accepted our newfound friends, the dogs remained relaxed.

Finally, the one I was talking to stood and motioned to the others, and then all three left. The older one made a running motion toward the watchful grizzly, sending the bear on a gallop away from his hopeful meal. I then watched as the trio of Čhiyé Tȟáŋka lumbered in the direction of the horizon and disappeared.

We took what meat we could load on each dog's travois and left. My wife's sister, Pȟáŋžela Napé, came up to me and asked, "Chaŋku Wašte, why do the Čhiyé Tȟáŋka smell so bad?"

"Well," I answered, "it's probably because they would rather drink their water than wash in it."

She stared at me in shock. Then, when I began to laugh, she joined me in the joke. My other three family members looked at us and asked what was so funny. Pȟáŋžela Napé told them, and soon everyone was laughing.

As we headed back to the encampment, Óta Heȟáka asked me, "What did Elder Čhiyé Tȟáŋka tell you?"

"It wasn't good news, my son. You've knocked down a hornets' nest in the land of the Ȟaȟátȟuŋwaŋ, and trouble is coming to our lands. He said we have to be prepared and that the outcome of this threat would be decided in a dark and bloody battle. That's all he could tell me. The rest is controlled by the Great Mystery.

"When we settle in our winter camp, I'll take out the čhaŋnúŋpa wakȟán (*chah-nuen-pah wah-kahn:* sacred pipe) that the Mother of Life, Ptesáŋ Wí (*tay-san wee:* White Buffalo Calf Woman), gave us during the year of starvation, and we'll light it and pray for guidance. Other than that, everything else rests in fate and the chosen path for us. Even though you were given a dream to attack the Ȟaȟátȟuŋwaŋ, it might not have been the right decision."

After we arrived back at the camp, I approached SápA Ziŋtkála and told him the story the Čhiyé Tȟáŋka had relayed to me. We decided to approach Nážiŋ Išnála, leader of the akíčita, and have him send the Kȟaŋǧí Yuhá (*kohn-gay yue-hah:* Crow Owners' Society) to find us a winter camp along the Kȟaŋǧí Ȟupáhu Wakpá, near where that stream connected with the Wakpá Atkúku, the big river. Even though that put us closer to the Ȟaȟátȟuŋwaŋ, it would help us react to their movements better.

We found Nážiŋ Išnála, and he quickly dispatched the Tȟáŋka Yuhá members to locate a winter camp for the community. SápA Ziŋtkála and I, realizing there was protection in numbers, decided to keep our two villages together during the winter. With the successful buffalo hunt, we now had enough food to get us to spring and sufficient hunters to add to the fresh meat during the winter months. Since we had arrived sooner at this camp than in previous years, we had more time to fish the two rivers to increase our supplies.

The Kȟaŋǧí Yuhá was a group of warriors that emulated the crow. Its members always endeavoured to be the first to strike in battle and wore stuffed crows around their necks. They were also responsible for searching out our winter camps. The akíčita had several warrior societies, which made it even more respected as a strong group of guardians.

It would take ten to twelve suns before all the buffalo meat was dried and processed. Once that was done, the women would tan the hides and make robes and clothing. The men would still follow the buffalo herd and try to pick off any stragglers the wolves and grizzlies failed to kill. Anything they could slay during their hunt, they cut up on the prairie and brought back with dogs and travois. It was then given to the women to dry on the racks.

The women cut the meat into long strips and hung them to dry in the sun. Once the strips were ready, they pounded them into flakes and mixed that in a hide bag with dried berries. Then melted fat was added. The meat would keep for a very long time and would be eaten out of the bag or cooked in water with wild onions and turnips.

Seventeen suns after the Kȟaŋǧí Yuhá men departed, there appeared on the horizon from the northeast three figures.

15

ALLIES GATHER

ZHASHAGI

Once my eyes adjusted to the light, I recognized our camp intruders. The leader said to me, "My Anishinaabe friend thinks he's so safe in our lands that he doesn't have to post a guard?"

"Well, Waughshe Anue," I replied, "if you killed us in our sleep, you wouldn't have gotten much more than what we were going to give you as gifts!" Waughshe Anue was the Ouendat chief we had helped in the battle with the Haudenosaunee.

The chief extended his hand and pulled me up from my sleeping spot. "We knew you were here yesterday when you came ashore. Some of our younger hunters watched as you landed on the peninsula, and they came running to me with the news. They thought we were going to be under attack by a group of spirit animals." He nodded at the three cousins.

"They're as fierce as they look," I said. "But they also sleep quite heavily. Get up!" I yelled, and the four slumbering warriors woke with a start as Misko barked repeatedly.

My companions got to their feet in a hurry with expressions of amazement on their faces once they saw the surrounding Ouendat.

I said to them that I thought the best we could expect was getting burnt at the stake now that we had been captured. Waughshe Anue and his men started to laugh, and after a while my sullen face broke into a grin. My four comrades exchanged glances and began to laugh nervously. They knew that if the men around us weren't friends we would all be thrown into the firepits.

I made quick introductions and brought out the war belt I was carrying. The Ouendat men all nodded in anticipation of my request. We gathered up our belongings, and I handed the bearskin to Waughshe Anue. He took it, thanked me for the kind offering, and threw it around his shoulders with a satisfied grunt. "Follow me, my friends," he said, and we headed off to his village.

It was nearing sunset when we reached the edge of their cornfields. In the distance, I saw the stockade surrounding their community. Scattered throughout the fields of corn, squash, and beans were wooden stands that the young boys sat on to keep watch and chase deer, raccoons, bears, and birds from their food source. Women and children were harvesting the corn by picking the cobs and putting them into baskets on their backs. Strolling by a couple of plants, I grabbed some beans and ate them raw. We had left without an early-morning meal, and hunger pains had started to nag me. I even snatched an ear of corn and ate it. It was very tasty and juicy.

Where the corn had already been harvested, they were burning the stalks and scattering the ashes on the ground to replenish the soil with needed earth food to help next year's crops grow.

The cornfields surrounded the village, and it took us a while to reach the front gate. When we entered the village proper, I noticed a pet bear roaming around tied to a leash with a young boy coaxing him with corn.

In the centre of the village was a huge heap of corn that had been harvested. More women, children, and Elders were pulling back the husks and braiding them together to be hung in the longhouses to dry. After drying, the women would scrape off the kernels, wash and dry them, and then store them in bark-lined pits. I even saw some women drying whole ears of corn on hot embers and stockpiling them whole.

The corn husks would be used to make corn dolls for young girls, baskets, and clothes. All the warriors, women, and children in the village were healthy and seemingly happy. The groups doing the harvesting laughed and sang the whole time they worked.

As we ambled farther into the enclosure, we came upon five men gutting two deer hung up on poles, surrounded by flies and eagerly watching dogs. The aromas of cornbread wrapped in husks baking in the hot ashes and corn soup boiling made my stomach growl.

My four companions and I passed a cooking fire where a girl was engrossed in making soup and boiling corn. She glanced up from her job and held a wooden bowl out to Nitaage Niibiwa, saying, "Ask your friends to stop and eat with me and my family."

We eagerly sat on our haunches, and the girl handed us bowls of hot soup, tea, and boiled corn. Soon one of the warriors who had been in the group that had brought us to the village joined along with two young boys and the warrior's wife and mother of all the children, including the girl who had invited us to eat. We enjoyed a fulfilling meal, answering questions about our travels and where we lived. The young boys smiled, listened to every word we said, and never uttered a word themselves. They were quite shy but cheerful.

The father's name was Ohskënonton' (*o-ski-non-ton'*: Deer), the brother of Achie, the Ouendat who had fought with us in the battle with the Haudenosaunee. The bear was Achie's, who had raised it from a cub after he adopted it one spring ago not long before we joined the Ouendat and their Omàmiwinini allies in the fight against the Haudenosaunee. Achie had been with the Omàmiwinini back then and still travelled with them.

That night we and the others went to a council meeting and presented the red war belt. Waughshe Anue took the belt and accepted it on behalf of the Ouendat Nation. He told us that any Ouendat who desired to go to war in the spring with us would be allowed to as long as enough warriors stayed to defend the families that remained.

"Are the Omàmiwinini in the land of the Ouendat?" I asked.

"No, they left after our Feast of the Dead and journeyed to a river that empties into a bay the Haudenosaunee call Kenhtè:ke," Waughshe Anue said. "It's on the northeast end of an island at the end of the last of the big lakes. If you must go to find them, I'll send two men with you."

"Yes," I replied, "we need them also!"

"If you go south now, you'll have to be prepared to winter there," the Ouendat chief said. "If that's what you decide, my young men will be ready to leave with you at spring breakup to make war on the Nadowessioux."

"We would like to rest one more day and then head out to where the Omàmiwinini are. When we left our homes, we fully expected to spend the winter in these lands."

The next day we traded our copper for moccasins, heavier clothing, extra food, and arrows. The two warriors who were leaving with us were called Otawindeht (*o-ta-win-dat*: Otter) and Skenhchio (*sken-shoe*: Red Fox).

The morning of our departure our hosts fed us well, and the young daughter of Ohskënonton' gave us a leather bag full of leaves and said, "We call this evergreen, and if you drink the tea from the leaves, it will give you strength and take away your aches and pains."

"Thank you," I said. "Here is a bear claw to remember me by." I took it from my neck and hung it around hers. When we returned through here in the spring, I thought, I would ask her father for her hand. She was probably fifteen or sixteen summers old with a smile that lit up her face and melted my heart. When my companions and I left the village shortly after dawn, I felt different, happier, and hopeful for the future.

The seven of us and Misko made good time in the early going. The Ouendat had many trails connecting their villages and they were well worn. With the two young warriors leading us, we ran unhindered through the network of paths. It took us a day and a half to leave the immediate Ouendat territory, staying one night in a village of about five hundred people. There we again showed our war belt and were told that warriors would join us on our spring return to the land of our people.

Eventually, we came to a lake and paddled across it without any problems, catching a few fish in the process. That night, when we camped, I made tea from the leaves the girl had given me. Thinking of her, I became embarrassed. I didn't even know her name. I was so caught up in her beauty that I had never thought to ask. As we sat by the fire, I asked Skenhchio, "What is the name of the daughter of Ohskënonton'?"

He grinned and said, "Yatie' (*sha-tip*: Bird). Why the sudden interest, my friend?"

"No reason. She gave me these leaves for tea and I never knew her name."

Otawindeht spoke up and said, "I'm sure she liked the bear claw you gave her."

The three cousins', Nitaage Niibiwa, and the two Ouendat guffawed. I merely smiled and drank my tea.

Skenhchio finished his tea, crawled under his fur robe, and advised the rest of us, "Two more suns and we'll be near our friends. Rest up!"

16

HOW THE MOSQUITO CAME TO BE

ANOKÌ

The great Mi'kmaq warrior Crazy Crow returned to our Omàmiwinini camp just after the first frost. He had taken it upon himself to be our constant scout in this newfound area where we were hunting and fishing.

"Kìnà Odenan!" he called out to one of the Warrior Women as he entered our winter camp.

She looked up and asked, "What is it, Crazy Crow?"

"A half day to the west of here there is a river — the Sagottaska (Moira) — that empties into this bay. A group of Haudenosaunee is camped there, netting fish and drying them. I don't think they have plans to come down here, but we should send two scouts each day to watch the waterway until freeze-up."

"Agwanìwon and I will take a look tomorrow," Kìnà Odenan said. "Thank you very much for your report.

Wàbananang, Pangì Mahingan, and Ki'kwa'ju killed a deer this morning, so there's fresh deer on the spit in among the dwellings. Help yourself."

Crazy Crow licked his lips. "Many thanks."

I spent the day of Crazy Crow's return with the two Ouendat warriors, Achie and Önenha', gathering wood for our winter supply, a task the two Warrior Women chiefs, Kìnà Odenan and Agwanìwon, had assigned us. We found lots of deadfall and fastened a pole sled to my dog, Nìj Enàndeg, to cart it back, two of us taking turns pulling another sled while the third scouted. Dawn to dusk we worked and managed to collect an enormous pile of wood. In fact, we amassed so much that we surrounded our five huts with a shoulder-high fence with a small opening to enter.

Kànìkwe laughed when he saw what we had done. "You have enough wood for us to stay two winters!"

Uncle Mònz's face had healed, but the scar he had earned in the battle with the Haudenosaunee made him seem even fiercer. His wife, Wàbìsì, who was also my father's sister, had made sure he was well looked after. Both Mònz and Wàbìsì had been in mourning for more than a year. She had given birth to a dead son. The umbilical cord had been wrapped around his neck and had cut his air off. The birth woman had told Wàbìsì that he had died in the womb. Mònz had been sullen and in mourning ever since. He only seemed happy when busy at some task that took his mind off the death. Mònz treated everyone kindly, but we knew he was hurting.

Wàbìsì, as sad as she was with the loss, concentrated on taking care of Mònz. They both enjoyed hunting with the two Mi'kmaq warriors, E's and Jilte'g.

The twins, Makwa and Wàbek, accompanied by their wives, Àwadòsiwag and Ininàtig, had left a couple of days ago with Mitigomij to try to find either a moose or an elk to slay and bring back to camp. A big animal like that would keep hunger away for a very long time.

About once or twice every ten or eleven suns we were able to kill a deer. Its meat didn't last very long with our group, plus we had about twenty dogs that were ravenous most of the time. We had been eating well, so the dogs got intestines and bones to gorge on. If our food supply lessened during the winter, the dogs would be lucky to get that much and they themselves might end up being our nourishment.

The days were getting shorter and the nights cooler and along with this change the bugs disappeared. The Ouendat and I had made sure everyone had lots of firewood piled outside their lodges. Kìnà Odenan chuckled every time we came in with loads of wood. We were now down to three or four trips a day because of the lack of daylight, and we had to go farther away to find deadfalls.

Kìnà Odenan looked at us one day and said, "I have to admit that the three of you take your jobs seriously. You've been at this for over a moon. How about I say that's enough wood and tell you to spend your days fishing? I'm sure that if you take that job as seriously as wood collecting, we'll have an ample supply of fish. I'll get Kànìkwe to erect some more drying racks in addition to the ones we've been using since we got here. He's getting bored setting snares for rabbits. It's time for him to expand his abilities."

"One more load," I said. "We left a pile in the woods that we want to bring out."

"All right," she replied, "and tonight come to our lodge. Kànìkwe says he has a story to tell."

That night we sat and ate fish and venison and drank spruce tea in the lodge of Agwanìwon and Kìnà Odenan. My wolf dog lay beside me, while dogs that were close companions to other warriors were sprawled behind the seated group.

"Does anyone here know where the blood-takers, the sagime (*suh-gih-may*: mosquito), come from?" Before anyone could say a word he came right out and said, "Well, I'm going to tell you!"

That brought a chuckle from a few of us because we all knew Kànìkwe wasn't going to give anyone a chance to ruin his story.

"It all began many, many years ago when Turtle Island was still young," Kànìkwe began. "The Nipissing, Ouendat, and we, the Omàmiwinini, lived very close to one another. At that time our numbers weren't as great as they are now and we needed the protection of one another from our enemies to the south and the creatures in the forest that preyed on us when we let our guards down. Whenever we hunted, always one or two hunters from each tribe went out together. That way we learned to share and feed all equally. This worked for many years, and soon we realized that our numbers were increasing and we would have to find larger territories to feed our growing population.

"One spring it was decided the three nations would go their separate ways in the fall. Then something strange started to happen. Hunters went out and never returned. Our people would go out and search for them but couldn't find any trace of them. For a long time we thought it was our enemies, but there was no sign of our foes coming through the area. We had to keep sending hunting parties out, because our people were now starving from lack of food. Berries, fish, and small animals couldn't feed everyone.

"Then one day an Ouendat warrior returned without his companions. His eyes were full of fear and he was gasping for air. He told a story that sent chills throughout the camp. A monster had captured and eaten his companions right in front of him. He had only escaped by jumping off a cliff into a lake, Mazinaabikinigan (Lake Mazinaw), that they had paddled across. The monster didn't chase him, and the Ouendat made it back to the camp safely.

"The next day they left twenty warriors guarding the camp and over a hundred others headed out to hunt down the monster. When they got to the area where the men had been disappearing, they dug a big pit and covered it with branches. Then all the warriors disappeared into the surrounding forest except for eleven who made a fire next to a rock cliff and sat with their backs to it, roasting a haunch of deer. Soon they heard a tremendous roar and a huge twelve-foot monster dripping saliva and blood from his mouth came into the small clearing. He was carrying half a bloody man, one of ours who must have been taken in the forest. Glaring at the warriors against the cliff, he growled, 'I have you cornered and you'll be my meal today!'

"The monster then stepped toward them and fell into the pit. The creature's roaring and screaming sent chills down the spines of everyone. The men all rushed from out of the woods and stood beside the pit, spears and arrows ready to slay the monster.

"'If you think killing me will stop the blood-taking, you're wrong,' the beast snarled. 'I'll still take the blood from your bodies.' Then the monster started to laugh.

"Hundreds of spears and arrows pierced the beast's enormous body, and when he died his carcass broke into thousands and thousands of small flying bugs that attacked the men, biting them and extracting blood from their skins. The warriors left for home tortured by these tiny insects.

"No monster like this was ever heard of again, but he gifted our lands with the bloodthirsty sagime!"

Kànìkwe rose from his position at the fire, filled his drinking vessel full of tea, and headed for the doorway of the lodge, stopping suddenly and saying, "Safe dreams." Then he laughed and continued on his way out of the lodge.

We looked at one another nervously, threw some more wood on the fire, and decided to sleep for the night in the lodge of Agwanìwon and Kìnà Odenan.

The next morning Achie, Önenha', and I started to rebuild the fish weirs, making them from stone and wood and putting them in the spots where we'd had them the spring after we arrived. There were a few nets also left from that time, which we repaired. The rapids and surrounding area were a popular place for fish of all types in these fall months. We took turns minding the nets and weirs, and when not doing those chores, Kànìkwe and the three of us enjoyed spearing fish.

Our community was a rare one because there were no children, which meant that a lot of chores normally done by young boys and girls had to be shared among all the adults. Tending fires, feeding the dogs, collecting berries and roots, plus cleaning fish and hanging them to dry were jobs everyone in camp took on. We always had to stop before sunset and clean the fish.

Nìj Enàndeg, my wolf dog, guarded the piles of fish that we tossed onto the shore. Even the fish that flopped around, headed back to the river, Nìj Enàndeg caught with his mouth and brought back to where he watched over them.

None of the other dogs even attempted to steal one. Nìj Enàndeg made sure of that. After a few days, the camp dogs learned to stay away from my wolf dog and only came around when the fish were being cleaned. This was feeding time for them, and they all got to eat their fill between the snarling and short fights over the guts. Small fish were always thrown back into the water with the hope that they would grow. Within four days we had all the drying racks full and we erected more.

After about a week Mitigomij and his small band of hunters returned. They had killed a moose and had brought all the meat back along with the help of the five dogs they had taken with them. As they entered camp, I watched the shadowy figure of Makadewà Waban, Mitigomij's panther, skirt the camp and leap into a tree to watch over his lifelong companion and the small village site.

We had made our permanent summer and winter camp above the falls on the north side of the river just before the torrent swerved toward the cataract. It gave us added safety because the river was fairly straight there and we could see anyone moving in from the northeast. Plus, if intruders came from the falls area, they had to leave their boats, giving us a good view southwest from the top of the falls and rapids.

Our people had also built a tree stand high above the camp area that overlooked both sides of the river. We all took turns up there during the daylight. The lookout time was divided into five shifts: two people split the morning and three handled the afternoon.

Whenever we fished below, we always had to carry our catches back to clean and put on the drying racks. To do that we used reed baskets and also long saplings with a short branch like a gaff still intact on the end. We slid the fish onto the sapling by sticking them through their gills. Then, when we returned the short distance to the camp, we each held one side of a basket and carried a sapling full of fish over the other shoulder.

One evening, after filling all the racks and before the frost and snow of namegosi-kizis (*na-me-go-sis-key-sis:* October), our group was awakened by the ear-splitting howls of Mitigomij's big cat. Everyone rushed out of the lodges with weapons in hand.

There, in the moonlight, was a female bear and her two cubs, which had grown to a fair size from the summer's bounty. Because the three of them had taken turns fending off the dogs, they had managed to strip two of the drying racks and gorge themselves on all the fish that had been there. The female we had to slay, but we were reluctant to kill the half-grown cubs. If we didn't, though, they would have kept returning to forage for food now that their mother was no longer alive to provide guidance.

Before the night was over there was a lot of snarling, growling, and roaring. In the end, we obtained a good supply of fresh meat, three warm robes, and hopefully no more bear problems. It was dawn before everything was back to normal, the animals had been butchered, and the dogs were settled down. A few of us tried to sleep for a few hours, while others who were too excited from all the unrest started their day.

About three suns after the bear attack I was out with Nìj Enàndeg scouting to the southwest along the river when I heard voices only a short distance from our camp. Motioning to my wolf dog, we scurried up an embankment and watched as seven warriors walked along the shoreline.

17

LAKȞÓTA WINTER CAMP

CHAŊKU WAŠTE

The three men on the horizon were from the Crow Owners' Society. They had come back to lead us to the winter camp at the joining of the rivers called the Kȟaŋǧí Ȟupáhu Wakpá and the Wakpá Atkúku. They told us that the area was safe and that the others had stayed behind to clear a camp area.

At the junction of these two rivers the water was calm with no rapids. There was good fishing and the protection of a large island sitting back from the forks and a smaller island right in the forks. Both rivers had bends before they came to the junction. The three Crow Owners' Society men said our winter camp would be situated on the southeast side of the river below the intersection, with a view of the bigger river, the Wakpá Atkúku, before it flowed into a bend to the south. The village could also see toward the exiting part of the bend on the Kȟaŋǧí Ȟupáhu Wakpá and could station warriors on both islands for protection.

Our combined villages of close to seven hundred people, with around two hundred warriors, were ready to move, but the column could only travel as fast as our slowest members. The Tȟokȟála (*tah-koh-la:* Kit Fox Society) warriors volunteered to patrol the perimeter of the column and assist stragglers, keep the line moving, and guard against unexpected problems, man or beast. These society members wore fox skins on their shoulders.

My nephew, Tȟatȟáŋka Kaťá, drew close to me and asked, "Why are both camps staying together for the winter, Uncle?"

"Óta Heȟáka and some of the braves made war on our enemy, the Ȟaȟátȟuŋwaŋ, in the spring. The other leaders and I think they'll attack us in the future and that to survive we need safety in numbers."

"I'll help protect our people," Tȟatȟáŋka Kaťá insisted. "Óta Heȟáka said I can go to battle with him now that I have my warrior name. I'll help to defend!"

"I know you will," I said cautiously.

Our Lakȟóta moved as fast as possible. With that many people and more than three thousand dogs, we strained to make good time during daylight. Three times we had to stop: twice while women gave birth and once to bury an Elder woman who passed away during the fourteenth night on the trail. With our column in no particular danger from attack or no real rush to get to our winter camp, the birthing women had traditional births in privacy. Once they came back to the column, the women had comfortable travois with cushions of buffalo robes and deerskins prepared for them and their babies. The proud fathers walked alongside their wives and newborns. One of the birthing mothers had two other young children, and they took turns riding the pole sled with her. The father had arranged to have two of his strongest dogs harnessed to the travois, and they pulled the added weight with no problem. Both women who had given birth were well looked after by the other wives.

The Sotkàyuha (*shoh-dkah-yuh-hah*: Bare Lance Owners' Society) was made up of young warriors who carried bare lances and had yet to collect war honours. They were assigned to do the hunting each day and took great pride in supplying this service. They kept the column in continual supply of wild game, preventing the depletion of the buffalo meat that was being transported to keep this large number of people alive through the winter.

The column was strung out as far as I could see, and other than just the one death, the only serious injuries were a few sprained ankles and one young boy who stepped in a gopher hole and broke his leg. Two dogs were hooked up to a travois to drag him along with the rest of the line.

Finally, after almost one full moon, we reached the winter camp. The Crow Owners' Society warriors had been watching for us and two days previously had come into the travelling camp. They told the akíčita that a shallow ford had been found where we could cross. It took most of the final day to ford the river.

The dogs were released of their travois, and everyone carried the robes, meat, and living essentials through the water, keeping everything dry.

Small children were transported on shoulders, Elders were guided by warriors, and the dogs swam. There was lots of laughter and talking. Some of the older children splashed and carried on as they took their time. It was a warm fall day and no one minded the cool water.

Once the women reached the other side, they started to erect the lodges. Since we only had about two hundred warriors, they would have to hunt, fish, and scout the area relentlessly. The young boys' job was to collect firewood on a continual basis.

By the first night, close to two hundred teepees were erected and the smell of the cooking fires enveloped the whole camp. The din of the day had calmed down and everyone was eating and resting. There were many tasks to do before the first snowfall, and our survival depended on staying warm and being fed. We needed more than the buffalo meat to sustain us. All the young girls and women scoured the surrounding area for roots and berries, while the young boys kept bringing in piles of wood to stack near the lodges and to put in a communal pile. Hunters were out every day and Elders fished along the shoreline. We also needed birchbark canoes, and several men were busy making them.

Every day Tȟatȟáŋka Kaťá left after the early-morning meal, and we didn't see him again until just before sunset and the evening meal. He was helping the other boys collect firewood and set small-game snares. My son, Óta Heȟáka, was gone days at a time hunting game, while my wife, Wawát'ečala Iȟá, and her sister, Pȟáŋžela Napé, were busy making winter clothes and cooking and tanning the rabbit and deer hides Tȟatȟáŋka Kat'á and Óta Heȟáka brought in. All the meat had to be dried and mixed with berries and fat to prevent rotting.

One day SápA Ziŋtkála and I took a canoe and paddled upstream on the Wakpá Atkúku toward the northeast bend in that river. "Chaŋku Wašte," SápA Ziŋtkála said, "this is where the Ȟaȟátȟuŋwaŋ will come from when they arrive in the spring. We need to have warriors up here watching and then a defence on the islands to protect the village."

"I agree, SápA Ziŋtkála. They'll move their force down this river swiftly. They'll also undoubtedly outnumber us. We'll need scouts around this bend in the river to avoid any surprises."

"Let's go back toward the village and up the Kȟaŋǧí Ȟupáhu Wakpá."

Paddling around the bend, we turned northwest. The day was sunny and the river calm. We took our time to enjoy the surroundings. Reaching a bend in the river, we heard voices and were quickly surrounded by a vast number of canoes.

18

PREPARING FOR ANOTHER WAR

ANOKÌ

Taking a closer look at the seven warriors, I realized that two of them were Ouendat men I had seen in the village of Ossossanè where I had once stayed. The other five were Anishinaabe warriors, and one of those with a dog at his side had a familiar face.

"Zhashagi!" I cried from my vantage point.

Zhashagi and the others turned with their weapons at the ready as Nìj Enàndeg and I scurried down through the brush. When I got to the bottom, my arms had streaks of blood oozing from where they had been scraped by thorn bushes.

Seizing me in a big embrace, Zhashagi asked, "Anokì, how are you?"

"I'm fine as long as you don't crush me in this bear hug."

"Sorry! In my excitement seeing you, I got carried away. Please, meet my companions." He then pointed at each warrior in turn. "Apiitendang Makwa, Gich Bizhiins, and Gizhiibatoo Inini. The other Anishinaabe is Nitaage Niibiwa, who joined us during our voyage here. The Ouendat men, Otawindeht and Skenhchio, are our guides on this trek to find your people."

Everyone nodded in approval at the introductions. During this time, I noticed that their weapons were bloodstained from a recent encounter. I didn't see any animal carcass that they were transporting. Since they didn't mention anything about what had happened, I assumed it wasn't of any consequence.

As we walked together, Zhashagi asked, "What about those three fierce warriors, Mitigomij, Glooscap, and the one they call Elue'wiet Ga'qaquj, who talks to crows?"

"All except Glooscap are with us," I answered. "Glooscap, Apistanéwj, Nukumi, and their dogs returned to the lands of the Mi'kmaq."

Before entering the camp I hooted an owl call to announce my entrance.

Our two Warrior Women chiefs, Agwanìnon and Kìnà Odenan, approached us and welcomed the newcomers. "Come in and eat," Agwanìnon said. "We have moose and fish cooking on the fires and tea boiling."

Everyone happened to be in camp at this time, so we were a crowd around the cooking fires as we ate. After the meal, Zhashagi began to speak. When he held up the red war belt, we knew what he wanted from us. He told us the story of the ambush by the Nadowessioux and what the Anishinaabe plans were this coming spring.

After Zhashagi finished talking, Agwanìwon stood and said, "I can only say for myself that I will go with you to make war on the Nadowessioux. As for the others, it is their decision."

When she sat back down, all of our group stood and raised their weapons, signifying their intentions to follow her.

Once everyone had said their piece about following the Anishinaabe into war, Crazy Crow brought up the subject of my puzzlement. "I see your weapons have the red stain of death on them. Did you slay an animal and devour it before Anokì met you?"

The Anishinaabe called Nitaage Niibiwa said, "No animals, just Haudenosaunee. We came upon a group fishing and drying their catch about a half day east of here at the mouth of a river (present-day Moira River, Belleville, Ontario). We thought they would be a threat to you because the Ouendat guides said your campsite would be close to where the Haudenosaunee had set up their hunting camp.

"We sat and watched them for a while before we made the decision to kill them. They had one young boy guarding the camp, and he was more intent on skipping stones across the river. I shortened his stay here with a well-placed arrow. Once we took care of him, we surprised the rest of the camp. There were three warriors and six women. It was quick and bloody work.

"One of the men might have survived, but I think he drowned. I clubbed him and was taking off his hair. I could hear his teeth grinding as I did this because my knife was dull and it wasn't cutting very well. When I was done, I set about finishing him off, but he rolled into the water as I turned my back to pick up my club. The current then took him away. Figuring he would either bleed to death or drown, I didn't bother to go after him. We were hungry, ate our fill of their food, and cached the rest."

Our group looked at one another as we shook our heads.

"We've been watching that fish camp for two full moons," Mitigomij said. "They were no threat to us because they stayed in that area and didn't know we were here. They hadn't prepared their lodges for a winter stay, and the last time we checked on them it looked as if they would have been gone before the next moon. Now someone will miss them when they don't return, then come looking for them in the spring. Sooner, if that hairless victim survived his river plunge and was able to make it back to his lands."

"No one could survive a wound like that," Nitaage Niibiwa said.

There was a roar of laughter to the left of me and then the rest of our group started to chuckle.

Kànìkwe rose and said, "I survived a scalping and have lived to tell about it." To prove it, he took off his fur hat.

Our visitors stared at his scarred head in astonishment.

"What do we do about this problem then?" Zhashagi finally asked.

"If we leave now," Kìnà Odenan said, "a lot of the food we've dried and stored would have to be left behind because the dogs couldn't pull sleds through the bare ground of the fall woods. If we wait until the snow comes and build enough odàbànàk (*oh-dah-nahk:*

toboggan) sleds, we could take all our furs and food supplies back to Ossossanè. We might have to walk around the lake the Ouendat call Ouentironk (Lake Simcoe), which would add another day to our travels. There will be enough of us breaking trail for the dogs that they won't have problems pulling their loads. We had planned to stay until spring, but with the killing of the Haudenosaunee at the fish camp and the Anishinaabe needing us by the start of the summer, it's better that we leave with the first snow. Mitigomij and Crazy Crow, we need the two of you to watch that the Haudenosaunee don't come before the first snow and surprise us. They'll come from the west and have to carry their boats through that long carrying place on the north side of the island. That's the only entrance for them to this river unless they come all the way around the island and enter through the bays. Either way we'll see them if and when they come up this river. We'll plan for winter travel unless the Haudenosaunee come, and then we might have to plan for death."

For the next few moons we worked on our weapons and making àgimag (*ug-ga-mug*: snowshoes) for ourselves. All autumn there was no sign of our enemy. The first snowfall came and then after that a big blizzard. It was time to go.

There were twenty-five of us plus more than twenty dogs. Dogs, men, and women were all laden with packs. Mitigomij, though, and his big panther disappeared every morning and were our eyes on the trail. Crazy Crow and the three Anishinaabe Spirit Warriors guarded the column on all sides and carried lighter packs.

The snowshoes enabled us to make good time and in turn broke the trail well enough that the dogs had no trouble. We had to keep a close eye on their paws and all of them eventually ended up wearing leather covers on their feet to protect them from the cutting snow. A few of them had bloody dew claws, but on the whole they stayed healthy.

One of the females had a litter of pups, and we had to put her on a sled with them. Nìj Enàndeg pulled her, mainly, I thought, because the pups looked a lot like him. By the time we got to Ouentironk, two of the dogs had died and we had to abandon their sleds. Their loads were divided among the other dogs. The animals that were carrying food had their loads lightened every night to feed us. We made lean-tos of cedar boughs for shelter every night, and one evening we stayed in an abandoned village.

As we stood on the shore of the lake, we had to decide whether to take the canoes over through the open areas and then pull them on the ice or to walk around the lake. There had been a cold snap for a few days, and the lake was starting to freeze, but my mother and the two Warrior Women thought the water would be too cold and the ice too thin yet to walk and drag everything across. So the decision was made to walk around the lake along the eastern shore toward the north.

Once we made it around the lake, I noticed that Mitigomij and Crazy Crow had disappeared. They were off on some adventure that we would learn about whenever they showed up again. The two of them together were formidable foes to face in this country, which they knew so well.

The good thing about walking in the winter was that there were no bugs, but it was essential to keep warm. I had seen people who froze to death in the woods after sitting down to have a quick nap, only to be found later that winter partially eaten by wolves, lynx, and foxes.

Once we left the shores of Ouentironk, we made it to Ossossanè in two days. We had slogged for fourteen suns through the woods with no loss of life other than a few dogs, but they were replaced by a litter of eleven pups. When we arrived at the village, the female dog got out of the sled and the pups waddled behind her. Nìj Enàndeg kept a close eye on them.

Mitigomij arrived in Ossossanè a week later. He said that the Haudenosaunee had, in fact, come to the fish camp. About sixty in all, they paddled down the bay and found our camp. The water was still ice-free there. They saw our tracks, had a big discussion, but didn't follow for two reasons. They had no snowshoes and they found the bodies of two warriors who had entered the forest to relieve themselves. One had been mauled by a big cat, the other had been slain and had crow feathers strewn on his body.

Then Mitigomij recounted what had been said by the Haudenosaunee. "I overheard the leader say to several of his men, 'Taking on that shape-shifter the bark eaters call Mitigomij and his black panther is one thing, but they're with Tsyòkawe Ronkwe (*jo-ga-we roon-gway:* Crow Man, the name the Haudenosaunee call Crazy Crow), and that's more than I'm willing to take on with only these few men. We'll leave and pick another day to die!'

"Another warrior answered, 'But we're sixty warriors!'

"'Fifty-eight now! I've seen these two in battles out in the open destroy our warriors with smiles on their faces. Now they're hidden and starting to pick us off like rabbits in a snare. No, my friend, like I said, I'll die another day!' replied the leader."

Zhashagi turned to Mònz, my uncle, and asked, "How did Mitigomij get close enough to the Haudenosaunee to hear them say all this?"

"Mitigomij has many powers that he keeps hidden," Mònz replied. "He and that black panther have had many adventures together and have saved our lives numerous times. We don't ask questions of the ageless one. His brother, Mahingan, knew of his powers but kept them a secret, so we don't ask. Plus with the added companionship of Crazy Crow, the two of them are deadly together!"

Our Omàmiwinini group was told that Zhashagi intended to ask an Ouendat girl, Yatie', daughter of Ohskënonton', to marry him, but to Zhashagi's disappointment she had married while he was away. Skenhchio, one of the Ouendat guides who had brought Zhashagi to us, told Pangì Mahingan and me this news.

"He had only met her the day before we left to find you and your people," Skenhchio said. "It was more like he was smitten by her beauty than anything else. He didn't even know the girl. Plus if he had married her, he would have had to live with her family. The man has a battle to fight. Falling in love is a foolish thing when you might be facing death in the coming summer. Anyway, he shouldn't be too heartbroken. They had hardly even spoken. In fact, he had to ask us her name when we were on the trail. So it can't be that much of a loss, can it? He gave her a bear claw when we left — hardly a declaration of love!"

When he told me this, I laughed and Pangì Mahingan smacked me on the side of the head, saying, "Have some compassion for this poor man. His heart has been broken. I'll remind you of your actions the first time you fall in love!"

Skenhchio started to laugh and ducked as Pangì Mahingan half-heartedly swung her spear shaft at him.

My mother came over to us and asked my sister, "Are these men giving you trouble? If they are, I'll take care of them." She drew her knife and smiled.

I glanced at Skenhchio. "This is one woman you don't want to fool around with when she takes her blade out. See what kind of trouble a mother and sister can bring men?"

Skenhchio and I chuckled and then took off running with the two laughing women chasing us. We passed Zhashagi and he asked as we went by, "What's the cause of all this commotion?"

"You!" Skenhchio shouted, and we kept on running, much to Zhashagi's puzzlement.

Since we had brought so much food back with us, Kìnà Odenan, Agwanìwon, and my mother hosted two feasts in the three full moons we were in Ossossanè. Crazy Crow and Mitigomij spent their time away from the village doing whatever they did. The rest of us hunted, ate, and slept. Pangì Mahingan, Ki'kwa'ju, E's, and Jilte'g went out hunting one sunny day near the spring moon of kà-wàsadotòj (*kah-wah-suh-koh-tooj*: April). Six suns later they came back with a huge wàbidì (*wah-bi-dee:* elk). That night there was another feast, and the elk skin was presented to our hosts for their kindness in sheltering us for another winter.

The days were getting longer and the sun warmer. Snow still lingered on the forest floor, but on the unprotected areas that lacked tree cover the whiteness had disappeared. Then, one sunny day, Waughshe Anue, Zhashagi, and our two chiefs, Agwanìwon and Kìnà Odenan, told everyone that the Ouendat volunteers, the Omàmiwinini, and Zhashagi's men would leave for the land of the Anishinaabe. We had to be prepared to depart the next day. There would be one hundred and seventeen Ouendat warriors from the surrounding villages, our eighteen, and the five Anishinaabe along with favourite war dogs. The Ouendat had prepared the canoes the previous fall, and they were waiting for us at the lake. Thirty canoes would transport us to our destiny in a far-off land. I counted Crazy Crow and my uncle in our group, even though we hadn't seen either of them for most of the winter. When the time came, I knew they would appear from the darkness of the forest to watch over us.

That night was filled with excitement, dancing, and striking the war post. Everyone ate heartily and told stories of past battles. Sleep came quickly for me, comforted by the warmth of Nìj Enàndeg beside me.

19

THE BLOOD SUN

ANOKÌ

Kìnà Odenan and Agwanìwon circulated through the camp before sunrise and collected our scattered group. There would be sixteen of us. Achie and Önenha', even though they were Ouendat warriors, had been travelling with us for so long that they would never consider not being in our tight-knit group. Mitigomij and Crazy Crow, we all knew, would show up sometime in the future.

Agwanìwon told us that the war party would run at a swift pace through the forest. Our group would guard the rear, and we were only to take enough food to last ten days. Hunters would be put ashore along the route to keep us in meat, and while we were in the canoes we would fish and shoot waterfowl. Nìj Enàndeg knew something was about to happen and didn't leave my side while I got ready for the journey.

As we left the camp, I sniffed the faint aroma of corn soup being brewed intermingling with the scent of burning wood. Walking out the gates, I turned to glance back and watched as the glowing fires faded from sight along with the village smells.

The first part of the column was almost through the fallow cornfields when the sun crested over the tops of the trees, highlighting the steamy breaths of the warriors as they silently loped single file. Once the sun broke the horizon, the earth turned white from the frost. It was still in the early days of wàbigon kìzis (*wah-bi-gon key-zis:* May). Even though the days were becoming warm, daybreak still had that early spring coolness, creating a white blanket of frost the moment the sun rose above the trees.

With the rising of the sun, the air around us became filled with the deafening sound of male songbirds greeting the early light with their high-pitched songs, trying to impress the females with the quality of their singing. It was a wonderful feeling to hear the birds and watch the sun rise.

Since we were the last of the long line to leaving the village, I turned to Pangì Mahingan and Ki'kwa'ju and said, "With the rising of the sun, we have enough light to make sure we can walk around all these dog droppings."

"Too late for me!" Ki'kwa'ju replied, raising his heel.

My childhood villages never had a problem with dog dung because we didn't live in a stockade and the dogs went into the woods more times than not to defecate, plus we moved our villages frequently. Our dogs probably picked up the habit of going into the forest from watching our people enter the bush and squat to do our jobs. The dogs, however, didn't turn a heel in the dirt to make an indentation beforehand to bury the droppings after the job was done as we did.

The Ouendat seemed to have an abundance of this problem in their stockades and assigned young boys to scrape it up and take it into the woods for disposal. Today, though, with the rising sun and white frost, the lumps stood out on the ground like small corn hills.

The dogs we took on this trip were fierce ones and weren't expected to pull pole sleds; unlike normal working dogs, these animals were bred to fight alongside their owners.

Waughshe Anue led us past the village women and children who had assembled in the fields to see us off. The warriors who stayed behind to guard their lands had also gathered to yell and whoop as we entered the forest.

A brisk pace through the forest and beaver meadows was set for us by Waughshe Anue. In the early-morning mist as we passed beaver ponds, we startled flocks of ducks and geese, awakening them from their night's sleep.

As the sun warmed the day, most of the warriors stripped to just breechcloths and moccasins, tying up the rest of their clothes and fastening them to the backs of their dogs. Once suitably unclothed, everyone applied whatever they could find to their bodies to keep the spring bugs from biting.

While we ran, I ate a handful of corn along with a mouthful of the pikodjisi (blackfly) that were so numerous. Washed down with a sip of water, the corn eased my hunger pangs. The only sounds I heard as I raced were the quick breaths of the runners, the panting of the dogs, and the noisy announcement of our presence from the surrounding trees by vigilant jays.

Looking ahead, I noticed steam rising from the sweaty bodies as we sprinted through the morning coolness. The aroma of the pine trees and the crisp scents of spring awakened my senses, giving my body renewed strength and life.

At the noon sun we stopped by a swift-moving spring runoff and drank our fill. There was very little conversation as warriors hastily ate and shared what they had with their dogs.

Mònz approached and said, "Nephew, if during this adventure to the setting sun I should suffer a warrior's death, please look after Wàbìsì for me."

"She's family, so you know I will," I replied.

Mònz had painted his facial scar red, making him appear even more frightening. His voice was still strong and he carried himself tall and erect as always, exuding the same confidence we all knew. But as he turned to walk away, I wondered if he knew something about what was coming.

Waughshe Anue then whistled sharply, and everyone got to their feet and followed him into the forest and the path leading to the canoes. Kìnà Odenan, Agwanìwon, my mother, and Kànìkwe trailed the column along the sides in the forest, keeping watch for bears and enemies. Our women warriors were always the first to volunteer for anything. The Ouendat men held great respect for our women and treated them as equals on the hunt and during battle.

We continued to run for the rest of the day, never needing to stop. Once in a while we passed a warrior relieving himself alongside the trail, but he soon caught up and resumed his place in line. Because we were the last in the column, if one of us had to step aside to heed nature, our people who were scouting on the sides made sure the straggler was watched over until he caught up again.

The sun was just starting to change colour and drop into the west horizon when I sensed the tang of water as well as the smoke of a campfire. Waughshe Anue halted the column. The smell of the fire set off alarms all down the line. Warriors readied spears and strung arrows in their bows. My mother and Kànìkwe rushed to the front of the line and told Waughshe Anue they would find the source of the fire, then quickly headed into the forest off the warrior path.

My mother was one of the most skilled fighters with knives I had ever seen. She could cut an enemy up in the blink of an eye. Kànìkwe, too, was an expert and agile fighter. I knew they could handle anything ahead of us. But just in case, I said to Nìj Enàndeg, "Go with them!" Without hesitation the dog followed my mother, who turned and touched the half wolf's head when he caught up with her. Then the three of them entered the dark forest, vanishing into the shadowy light.

20

ON THE CROW
WING RIVER

CHAŊKU WAŠTE

The canoes surrounded us as we entered the bend of the river. SápA Ziŋtkála went for his weapon, but I touched his hand and shook my head. "They're friends, the Itázipčho (*ee-dah-zeeb-koh:* Sans Arc), from north of here. The Itázipčho are known to be very generous and never mark their arrows when hunting, enabling all to share in the bounty. Due to their generosity, the holy woman of our culture, Ptesáŋ Wí, gave them the sacred pipe because she knew they would share it with the other tribes of the Lakȟóta. Their name's true meaning is "No Markings," meaning no markings on their arrows."

"I've heard of these men, Chaŋku Wašte," replied SápA Ziŋtkála, "having met some the past few years, and as you say, they're a very kind and open-handed people."

"Chaŋku Wašte, it's me, WičákȟA (*wee-chah-kah*: Speak True)," a voice piped up.

As I looked toward my old friend, I noticed that all the warriors with him, twenty in total, carried crooked lances wrapped in wolf skin and had otter fur around their wrists and necks. They were the Íȟoka (*ee-hoh-ka*: Badger Society), known for extreme ferocity in battle.

"WičákȟA, you've brought the best of the best with you," I said. "Is this just a visit?"

"No, my people heard you might have troubles this summer, so we're here to help our friends!"

"Many thanks, my friend. Please come to our village and we'll find lodging for your stay. Your help is sorely needed."

Once we reached the shore of the village on the east bank of the Wakpá Atkúku, my people came toward us whooping and singing to welcome our friends. The women, children, and warriors all had smiles on their faces. Knowing that the Itázipčho thought so much of their brethren that they sent their Badger Society warriors gave them a great sense of relief.

"WičákȟA, when the day comes for battle, I want your warriors to be the last line of defence guarding the women and children," I said.

"I would expect nothing less in the battle than to do this for you. My warriors are war-hardened against the Ȟaȟátȟuŋwaŋ over the years and know the foe they face."

The women fetched chunks of fresh venison and buffalo that had been brought in by hunters over the past few days. Then they built the fires up to cook for the visitors. Stories of past battles, drumming, dancing, and food kept everyone up until dawn. What fear the future would bring was put aside while we celebrated with good friends.

21

ON THE SHORE
OF ATTIGOUATAN
(GEORGIAN BAY)

ANOKÌ

As I later learned, Kànìkwe, Nìj Enàndeg, and my mother, Wàbananang, followed the scent of woodsmoke. When they neared the edge of the woods and the shoreline where the canoes were hidden, they heard the faint flapping of wings and then a black shadow swooped down from the forest canopy and landed on Kànìkwe's bald head. As soon as that happened, an unmistakable laugh echoed in the woods.

"Crazy Crow!" my mother shouted. "Come out here and feel the sharpness of my blades!"

"Even I'm not foolish enough to give the warrior wife of the great Mahingan a chance to carve me up as she's done to so many unsuspecting enemies," Crazy Crow said, then roared with laughter. "I've seen your knife work and I don't want to be on the receiving end of it!"

Crazy Crow then appeared from the shadows and gave my mother and Kànìkwe huge hugs, sending the crow perched on the bald one's head fluttering into the trees, its sinister cackle resonating through the forest long after it was gone.

"Kànìkwe," Crazy Crow said, "go back to Waughshe Anue and tell him all is well here and that you've found some old friends who have an evening meal waiting for them. Wàbananang, please follow me. Mitigomij and I have two fine deer on spits waiting for someone to take a first taste to see if they're ready. Your expertise with knives will come in handy taking a slice off. We also have lots of spruce and cedar tea boiling in birchbark vessels."

"Crazy Crow, the two of you never cease to amaze me!" my mother replied.

As they broke through the forest line and stepped on the shore, my mother noticed Nìj Enàndeg turning to look up into a tall tree. When she followed the dog's gaze, she spied the black outline of Mitigomij's magnificent panther. She then turned her attention to where her late husband's brother was standing between two spits, rotating them over separate fires. My mother now felt sudden warmth course through her body, knowing that Mitigomij and the great Mi'kmaq warrior Crazy Crow were now among them.

When the warriors started arriving, my mother was tending the boiling teas. They didn't need to be asked twice to come forward and cut off slices of venison and dip their drinking vessels into the tea containers. Before they came back for seconds, many of the Ouendat went into the forest to retrieve the hidden canoes and bring them out to the shore. Our Omàmiwinini group then built more fires for the evening.

The canoes, tipped on their sides, would serve as places to sleep for many of the warriors this evening. Others built quickly erected lean-tos close to the fires for their night shelters. Evening guards were assigned, but with so many dogs in the camp and Mitigomij's powerful panther companion, Makadewà Wàban, lurking in the shadows, there was little chance any man or beast could surprise this camp.

That night, as the fires burnt, Mitigomij sat beside Crazy Crow and asked everyone as they warmed themselves, "Would you like to hear how I saved the Crow Man's life this winter?"

Several of the gathered warriors spoke in unison, saying, "Yes, we'd like to hear how one great warrior saved another great warrior's life!"

Crazy Crow cleared his throat, nervously laughed, stood, and then came and sat beside me to hear Mitigomij's tale.

Mitigomij's Story

It all started when we decided to hunt separately, figuring we would have better luck covering twice the area. It was bitterly cold, and we had to shield our faces with our fur scarves, only letting our eyes peek out from the protection against the harsh wind. I was gone five suns and had very little luck — one scrawny rabbit that Makadewà Wàban and I shared. Hardly enough for myself, let alone a full-grown panther. The evening of the fourth sun I was able to dig into a large drift, making a warm sleeping burrow just large enough for myself and the cat.

That morning we were awakened by a noisy crow sitting at the opening. Figuring my good friend had made a kill, we quickly followed the bird as it led us through the forest for most of the day. The snow was very deep, but my snowshoes enabled me to keep up with our overhead messenger. The sky was bright blue, and the only noises in the forest were the branches snapping in the cold, the intermittent knocking of woodpeckers searching for a meal, and the occasional displeasure of a jay whenever we happened into its area.

It was very close to dusk when we arrived in a clearing where there was a loud gathering of crows around a frozen moose carcass. The crows were diving at a pack of seven wolves that were intent on obtaining a meal from the dead animal lying in the blood-encrusted snow. After a loud scream from Makadewà Wàban and a yell from me, the wolves reluctantly slinked off. As I approached the carcass, I wondered where Crazy Crow was. The crows were here, and if he had slain this moose, he should be nearby.

As I got closer to the moose, I heard what I thought was the muffled sound of my name but couldn't figure out where it was coming from. It seemed as if someone or something was uttering it from a deep hole. Looking around, I continued to have trouble discerning the source of the noise until Makadewà Wàban sat down and stared at the animal's chest. I knelt, looked hard, and there he was — Crazy Crow — inside the moose's belly, which was frozen stiff!

Once I cut him out, he told me that after he had slain the animal and gutted it, he was chilled to the bone, so he had crawled inside to get warm and had quickly fallen asleep. He was awakened the next morning by the wolf pack and the crows noisily fighting over the carcass and him. The body of the animal was so frozen that he couldn't get out. The wolves were determined to have a meal from the dead animal, and the crows were just as resolute in keeping them away from him. Crazy Crow had been inside the moose for two days before I was led back to save him. That's the story!

ANOKÌ

Crazy Crow stood and said, "You haven't known the closeness of death until you've spent two days in the belly of the beast!"

Everyone laughed, and many said that was the best survival story they had heard in a long time. Some of the warriors dipped their cups in the tea container and others, including me, left the fire to go to their sleeping areas.

The next morning I felt a foot dig into my side, startling me from a deep sleep. "Anokì, time to wake up!"

I opened my eyes to see Ki'kwa'ju, my sister's husband. He was warming some of the previous night's venison on five or six sticks stuck in the ground and hanging over a fire.

Pangì Mahingan and my mother were boiling tea. Both looked at me and my mother said, "Since you've had so much sleep, you can load the canoe and take the rear to steer."

Smiling, I got up and ran into the woods to relieve myself of the buildup of my evening's sleep collections. Once all that pressure was relieved, I was able to function better. When I returned to the fire, I dipped out some tea and stuck my knife in the meat, taking a chunk off one of the sticks.

"Agwanìwon has told us we'll be travelling on the north shore and going through the strait between the big island and the mainland," my mother informed me. "We'll stop at the rapids between the two big lakes and try to take as much fish there as we can. After that, as we enter the big lake, Gichigami, hunters will be dropped along the north shore to hunt and will be told which predetermined places to meet up at."

As we were eating, Zhashagi and his dog, Misko, came to our fire. He had five filleted fish on a couple of sticks and stuck them in the ground over our fire to share with us. Opening his hand, he tossed some fish guts to Nìj Enàndeg, who eagerly gulped them down. The two dogs sniffed each other and then settled together on the ground. Zhashagi wiped his hand that had held the guts on Misko, which in turn caused my dog to lick Misko's fur clean of the fish taste. The five of us sat there and laughed while Nìj Enàndeg groomed Misko.

Zhashagi gazed at the fire, then said, "The journey begins today in earnest." He dipped out some tea and continued to brood at the fire.

We broke camp, doused the fires, and picked our canoes to push into the early mist on the water. The Anishinaabe warriors led the way, with our group of Omàmiwinini between the divided Ouendat warriors.

My mother called out, "Anokì, make sure you get us a good boat with no leaks and at least one paddle for yourself! We're going to spend our time fishing and sleeping."

I selected a well-made Ouendat canoe and brought it to our campsite. Dropping it at the edge of the water, I tossed my weapons in the back where I had been designated to sit and steer. My mother, sister, and Ki'kwa'ju quickly got into the boat along with Mitigomij and Nìj Enàndeg.

"Uncle," I asked, "where's your black companion?"

"Don't worry. He'll never be far away."

Thinking back to my younger years, I might have seen Makadewà Wàban only once or twice in a boat. When we camped at night, he always showed up. The Haudenosaunee feared this animal friend of my uncle, who they called Kahastines, and believed lived in the under waters of the lakes. Many of our people also believed this and called him Gichanami'e-bizhiw. Even I had started to believe the legend, mainly because I couldn't explain his disappearances and reappearances.

The bright sun began to burn through the mist, skipping fractured beams of light off the water and through the steamy morning haze as we left the shore. The only ripples on the water were made by the bows of our canoes and the dipping of our paddles.

Designated warriors patrolled ahead along the shoreline to ensure our safety. Another boat was given the responsibility of making certain no one ran into problems, usually as the result of a leaky boat.

On the first day we paddled toward Manidoowaaling Minisi (Manitoulin Island) and then entered the channel between the big island and the north shore. Travelling through this system of islands sheltered us from the lake winds.

Once we were halfway into the channel, some of the boats went ashore and dropped off seven or eight hunters. They would stay along the bank, hoping to find game that might come down to drink.

During the day, a few of the warriors shot waterfowl with arrows or fished. It wasn't really enough fresh game and fish to feed this large group, but mixed with the corn we all carried, the day's catch made for a tasty soup with small chunks of meat.

Passing by one of the islands at mid-afternoon, we were entertained by the antics of a group of otters. There had to be more than a dozen of them. Some swam alongside the boats, and a few of the warriors threw them fish and watched them manoeuvre to retrieve the handouts. The otters all seemed to come from a nearby island. Once we approached the end of that island, we stopped our boats and continued to observe the playful animals slide down a muddy trough running off the side of a hill and into the water. Once in the lake, they dived for fish, and the younger ones scampered back up the hill to slither down again. I had seen bears glide down a snowy hill in the early spring, but the otters were much less dangerous to watch.

Near the end of the day we approached an island at the mouth of a river (Aird Island at the mouth of the Spanish River). Except for the canoes that went back toward the main shore to pick up the hunters at the predetermined spot, the rest of us went ashore on the island.

We got out of our canoes and many of us bolted into the forest to empty bladders and intestines. The dogs rushed around doing their jobs and then chased and caught small rodents for hastily arranged dinners.

Fires were started to make our meals and also to guide the other canoes to us if darkness set in before they returned. Just as the sun was setting, lighting the waters around us with a deep red glow, the hunting party arrived, paddling through the shimmering waters and appearing as if they were exiting a burning landscape.

When they approached the shore, a cheer rose up among everyone. Hanging over the side of the lead boat was a large moose: enough fresh meat for everyone and ample bones for the dogs.

With many eager hands to help, the moose was gutted, skinned, and apportioned out in a short time. Mitigomij took a large bone and a fist-sized piece of meat and strode into the treeline, reappearing a short time later. There was no need to question where he went; the black one was there and Mitigomij did what he had done for years — looked after his friend. They had taken care of each other like that for many years. The cat was older than I was, but he still seemed like a young cougar given his stamina and deeds.

The night's sleep was restful except for the usual bugs that tried their best to eat us alive. The next morning I happily rose before everyone else, started a fire, and went around poking everyone with my feet to rouse them from their deep slumbers.

We were able to reach the area the Anishinaabe called Baawitigong (Sault Ste. Marie Rapids) around midday. Here we would spend seven to ten suns spearing and netting enough fish to dry to sustain us on our remaining travels. We wanted to reach the land of the Nadowessioux during the moon of miskomini-kìzis (*mih-skoh-mih-nih-kee-zihs:* July) strong, able, and well fed. It took a lot of food to keep this many warriors satisfied. While most were fishing, others were off hunting game.

After five suns, the drying racks were full and it was a seemingly perpetual job to maintain the smoking fires. The smoke was essential to speed up the drying of the meat. It also helped to create a crust that kept flies from laying eggs in the flesh. Until then it was a constant task to walk around and wave the flies off the meat. The quicker the meat was cut into thin strips and hung over the fires, the easier it was for this to happen. The meat had to be hung high enough so that it didn't cook but still gave us the end result we wanted.

Ten days later the war party had enough meat to get us to Zhashagi's village. Before we left I approached Agwanìwon, Zhashagi, and Waughshe Anue and asked a favour of them. "A few of the Omàmiwinini warriors and I would like to travel the north shore to the big island at the end and enter the bay behind it. There's a large lake north of there that Nitaage Niibiwa calls Animbiigoo-zaaga'igan (Dog Waters Lake — Lake Nipigon). He said that the elk are huge up there. We want to go there and kill one and bring the hide to Zhashagi's friend, Misko Zhiishiib (*mis-ko zhe-sheep:* Red Duck), at Mooningwanekaaing (Madeline Island)."

"You have twenty suns to do this," replied Agwanìwon. "You must arrive at the peninsula of Keewaynan (*kee-wi-wai-non-ing*) by then. We want to attack the Nadowessioux in the heat of the summer and then be able to get back to Ossossanè before fall. Twenty suns, Anokì. We leave without you and your hunters if you're not there by then!"

"We leave now!" I said.

22

A BATTLE UNLIKE
ANY OTHER

CHAŊKU WAŠTE

"For weeks, Óta Heȟáka," I said to my son, "our warriors have been scouting the two rivers. There are no signs of the Ȟaȟáthuŋwaŋ. I'm beginning to think they won't attack us this year. It's now the first suns of wípazukȟa-wašté-wí (*wi-pah-zoo-kah-wash-tay-wi:* June). The attack on the river last year might have sent them into hiding and maybe they have no stomach for any more bloodshed. We're spending too much time looking for ghosts. The camp is well protected here. I don't think we have anything to fear. I'm going to talk to the akíčita and change our focus to hunting for the next while."

"Father, let me take Tȟatȟáŋka Kat'á and some of the other Sotkàyuha warriors in the days toward the end of this moon and start looking again. They're coming. I feel it!"

"The Sotkàyuha are young and not battle-tested," I said. "None of their lances have any war honours. They're not yet warriors."

"Father, it would only be to scout. We wouldn't be strong enough even to ambush the Ȟaȟátȟuŋwaŋ if we found them. I promise that if we see them I'll come back immediately with the warning!"

"All right, in fifteen suns you go out with them to search out our enemy. In the meantime, train them in the art of canoeing and shooting from the boats so they can at least defend themselves."

"Thank you, Father. We'll make the village proud."

ANOKÌ

"There are the islands ahead, Anokì," Nitaage Niibiwa said. "We'll stay along the shoreline and it will bring us into a bay and from there we go up the river to the lake called Animbiigoo-zaaga'igan. There are several carry-rounds where we have to take the boats from the water, but they're easy. Once we get near the lake, we'll go ashore. The elk aren't plentiful there, but they're big!"

There were two canoes in our group. Nitaage Niibiwa, Pangì Mahingan, Ki'kwa'ju, and I were in one, while my cousins, the twins Makwa and Wàbek, along with their wives, Àwadòsiwag and Ininàtig, the daughters of the Wàbanaki warrior Nigig, were in the other. Nìj Enàndeg and three other dogs were also with us.

"Nitaage Niibiwa, we're into our seventh day," I said. "We have to find one of these huge beasts quickly now that we're finally here!"

"Patience, my friend. We'll be well rewarded."

With our two boats of skilled paddlers going upstream we got to our destination by nightfall of the next day. After hastily made fires and a meal of fish, we put ourselves to bed among the ravenous bugs. The next morning Nitaage Niibiwa led us along a game trail in the woods. I blazed trees as we went along so that we wouldn't get lost. Every once in a while Nitaage Niibiwa halted to make an elk call. He was very good at that, enough so that even the dogs stopped and sniffed the air for the animal.

"This is a beautiful land, Anokì," Makwa said.

"The scent of the forest mixing with the smell of the wind off the lake gives me a sense of calmness, plus walking on the pine needles is so easy on my feet and legs," added Wàbek.

"My cousins, the two of you are acting oddly, like you're somewhere else," I said. "This country is no different than any other we've been in. Talking about smells and how easy the ground is on your feet? Are you hallucinating?"

"No, we're not!" they both insisted at the same time. "We're going to be fathers!"

"Oh, my!" I exclaimed, then grabbed and hugged each of them. Turning to look at their wives, I saw the two women blush. "Who else knows?"

"Just you and us," Ininàtig answered.

"When?" I questioned.

"Six more full moons," replied Àwadòsiwag.

"Well, I know two warrior women who will be staying at Zhashagi's village when we travel to the lands of the Nadowessioux."

"Anokì, we will never leave our men!" Ininàtig said fervently.

"We fight by their sides always!" Àwadòsiwag added emphatically.

"All right, all right," I said. Mitigomij, I told myself, would know about this and would handle it his way. They would be well protected.

"Quiet," Nitaage Niibiwa suddenly said.

We were at a beaver pond west of the Makadewaagami-ziibi (*mak-a-day-eh-wa-gami-zee-bee*: Blackwater River near Beardmore, Ontario). I squinted and gazed across the pond where I spied a faint shadow in the treeline on the other side.

Nitaage Niibiwa then made the call of a bull elk. Immediately, a real elk stepped out and returned a warning cry to the interloper. He was huge! Nitaage Niibiwa called again, and the elk started to splash through the shallow water of the pond, making his way to drive his rival off.

The eight of us crouched in the shadows of our treeline and watched, waiting breathlessly as the animal moved into range. Water splashed onto the elk's muscled withers as he uttered another loud scream of challenge. His head was held high and his nostrils flared, trying to pick up a scent. The wait seemed endless. I looked at the dogs lying on the pine-needled forest floor quietly panting and trying to stay cool.

Then, suddenly, the elk was in range. All of us stood at the same time and fired our arrows — eight shots, eight hits. The huge beast's front legs gave out in mid-stride and he went headfirst into the shallow water, sliding toward us and splashing water into the air. I watched sunlight glisten off the beads of airborne water and listened to the final grunts of the dying creature.

We all shouted with joy at our success and then rushed to the elk to cut its throat and bleed it out. Even the dogs were caught up in the excitement, barking and howling. Their enthusiasm might have been fuelled by their canine knowledge of a future meal of entrails.

I turned to Ki'kwa'ju to slap him on the shoulder and express my happiness, but he wasn't there. Instead, he was standing beside a rock on the other side of the narrow treeline between the river and the beaver pond where he was laying his shield, sword, and axe on the ground.

"What are you doing, my friend?" I asked.

"Leaving my old life behind. I'm no longer an Eli'tuat (*el-e-do-what*: Men with Beards). I'm an Omàmiwinini. I'm married to an Omàmiwinini and I live with the Omàmiwinini. So that's who I am now! Someone many years from now will find these weapons and know that a Viking came this way but left his past here to walk another path. Besides, I was tired of carrying them around and I'm much more skilled with the lance and arrow!"

"Come, my brother, we have an animal to butcher."

It took all of us to drag the kill onto some dry land to cut it up. The three women busied themselves making pole sleds for the dogs to cart parts of the kill. The rest of us would carry as much as we could. The remainder would be left for the wolves. Nìj Enàndeg would have the elk skin on his sled.

We camped that night along the river and feasted on the fresh meat. Wàbek led a ceremony thanking Kije-Manidò for his gift of the elk and to assist the elk's spirit in its travels. During the night, we took turns feeding the fires smoking the meat. As with the fish, we needed a crust on the meat to prevent flies from laying eggs in the carcass.

The next day we reached the canoes and struck out to keep my promise to get back within twenty suns. We had been gone twelve suns now, and Nitaage Niibiwa said that we were only three or four days from Misko Zhiishiib's village. We would have time to spare.

ÓTA HEȞÁKA

During the start of the čhaŋpȟásapa wí (can-pa'-sa-pa wi: Moon of Cherries Blackening — July), I had taken eighteen young men of the Sotka'yuha, as well as Tȟatȟáŋka Kaťá, out on scouting trips up the two rivers, alternating each day from one to the other. We always came back with fish, waterfowl, and the odd deer on our outings. The boys were learning the art of the hunt and canoeing quickly. We travelled in five canoes, and I was careful always to put an experienced boy in each canoe.

It was now midsummer and sixteen days into what we called the cherry-blackening moon. The rivers had been calm and the afternoons sunny and cloudless. The smell of the freshness of the rivers added to the joys of being alive during this time. Today we were on the wide river called the Wakpá Atkúku.

"Óta Heȟáka," Tȟatȟáŋka Kaťá said, "I don't think our enemies will strike. It's getting late in the summer and we haven't seen any sign of them. We're living in fear over nothing!"

"We aren't living in fear, T̃hat̃háŋka Kat'à. We're being cautious. There are women, children, and Elders to protect here. It's our duty to make sure we're not taken by surprise. I don't fear our enemies. Do you?"

"Yes, I'm a little fearful because I've never experienced warfare before."

"Use your fear as an ally in your battles. Make it work for you in these times. It will lead you to many victories!" I looked around at the boys in the canoes. They were lazily paddling upstream. Their weapons lay at their feet.

Each day we departed the village fifteen warriors always left camp after we did and walked along the shore's treeline, hidden in the shadows in case I needed them. I had confidence in the boys to stand and fight, though they would be no match for battle-hardened warriors in a head-to-head fight. We were just coming up to the first bend north of the village where part of the river flowed to the south, straightened out, and then went into another bend northeast. Rounding the curve, we were halfway through the straight part of the river. T̃hat̃háŋka Kat'á was in a boat in the front, and I brought up the rear to make sure everyone was safe.

As we started into the bend to the northeast, a huge flock of ducks climbed toward us from upstream. They had been spooked by something, perhaps my scouts on the shore …

ANOKÌ

Our hunting group had caught up with the Ouendat force on the peninsula of Keewaynan one sun away from Misko Zhiishiib's village where they were collecting copper and fishing near the shore. That evening we feasted on elk meat and listened to Zhashagi tell us about his people's battles with the Nadowessioux.

When we arrived at the shoreline of Misko Zhiishiib's village with one hundred and sixty-five warriors and thirty dogs, it was like walking into a swarm of bees. People ran about hailing old friends, dogs barked, children and women laughed, and a few of our greeters pounded on drums to welcome us.

After spending the night at Misko Zhiishiib's village, feasting and drumming, we left at dawn and arrived at Zhashagi's community before dusk.

With the Ouendat from the south and the warriors from the surrounding Anishinaabe nations, we now totalled about three hundred and fifty fighters — an enormous number of men to move downriver, which had to be done swiftly and stealthily if we hoped to catch the Nadowessioux unaware.

Our canoe was beside Zhashagi's as we pulled our boats ashore. While we were doing this a tall warrior whom I immediately recognized stepped out of the teeming mass of people accompanied by two young men. The warrior walked up and grasped Zhashagi in a huge embrace.

"Omashkooz, it's such a pleasure to see you so healthy!" exclaimed Zhashagi. He then glanced at the two young men with his brother. "It doesn't look as if my brother was eating dog this winter. I take it your hunting was successful."

Omashkooz laughed. "Brother, they supplied me and my wife with more than enough. We were giving food away!"

The boys shyly looked up and smiled.

"You've upheld your part of the bargain and now I'll uphold mine," Zhashagi said. "Prepare yourselves to leave for battle tomorrow and gather your weapons!" "Before you go, though, this is my friend, Anokì, son of the great Omàmiwinini chief Mahingan. Anokì, these are two first-time warriors, Mayagi-bine and his brother, Bikwak."

The boys nodded in my direction, and Bikwak said, "It's our pleasure to meet you. Omashkooz has told us many things about you and your people, especially the warrior Mitigomij."

I laughed. "He might be exaggerating some of his tales."

Zhashagi studied the two boys. "I'm sure Omashkooz has told you what's expected of you as first-time warriors, but let me tell you a few things, too. You can never get your feet wet getting in or out of a canoe on this trail. You must wear black war paint as a novice. You can't suck the marrow out of the bones of any animals slain and eaten on this journey. Finally, you can't sing death or war songs on this path to war. Do you understand?"

"Yes, Zhashagi, we do," they answered together.

"Fine. Then go and prepare. You'll be riding in the same canoe as Omashkooz and me. We leave tomorrow. Today is eleven suns into this moon. It will take us four suns to reach where our scouts say the Nadowessioux are — downriver at the junctions of two rivers, the Gaagaagiwigwani-ziibi and the great Misi-ziibi."

I watched as Zhashagi then turned to his brother and grasped him around the shoulders. "Tomorrow is the start of our revenge, Brother! It's been over a year. We're healed and healthy. Our slain warriors will have their deaths honoured!"

I smiled at Zhashagi and his brother. "I'll let the two of you catch up some more. I have to join my people."

That night the drums beat until late, with the war post struck so many times that it ended up in splinters. There was ample food to eat, and during the evening the women came to each warrior and handed him enough food to last five days on the trail. The village had been sending out hunting parties for many suns to collect enough food to feed all the warriors once they arrived.

Omashkooz got to his feet as the celebration neared its end. "We'll have eighty canoes to carry our force down to the Nadowessioux camp at the junction of the Gaagaagiwigwani-ziibi and Misi-ziibi. We must make it in two days cross-country to where our boats have been made and are stored near the Negawi-ziibi (Sandy River). From there we'll access the Misi-ziibi. Once we leave there, we'll only be stopping at night when there's no more daylight. There will be three scout canoes ahead of us at all times to make sure we aren't surprised on the river. We'll be gone tomorrow at daylight."

Once he finished speaking, a tremendous roar filled the village, startling the dogs and causing them to howl and bark simultaneously. The noise was so sudden and loud that some of the younger children began to cry and had to be comforted by their mothers.

The next morning we left at dawn. Zhashagi said that about thirty of the women and ten men who had been asked to stay behind from his village would follow in about two days to go to where the canoes were waiting and make camp there. They would be there to help with the wounded on our return, and the warriors would hunt and have fresh game for us when we arrived. Running with my Omàmiwinini friends and relatives, we made great time with a steady lope on a warrior trail, reaching the boats at sunset on the second day. Two deer had been taken just before we got to the camp, and they were divided among all the warriors, with the dogs given the bones to fight over.

That night it rained, and when we woke in the morning, my eyes were greeted on the north side of the river by a blanket of pink flowers of the mashkode zhigaagawinzh (*mush-co-day shi-ga-ga-wash:* prairie onion). The pinkness of the flowers' petals was highlighted by the sunlight glistening on the remnants of the evening's rain. It was a wonderful and calming sight. I only hoped that it was a sign of good things to come to our group in the days ahead.

After quickly eating a meal of cold meat and drinking some hot tea, we left in the canoes shortly past sunrise and made good time paddling downriver with the current pushing us. I was in a boat with E's, my mother, and the two warrior women chiefs, Àgwanìwon and Kìnà Odenan, along with their constant companion, Kànìkwe. I smiled when I noticed Mitigomij in the same boat as the twins and their wives.

They all looked at me, and Wàbek asked, "You told him, didn't you?" Then he laughed.

They were well protected with Mitigomij and Crazy Crow. Close by on the shoreline Mitigomij's big cat would be roaming. Mònz, Wàbìsì, Pangì Mahingan,

Ki'kwa'ju, and Jilte'g were together in another canoe. The two Ouendat warriors, Achie and Önenha', were with Zhashagi, Omashkooz, and the two Anishinaabe novice warriors. Each canoe also had dogs in it.

We stopped at the noon sun and ate a hasty cold meal and relieved ourselves in the woods. When we halted again at sunset, the sky was fiery red and there was no wind.

"That sky is a good omen," Waughshe Anue said.

I certainly hope so, I thought.

"Anokì," called out Kìnà Odenan, "we've been assigned near the front tomorrow. The Anishinaabe will man five scout boats. Zhashagi and his brother's boat will be one of them. Our two close Ouendat friends are with Zhashagi, and they're excited about being in the front where the first action will probably be initiated."

That night I didn't sleep well. Nìj Enàndeg seemed to sense my nervousness and lay closer to me than usual. The next morning the cooking fires had ample tea and food, but most of it went untouched. Warriors silently put on their paint and handled their weapons. The dogs that morning received an abundant supply of the food that hadn't been eaten by their masters.

The early morning was very warm. The river had no ripples, the sky was cloudless, and a faint mist rose from the water. When I took in the scent of the pine forest, it cleared my head of any ill thoughts. Quickly drinking a serving of tea to settle my stomach, I also grabbed a piece of meat from the cooking fire. Tossing some meat to my dog, we silently settled into the canoe and pushed off along with the others.

"Anokì," my mother whispered, touching my shoulder, "I'll see you in the afterlife or have tea with you tomorrow. Either way it will be a happy reunion."

I turned and smiled at her, then patted Nìj Enàndeg on the head. He glanced up and I said, "Watch over me, old friend."

As the noon sun burned down on the river, I felt the heat of the day on my bare skin. The flies must have been staying in the shade because they weren't probing for their usual taste of blood from our naked bodies. In the distance a flock of ducks ascended into the air as Zhashagi and the other four lead canoes scared them from their day's feeding on a bend in the river.

I heard Zhashagi turn to his brother and say, "I don't like what just happened with those ducks!"

The words had barely left his mouth when they rounded the bend right into the path of five canoes loaded with Nadowessioux.

Both groups of warriors were momentarily caught off guard by the sudden surprise of each other's appearance. But the inactivity was soon broken by a whoosh of arrows from the south shore, causing the nearest Anishinaabe canoe to flip over and take on water as the men in the boat were struck with arrows.

Zhashagi obviously realized we were now in a lot of danger. His boat made for the closest enemy canoe, pulling up alongside so the two Ouendat warriors could react quickly. Achie plunged his spear into the neck of a shocked paddler, sending him over the side, while Önenha' struck a young boy across the forehead with his war club, making a sound like the cracking of an egg. The enemy boy stood up, screamed in pain, and fell out of the boat, disappearing into the murky depths.

Zhashagi then yelled over his shoulder, "We have to turn the canoe!" As the words left his mouth, a youth on the enemy boat reacted swiftly and fired an arrow that caught Mayagi-bine in the face. Zhashagi twisted just in time to see the boy slump forward onto his lap, spattering blood down his thigh and leg. Omashkooz in the rear of the canoe quickly let fly an arrow that whizzed by his brother's head and caught another young enemy boy in the chest, sending him over the side and flipping the boat and its occupants. More arrows were arriving from the south shore, and this time they reached Zhashagi's boat. The arrows hit the side with loud thumps and exited into the canoe's interior, all above the waterline.

ÓTA HEȞÁKA

I watched the battle unfold in front of me as an enemy canoe and one of our Lakȟóta boats flipped over from the initial attacks. Quickly, I turned to Ťhatȟáŋka Kaťà and said, "Turn around, get back to the village, and warn my father and the rest of the warriors!"

"No, Óta Heȟáka, I stay and fight with you."

"Go!" I ordered. "The village is more important. Go now before we're overtaken. The rest of the Ȟaȟáťhuŋwaŋ are in sight. Go!"

Ťhatȟáŋka Kaťà obeyed me and turned the canoe around. As he did, the boy at the back took an arrow between the shoulder blades and fell sideways off the boat. Luckily, he didn't capsize the canoe as he tumbled out, and Ťhaťháŋka Kat'à made his escape down the river with his companions.

Looking back, I saw the enemy closing in fast with ten of their canoes spilling onto the shore to attack my warriors there. All that were left on the river from my group was my boat and one other with four youths in it. I yelled at them to follow me. It was suicidal to stay there with these boys and try to hold the swarm of canoes coming down the river at us.

I turned my canoe around, came alongside the other remaining boat, and told the boys to get in with us. That would give me six paddlers and allow another older boy and me to fire arrows behind us, aiding our escape. As we were taking the others onto our canoe, a boy was hit with two arrows, one in the leg and another in the throat, spilling blood on me as I was helping him into the boat. I released him into the water and yelled to the boys to paddle as hard as they could. Then I fired an arrow at the closest boat, just missing the warrior in front. Our eyes met, I recognized him from the river ambush, and then felt an arrow slice my right shoulder, taking a good-sized chunk of skin with it as it grazed the bone.

"Paddle!" I screamed, fitting another arrow into my bow.

ANOKÌ

I watched as Zhashagi's arrow sliced through the Nadowessioux warrior we knew as Óta Heȟáka. The enemy's arrow had narrowly missed Zhashagi before he had let his fly. He turned to his brother and cried, "Omashkooz, let them go! Another boat escaped before this one ahead of us and the enemy village will know we're here. We must decide now how we'll attack them." Zhashagi's boat was down to just his brother and Achie and Misko. The two young novice warriors were both dead along with Önenha', the Ouendat.

When the initial attack had come from shore, my companions and I were too far back to return fire. We watched as Zhashagi and his men sustained many losses and fought off the canoes on the river. Everyone strained at their paddles, trying to get close enough to attack. As we neared, the warriors on the shore came out of the forest and started shooting at us. Their arrows found their marks with alarming accuracy. In our boat, E's took an arrow through his arm and slouched in the canoe. He pushed the arrow all the way through his bicep, never saying a word. Quickly, my mother tied a piece of leather above the wound and turned it tightly with an arrow to shut off the blood flow. Then Kànìkwe spread honey on the wound as E's slumped in the boat. The canoe was riddled with arrow shafts, and a couple had pierced at the waterline, allowing water to seep in.

I glanced toward the shore to see that the enemy had suffered some losses along with a few wounded from the return fire of our force. Of the fifteen Nadowessioux who had come out of the forest, only about ten were still standing. All of them had long sashes hanging from their waists, and now they took their long spears and drove them into the sashes, pinning themselves to the spot along the shore.

"What are they doing?" I yelled to the boat next to me, which was full of Anishinaabe warriors.

"I've seen this once before," one of the Anishinaabe warriors replied. "They're called the Mawátani (*mee-wah-dee-nee*) Society. See their owl headdresses? When members of their group are wounded, they stay with them and fight to the end or until others come and save them all. They'll fight to the death. They're the best of the best of the Nadowessioux! It's a great honour to slay one of these men. They're very brave!"

Our boats landed on shore and we rushed the defenders. I heard a slingshot snap behind my head and saw a stunned look appear on the face of an enemy warrior in front of me as he slid to the ground with a fist-sized hole in his head. Mitigomij had been quick and sure as always! Agwanìwon raced from my side as we approached a muscular man with a huge war club. He was amazingly fast and caught her full in the face, shattering her skull. Charging the warrior, I felt blood rush to my face, causing my cheeks to heat up. Ducking a swing, I hit him hard on the left kneecap as I passed. When he dropped to his good knee, I heard a blood-curdling scream that could have only belonged to Mitigomij's big cat.

Looking over my shoulder, I saw Kìnà Odenan and Kànìkwe rush the man from opposite sides, both hitting him with their war clubs at the same time. The sickening crunch of broken bones and the spattering of blood on my face made me realize this was a battle unlike any I had ever been in before. The man went down in a heap at my feet, and Kìnà Odenan repeatedly smashed the body even after it stopped moving. As tears welled in his eyes, Kànìkwe pulled her away from the mangled corpse. Kìnà

Odenan sobbed, then glanced up with the most frightful look I had ever witnessed. With terrifying ferocity, she rushed a wounded foe on his knees trying to pull an arrow from his shoulder. His hand was covered in blood where he had the arrow grasped, and his chest was bright red from his life fluids streaming down his chest with every beat of his heart. The wounded warrior looked up just as Kìnà Odenan reached him. The last thing he likely saw in this life was her blade slicing his throat with a single sweeping motion. She straddled the blood-soaked man and screamed like a panther, sending shivers up my spine. The sound echoed through the woods, drowning out all the noise of the surrounding battle. Combatants from both sides gazed in Kìnà Odenan's direction to see the Warrior Woman covered in the blood of her enemies. For many years to come, the expression on her face would haunt all who had beheld her.

Then I heard another panther scream and turned to see Makadewà Wàban hit an enemy warrior so hard that he was torn from his sash, landing the two of them in the water and changing it to bright red. The big cat stood over his prey and dared anyone to approach.

To the right of the cat, I watched helplessly as Wàbìsì took an arrow through the throat as she ran toward her husband, Mònz, who was struggling with a short, brawny warrior. I quickly ran toward my uncle, only to be cut off by a tall warrior who had pulled his spear from the ground and lunged at me. Raising my spear, I deflected his lunge and he stumbled slightly, but enough for Nìj Enàndeg to tear at the man's thigh, taking a huge chunk of skin and muscle from his right leg. As he crumpled to his knees, I drove my spear into his chest and then plunged my knife into his neck. The man shuddered through the two weapons impaling his body, and when I pulled them out, he collapsed onto the ground without a word.

Quickly, I collected my senses and pivoted to where Mònz had last been. When I saw that my uncle was dead with a spear run through his body, I bowed my head in respect. Standing next to Mònz's fallen body and straddling a Nadowessioux warrior was Mitigomij, holding a bloodied war club.

The fight was over so quickly that it seemed as if it had been a dream. When I surveyed the carnage, I saw fifteen Nadowessioux warriors lying dead along with twenty-two of our force either dead or wounded. Among the dead from our people were Agwanìwon, Mònz and his wife, Wàbìsì, and Önenha' the Ouendat, while E's was wounded. Our family never seemed to die peacefully; ours was the death of a warrior always.

We left our wounded with the dead, one group to watch over the other. There was no time to mourn just yet. Mitigomij convinced the wives of Wàbek and Makwa to stay and aid the wounded. The twins thanked their uncle as they climbed into their canoe. Once we were in our boats, we raced to where we saw Zhashagi near a bend on the northern part of the river.

As we approached, he said, "Our presence is now known. If we decide to continue, we'll run into a force that's surely waiting for us. There will be many losses and victory isn't assured. We're down close to thirty warriors slain and wounded already and haven't yet met the power of their main group of defenders. What shall we do?"

As Zhashagi talked, I watched as he glanced over my head toward the west shore. I turned and saw a large hare sitting on its haunches. It appeared to be waving at us.

Zhashagi stopped talking and paddled his canoe to the shore where the hare was. As soon as the canoe arrived on the shore, the animal vanished into the forest and a tall warrior emerged to greet Zhashagi.

"Zhashagi, you've been caught in the open and things don't look good for the future of your raid."

"No, Nanabozho, they don't," Zhashagi replied.

"Well, my friend, take your warriors and their boats across this narrow piece of land. You'll come to the other river and from there it will take you to an island that protects their village. They'll be expecting you down this river, not the other one. Use your knowledge wisely. Good luck, my friend." Nanabozho then turned and was swallowed up by the forest.

Zhashagi waved us to shore, and we carried our boats across the narrow division of the two rivers. Putting the canoes in the Gaagaagiwigwani-ziibi, we quickly came to the big island shortly after the noon sun started to bring down the afternoon heat.

Our force of more than three hundred was able to surprise the defenders on the island. They had their backs turned to us as we charged them at the treeline along the shore. The fighting was brutal. I fought alongside Mitigomij, Makwa, Wàbek, Pangì Mahingan, and Ki'kwa'ju. Along with Nìj Enàndeg and Makadewà Wàban, we raced from our boats and came upon three Nadowessioux warriors. When they spotted us, they turned and ran in the direction of where their main force was expecting us on the east side of the island. I watched as the trio of fleeing warriors sprinted into the clutches of Crazy Crow and his Mi'kmaq friend, Jilte'g. The two of them easily handled the shocked enemy warriors. Crazy Crow twirled his weapon made of two rocks joined by a leather strap around his head and took the legs out from under the first warrior. Running past him, he crushed the man's head with one swing of the huge club-spear he carried. Jilte'g then fired two arrows that dispatched the second Nadowessioux.

The final enemy warrior met Crazy Crow head-on, and the two of them crashed to the ground. Both men's weapons had flown from their hands upon impact and they engaged in a vicious hand-to-hand fight. They tore at each other like wild animals. The Nadowessioux warrior was a match for the Mi'kmaq legend. We were too many steps away to help, so I sent Nij Enàndeg. The huge dog hit the Nadowessioux in a headlong run, tearing him away from Crazy Crow. They rolled on the ground and the dog came out on top, but the enemy now had a knife and was about to plunge it into my dog when he was hit by a black blur hurtling out of the forest. It was over in a flash. The dog stood beside the big cat and howled while the panther screamed deafeningly. Both animals' muzzles were covered with blood from the day's events. Crazy Crow picked himself up from the ground, approached the two animals, and bowed to them. Then he turned to Mitigomij and me and thanked us.

The battle raged on. Other Nadowessioux from a smaller island in the channel to the east of this one had come to their fellow warriors' aid, increasing the defenders' numbers.

Zhashagi and his brother rushed by us and confronted two enemy warriors and a boy. Omashkooz struck the boy on the shoulder with his war club, spinning the youth to the ground where he rolled in pain. I then heard Zhashagi yell, "Óta Heháka, I'm here to kill you!"

At that moment the sky started to darken, and I gazed at the clear sky and saw the face of the sun begin to disappear behind a black shadow. Then there was a blow to my head and everything turned black.

When I woke, I was lying in a canoe on fur robes. My head throbbed and my dog lay beside me. Opening my eyes to the bright sunlight, I saw E's sitting there with a big smile on his face.

"He's awake!" E's cried, making my head pulse even more.

Then I felt a hand touch my shoulder and my mother's voice say, "I've been saving this for you. Remember I said we'd share tea together if we lived? It's cold, but it's tea."

I stared at her, then laughed. "Mother, what happened?"

"You took a blow on the head from a Nadowessioux who had snuck up behind us. Nìj Enàndeg tore a chunk from his arm, but the man escaped. At about the same time the sun started to disappear from the sky. Warriors from both sides became scared. We picked up our dead and wounded and ran for our boats. Mitigomij carried you. We thought you were dead, but once we got on the water and picked up E's and the others, we realized you were breathing but asleep."

"The sun disappeared?" I asked incredulously.

"Yes, and we were well clear of the Nadowessioux village before it came from behind the darkness. It was a sign from Kije-Manidò that we had to leave while we could."

"How many suns did I sleep?" I asked.

"Almost two," my mother replied. "We're now almost at the spot where we have to travel overland to get back to Zhashagi's village."

"How many more of our group died or were wounded?" I asked. "What about the rest of the war party?"

"Achie was slain on the island, but no others except those you already know about. Overall, from the whole group, we lost forty-seven warriors and sixty-two suffered wounds. The Nadowessioux must have had as many losses as us. The fighting was bloody until the sun disappeared. We buried all the dead the first day we stopped. We had no fear of our enemy following, so we took our time and did it properly. By the time everyone arrives home, there will be many wives, sisters, and mothers mourning in the Anishinaabe and Ouendat camps."

That night we stopped and the mood was very sombre. The women were waiting on the shore when we arrived and the hunters had eleven deer hanging to feed us. We would stay here for several suns to help the wounded heal and to regain our strength for the trip back to the Ouendat village, which would now take longer than two suns because of the extra burden of the wounded.

The day before we were to return to Zhashagi's village he stepped forward and said, "A few of my warriors, some of the women, and I have decided to go to our friends, the Omashkiigoo. From there we'll head toward the setting sun. Our Omashkiigoo friends have told us there are lands of tall grasses and then beyond that waji-wan (*wa-chew-wan:* mountains). If anyone wants to come with us, they're welcome."

That night we sat around the fire and talked about the future. In the end, it was decided that Crazy Crow, Jilte'g, E's, Pangì Mahingan, Ki'kwa'ju, and I would go with Zhashagi and his people. Crazy Crow said he only decided to go because if he and Mitigomij stayed together there wouldn't be enough enemies to share between them, and besides, he said, these young Omàmiwinini needed him and the two Mi'kmaq warriors to watch over them.

Mitigomij decided to return to our Omàmiwinini people because they needed him and he wouldn't leave the twins, Makwa and Wàbek, alone while their wives were with child. They were family, and the children they had coming would need guidance in the future.

Kìnà Odenan and Kànìkwe were still mourning the loss of Agwanìwon, and they said they needed to tell her family how she had died.

My mother, Wàbananang, decided to let us go. She said she was getting old and needed to be with her people along the Kitcisìpi Sìbì. She wanted her spirit to be near my father, Mahingan, when her time came to leave Turtle Island.

The next day there were hugs and tearful goodbyes, and we set off to the land of the setting sun.

On a bluff overlooking a small lake, two figures stood. Nanabozho turned to the tall hairy one whom the

Lakȟóta called Čhiyé Tȟáŋka and asked, "Why did you do that with the sun?"

"There was an Ouendat warrior in the battle who needed to live. His granddaughter will give birth to a great-grandson who will be named Dekanahwideh (*deck-aknee-wi-day*).

Nanabozho looked at him and said, "I never knew you could talk!"

"I didn't know how to sign the name Dekanahwideh," he answered, "so I had to."

They nodded at each other, turned, and went their separate ways.

Treat the earth well. It was not given to you by your parents; it was loaned to you by your children. We do not inherit the earth from our ancestors; we borrow it from our children.

We were here long before you knew us. We were not strong enough to hold our lands. Guns and disease and alcohol were our demise. However, it was the white man who drew up the treaties for us to sign. All any of us ask now is for you to keep your word on what you asked us to sign.

AFTERWORD

THE SOLAR ECLIPSE THAT stopped the vicious battle portrayed at the end of this novel actually took place in that area on July 16, 1330. It took two hours and seven minutes for the moon to travel across the sun's face from 1:03 p.m. to 3:10 p.m.

The final battle in the book occurred at the junction of the Crow Wing and Mississippi Rivers. More than four hundred years later a pivotal two-day battle also happened there between sixty Ojibwe warriors and a party of five hundred Lakȟóta returning down the Mississippi River from a raid on an Ojibwe village at Sandy Lake with female captives. After two days of fighting, the Lakȟóta retreated and most of the women escaped. The Ojibwe gun pits are still visible in the park there.

The Anishinaabe who left the Lake Superior region and settled in Manitoba, Saskatchewan, and Alberta became known in the nineteenth century as the Saulteaux (*soh-toh*) Nation. This was a name given to them by the French and means "people of the rapids," in reference to their origins in the Sault Ste. Marie region.

In this novel, the Lakȟóta youth Tȟáȟča Čiŋčá's (later Tȟatȟáŋka Kaťà) parents were killed by a grizzly bear. These bears have been proven to be able to smell an animal carcass from eighteen miles away.

Readers might be surprised to learn that the yellow swallowtail butterfly (*ozaawaa-memengwaa*) eats from dead carcasses. They obtain important amino acids essential to their survival and colour pigmentation and are mentioned in this book when Zhashagi returns to find the bodies of the warriors who died during the attack on the river.

The seven stopping places of the Anishinaabe in their migration from the eastern shores are as follows:

1. Montreal Island
2. Niagara Falls
3. Detroit River
4. Manitoulin Island
5. Sault Ste. Marie
6. Spirit Island in Duluth, Minnesota
7. Madeline Island, among the Apostle Islands in Lake Superior

The Crow Creek Massacre near Chamberlain, South Dakota, was a real-life event that happened in 1325. Archaeologists discovered 487 bodies at the site. There are a few theories of who committed the annihilation of these people. Perhaps my hypothesis will open up a different line of thought.

The discovery of the Norse axe, sword, and shield handle near Beardmore in Northern Ontario is another actual event. They were found by a prospector named James Edward Dodd on May 24, 1931. The artifacts currently reside at the Royal Ontario Museum in Toronto. The authenticity of the relics has always been in question. Perhaps my postulation will suggest that it really isn't a mystery, after all. My Native forefathers travelled to Turtle Island for centuries before the whites came. Anything was possible, even a wayward Viking!

There are mysteries all around us. The Crow Creek Massacre and the Beardmore relics are just two of them. I would like to think that perhaps I have opened the door just a bit for other possibilities and thinking.

The sharp stone arrowheads that Chaŋku Wašte, the Lakȟóta warrior, attaches to his arrow shafts before the buffalo hunt were made from volcanic obsidian rock. Chaŋku Wašte got the items from a Crow who would have received them in trade from Natives who had access to lava beds and lived near the Rocky Mountains.

Oh, and if readers don't know who Dekanahwideh is, they should look it up!

To see how a birchbark canoe is made, check out a ten-minute video at www.youtube.com/watch?v=OPnj-Dj3xR2g.

In Canada the present-day Anishinaabe-Ojibwe are the second-largest population among First Nations, surpassed only by the Cree. In the United States, they have the fourth-largest population among Native American tribes where they are known as the Chippewa, surpassed only by the Navajo, Cherokee, and Lakȟóta.

The average age for Lakȟóta speakers in the United States is 65 and there are 8,500 to 9,000 speakers remaining in a population in the United States of 102,200 (2000 U.S. census). The population of the Mi'kmaq in Canada is around 60,000 with 8,935 speakers left (2011 Canadian census). The Algonquins have 2,275 speakers remaining in Canada. The average age for Anishinaabe (Chippewa in the United States) speakers is 70, and they have around 6,000 speakers left in the United States. The Anishinaabe (Ojibwe in Canada) have 20,000 speakers.

This is the legacy of the residential schools!

European colonialism failed to respect Native culture when taking possession of indigenous lands. As far as Europeans were concerned, the "savages" had no particular need for land, when in reality Natives went to war to keep their lands against rival tribes. William W. Warren, in *History of the Ojibway People*, notes that Native families needed one square mile per family to subsist for food gathering.

Personally, I think the biggest genocide to suck the Native population into a vortex of despair and sadness for the past 130 years involved the policies of Sir John A. Macdonald, Canada's first prime minister, and his gathering of as many Native children as his government could lay their hands on and institutionalizing them into the horrors of the residential schools. He might have been the first prime minister of Canada, but he was also the first man to teach future generations of despots how to control a country with no degree of consciousness nor any humanity toward fellow human beings. Macdonald was and is undeserving of the accolades heaped upon his dehumanization of the Native population of Canada.

The colonists might have taken many Native people's lives with disregard, but when they stole their children, they stole all hopes of the Native families' future along with those children.

Sir John A. Macdonald gets far too much credit for what people think he did and not enough credit for the things he actually did, which affected the Native population of my country of Turtle Island for the past 130 years!

Miigwetch
Rick Revelle
Mashkawizi Mahingan Inini (Strong Wolf Man)

GLOSSARIES AND PRONUNCIATION GUIDES

For the Native-language glossaries that follow, the Native word comes first followed by the pronunciation in *italics* and then the meaning.

It is my hope that all those who read the three novels in my Algonquin Quest series will gain a better understanding of these dying languages and that they will learn to pronounce a few words that will stay with them in the coming years. All the glossaries have websites that readers can visit to discover these ancient languages which were spoken by real people before they were removed from their lands.

Miigwetch.

ALGONQUIN/OMÀMIWININI GLOSSARY

For an Algonquin Talking Dictionary, please see
www.hilaroad.com/camp/nation/speak.html.

Àbimì (*ah-bih-mee*)	Defend, guard
Àbita (*ah-beh-ta*)	Half
Achgook	Snake
Àgimag (*ug-ga-mug*)	Snowshoes
Agingos (*uh-gihn-goes*)	Chipmunk
Agwanìwon (*uh-gweh-nee-won*)	Shawl Woman
Akwàndawàgan (*a-kwon-da-way-gan*)	Ladder
Amik (*ah-mik*)	Beaver
Àmò-sizibàkwad (*ah-mow-siz-zeh-baw-kwad*)	Honey
Àndeg (*un-deck*)	Crow
Anìbimin	Cranberries
Anìbìsh (*ah-ne-bish*)	Tea
Animosh (*an-ney-mush*)	Dog
Anokì (*uh-noo-key*)	Hunt
Asab (*a-sab*)	Net
Asin (*a-sin*)	Stone
Asinabka	Place of glare rock (Chaudière Falls)
Asticou	Boiling rapids (also Chaudière Falls)

Àwadòsiwag (*ah-wa-dow-she-wag*)	Minnow
Awesìnz (*uh-way-seehns*)	Animal
Azàd	Aspen
Enàndeg (*en-nahn-deg*)	Colour
Esiban (*ez-sa-bun*)	Raccoon
Gichi-anami'e-bizhiw	Fabulous Night Panther
Gichigami	Lake Superior
Guhn	Snow
Haudenosaunee (*ho-de-no-sho-nee*)	Iroquois Confederacy
Ininàtig (*e-na-na-dig*)	Maple
Ishkodewan	Blaze
Kabàsigan	Stew
Kàg (*ka-hg*)	Porcupine
Kànìkwe	No Hair
Kà-wàsadotòj (*ka-wah-suh-koh-tooj*)	April
Kekek (*kay-kayk*)	Hawk
Kìgònz (*key-gounz*)	Fish
Kije-Manidò	Great Spirit
Kìjik (*key-jick*)	Cedar
Kìnà	Sharp
Kìnà Odenan	Sharp Tongue
Kinebigokesì	Cricket
Kishkàbikedjiwan	Waterfall
Kitcisìpi Sìbì	Ottawa River

Kitcisìpiriniwak	People of the Great River
Lenepi	Delaware
Magotogoek Sìbì	Path That Walks (St. Lawrence River)
Magwàizibò Sìbì	Iroquois River (Richelieu River)
Mahingan (*mah-in-gan*)	Wolf
Makadewà (*ma-ka-de-wa*)	Black
Makadewà Wàban (*ma-ka-de-wa wah-bun*)	Black Dawn
Makon (*mah-koon*)	Bear cub
Makwa (*mah-kwa*)	Bear
Maliseet	Malècite
Mandàmin (*man-dah-min*)	Corn
Manidò	Spirit
Mazinaabikinigan	Lake Mazinaw
Me'hiken	Mahican
Michabo	The Great Hare, trickster god, inventor of fishing
Mìgàdinàn (*mee-gah-dih-nahn*)	War
Migiskan (*mi-gi-skuhn*)	Hook
Mikisesimik	Wampum belt
Mishigami	Lake Michigan
Mishi-pijiw (*mih-she-pih-shoe*)	Panther
Misi-zagging	Lake Huron

Miskomini-kìzis (*mih-skoh-mih-nih-kee-zihs*)	July
Mitig (*mi-tig*)	Tree
Mitigomij (*mih-tih-go-mihzh*)	Red Oak
Mònz (*moans*)	Moose
Nàbek	Male bear
Name (*nu-me*)	Sturgeon
Namebin (*nu-me-bin*)	Sucker
Namegosi-kizis (*na-mi-go-si-key-sis*)	October
Nasemà (*na-sem-mah*)	Tobacco
Nigig (*neh-gig*)	Otter
Nìj (*neesh*)	Two
Nìj Enàndeg (*neesh en-nahn-deg*)	Two Colour
Nika	Goose
Nòjek (*now-shek*)	Female bear
Nukumi (*no-ko-miss*)	Mother Earth/ Grandmother
Odàbànàk (*oh-dah-nahk*)	Toboggan
Odawàjameg (*oh-duh-wah-shaw-megg*)	Salmon
Odenan	Tongue
Odìngwey	Face
Odjìbik	Root
Odjìshiziwin (*oh-jee-sheen*)	Scar
Ogà (*oh-gah*)	Pickerel, walleye

Omàmiwinini (*oh-mam-ih-win-in-e*)	Algonquin
Omìmì (*oh-me-me*)	Pigeon
Onagàgizidànibag	Plantain
Onigam	Portage
Ouendat	Huron
Pakìgino-makizinan (*pa-kee-gun-no-muh-kih* *-zih-none*)	Moccasins
Pangì (*pung-gee*)	Little
Pangì Mahingan (*pung-gee mah-in-gan*)	Little Wolf
Pênâ-kuk	Pennacook
Pibòn (*pi-bou*)	Winter
Pikodjisi	Blackfly
Pikwàkogwewesì (*pick-wa-go-gwes-e*)	Jay
Piminàshkawà	Chaser
Pimizì (*pim-me-zee*)	Eel
Pine	Partridge
Pìsà (*pee-shah*)	Small
Pìsà Animosh (*pee-shah an-ney-mush*)	Small Dog
Sagime (*suh-gi-may*)	Mosquito
Shangweshì (*shan-gwe-she*)	Mink
Shàwanong (*shah-wuh-noong*)	South
Shìbàskobidjige	Set a net under ice
Shigàg	Skunk

Shìshìb (*she-sheeb*)	Duck
Tendesì (*ten-des-see*)	Blue jay
Wàban (*wah-bun*)	Dawn
Wàbanaki	Abenaki
Wàbananang (*wa-ba-na-nang*)	Morning Star
Wàbek	Bear
Wàbidì (*wah-bi-dee*)	Elk
Wàbigon Kìzis (*wah-bi-gon key-zis*)	May
Wàbìsì (*wah-bee-see*)	Swan
Wàbòz (*wah-bose*)	Rabbit
Wàginogàn	Lodge, home
Wàgosh (*wa-gosh*)	Fox
Wàwàshkeshi (*wa-wash-ke-she*)	Deer
Wàwonesì	Whippoorwill
Wegimindj	Mother
Wewebasinàbàn (*way-way-buh-sih-nah-bahn*)	Slingshot
Wìgwàs Chìmàn (*we-gwahs chee-mahn*)	Birchbark canoe
Wolastoqiyik	Maliseet

ALGONQUIN/OMÀMIWININI PRONUNCIATION GUIDE

See also www.native-languages.org/algonquin_guide.htm.

VOWELS

Character We Use	Sometimes Also Used	IPA Symbol	How to Say It
a		Λ	Like the a in what.
à	á, aa	ɑː	Like the a in father.
e		e ~ ɛ	Like the a in gate or the e in red.
è	é, ee	eː	Like a in pay.
i		I	Like the i in pit.
ì	í, ii	iː	Like the ee in seed.
o	u	ʊ	Like the u input.
ò	ó, oo	oː	Like the o in lone.

DIPHTHONGS

Character We Use	IPA Symbol	How to Say It
aw	aw	Like ow in cow.
ay	aj	Like eye.
ew	ew	This sound doesn't really exist in English. It sounds a little like saying the AO from AOL quickly.
ey	ej	Like the ay in hay.
iw	iw	Like a child saying ew!
ow	ow	Like the ow in show.

CONSONANTS

Character We Use	Sometimes Also Used	IPA Symbol	How to Say It
b		b	Like b in bill.
ch	č	ʧ	Like ch in chair.
d		d	Like d in die.
dj		ʤ	Like j in jar.
g		g	Like g in gate.
h		h~ʔ	Like h in hay, or like the glottal stop in the middle of uh-oh.
j	zh, ž	ʒ	Like the ge sound at the end of mirage.
k		kh~k	Like k in key or ski (see soft consonants below).
m		m	Like m in moon.
n		n	Like n in night.
p		ph~p	Like p in pin or spin (see soft consonants below).
s		s	Like s in see.
sh	c, š	ʃ	Like sh in shy.
t		th~t	Like t in take or stake (see soft consonants below).
w		w	Like w in way.
y		j	Like y in yes.
z		z	Like z in zoo.

Anishinaabe/Ojibwe Glossary

For an Ojibwe Talking Dictionary, please see
http://ojibwe.lib.umn.edu.

Aabita-niibino-giizis
  (*a-bi-ta-knee-bino-gee-sus*)
July (Berry Moon)

Aandeg (*on-deg*)
Crow

Adik (*a-dick*)
Caribou

Adikameg (*a-dik-a-meg*)
Whitefish

Adiko-wiiyaas
  (*a-day-ko-we-as*)
Caribou meat

Animbiigoo-zaaga'igan
Dog Waters Lake
(Lake Nipigon)

Animosh (*an-eh-moosh*)
Dog

Anishinaabewi-gichigami
Lake Superior

Apiitendang Makwa
  (*a-pete-tan-den ma-kwa*)
Proud Bear

Asemaa (*as-say-ma*)
Tobacco

Ashkaakamigokwe
Mother Earth

Baaga'adowewin
Lacrosse

Baapaase (*baa-pa-say*)
Woodpecker

Baawitigong
Sault Ste. Marie

Bikwak (*be-kwak*)
Arrow

Dagwaagin (*dag-waa-kin*)
Autumn

Diindiisi (*tchin-dees*)
Blue jay

E-bangishimog
Spirit of the West Wind

Gaagaagiwigwani-ziibi
Crow Wing River

Gichi Bizhiins
  (*gich-e be-zeans*)

Big Cat

Gichigami-ziibi
  (*gich-e-gam-e-zee-bee*)

Great Lake River, present-
day St. Louis River

Gichi-Manidoo

Great Spirit

Gichi-ziibi (*gich-e-zee-bee*)

Mississippi River

Giizhizekwe Ikwe
  (*key-zee-zay-kway e-kway*)

She Cooks Woman

Ginoozhe (*kin-nose-hay*)

Pike (fish)

Gizhiibatoo Inini
  (*giz-e-baa-too in-in-e*)

Run Fast Man

Ininishib (*eh-nay-nish-hip*)

Mallard

Ininwewing-gichigami

Lake Michigan

Iskigamizige-giizis
  (*is-ki-gamo-azing-a-gee-zas*)

April (Sugar-
Bushing Moon)

Jiimaan (*g-mawn*)

Canoe

Jooweshk

Killdeer

**Kababikodaawangag
  Saaga'igan**

Lake of Sand Dunes
(Lake of the Woods)

Kagawong-ziibi
  (*kag-a-wong-zee-bee*)

Kagawong River

Keewaynan
  (*kee-wi-wai-non-ing*)

Keewaynan Peninsula,
Lake Superior

Ma'iingan (*ma-een-gun*)

Wolf

Makadewaagami-ziibi
  (*mak-a-day-eh-wa-
  gami-zee-bee*)

Blackwater River

Makadewigwan
  (*mak-a-day-eh-we-gwan*)

Black Feather

Makizin Ataagewin (*mak-e-zin a-tash-win*) — Moccasin game

Makwa (*muck-wa*) — Black Bear

Manidoowaaling Minisi (*mana-do-wah-ling men-eh-si*) — Cave of the Spirit (Manitoulin Island)

Manoomin (*man-oo-men*) — Wild rice

Manoominike-giizis (*man-oom-inik-gee-zas*) — August (Ricing Moon)

Mashkode-bizhiki (*mush-ko-dee-bish-eh-ka*) — Buffalo

Mayagi-bine (*my-a-gay-bee-neh*) — Pheasant

Mishaabooz — Great Rabbit

Misi-ziibi — Great River (Mississippi River)

Misko — Red

Misko Zhiishiib (*mis-ko zhe-sheep*) — Red Duck

Miskwaabik (*miss-kwa-bic*) — Copper

Mitaawangaagamaa — Big Sandy Lake

Mooningwanekaaing — Madeline Island

Mooz (*moans*) — Moose

Naadawe — Huron

Naadowewi-gichigami — Lake Huron

Nadowessioux — Snake (Lakȟóta)

Negawi-ziibi — Sandy River

Nenaandawi'iwed (*ni-na-an-da-wi-e-wed*) — Healer

Nitaage Niibiwa   Kill Many
(*ni-ta-gay knee-be-wa*)

Odaabaan (*ou-da-bah*)   Sled

Odishkwaagamii   Algonquin and/or Nipissing

Ogichidaa-nagamon   Warrior Song
(*oh-each-e-da-na-ga-mon*)

Omashkiigoo   Cree
(*oh-mush-key-go*)

Omashkooz (*oh-mush-goes*)   Elk

Ozaawaa-memengwaa   Yellow Swallowtail
(*o-zaa-wah-me-mean-gwa*)

Ozhaashigob   Slippery elm
(*ooh-sosh-eh-ga-a*)

Waa-miigisagoo   Wampum

Wajiwan (*wa-chew-wan*)   Mountains

Wanagekogamigoon   Lodges
(*wan-a-gay-ko-ga-me-goon*)

Wiikwandiwin   Seasonal ceremony
(*wick-wan-de-wan*)

Wiininwaa   Nourishment

Zaagibagaa-giiziz   May (Budding Moon)
(*zaa-gi-ba-ga-gee-sus*)

Zhashagi (*sha-sha-gee*)   Blue Heron

Zhiishiib (*zhe-sheep*)   Duck

Zhiiwaagamizigan   Maple syrup
(*zhe-wa-ga-miss-e-gan*)

Ziibiins (*see-peace*)   Creek

Anishinaabe/Ojibwe Pronunciation Guide

See also
http://ojibwe.lib.umn.edu/about-ojibwe-language.

Sounds and Orthography

Double Vowels

The *Ojibwe People's Dictionary* uses the double-vowel system to write Ojibwe words. This alphabet has become the standard writing system for Ojibwe in the United States and in some parts of Canada. Users unfamiliar with spelling in the double-vowel alphabet should consult the Search Tips page of the *Ojibwe People's Dictionary* for help in getting the best search results. The Ojibwe alphabet is as follows: *a, aa, b, ch, d, e, g, h, ', i, ii, j, k, m, n, o, oo, p, s, sh, t, w, y, z, zh*. Note that the double vowels are treated as standing for unit sounds and are alphabetized after the corresponding single vowels. The character ' represents a glottal stop, which is a significant speech sound in Ojibwe. The doubled consonants (*ch, sh, zh*) are also treated as a single-letter unit. This is important to remember when browsing alphabetically. Each vowel is given below along with a phonetic transcription, Ojibwe words containing it, and one or more English words containing roughly equivalent sounds. The letters standing for the sounds focused on are in bold.

Ojibwe Letter	Phonetic	Ojibwe Examples	English Equivalents
a	[ə]~[ʌ]	*agim:* "count someone!" *namadabi:* "sits down" *baashkizigan:* "gun"	about
aa	[a:]	*aagim:* "snowshoe" *maajaa:* "goes away"	father
e	[e:]~[ɛ:]	*emikwaan:* spoon *awenen:* who *anishinaabe:* "person," "Indian," "Ojibwe"	café
i	[I]	*inini:* "man" *mawi:* "cries"	pin
ii	[i:]	*niin:* "I" *googii:* "drives"	seen
o	[o]~[U]	*ozid:* "someone's foot" *anokii:* "works" *nibo:* "dies," "is dead"	obey, book
oo	[o:]~[u:]	*oodena:* "town" *anookii:* "hires" *goon:* "snow" *bimibatoo:* "runs along"	boat, boot

NASAL VOWELS

These are indicated by writing the appropriate basic vowel followed by *nh*. Before a *y* or a glottal stop ', the *h* may be omitted in writing. There are no direct English equivalents.

Ojibwe Letter	Phonetic	Ojibwe Examples
aanh	[ã:]	*banajaanh:* "nestling"
enh	[ẽ:]~[ɛ:]	*nisayenh:* "my older brother"
iinh	[ĩ:]	*awesiinh:* "wild animal; agaashiinyi, agaashiinhyi:* "[someone] is small"
oonh	[õ:]~[ũ:]	*giigoonh:* "fish"

NASALIZED VOWELS

Vowels are nasalized before *ns*, *nz*, and *nzh*. The *n* is then omitted in pronunciation. A few examples are: ***gaawiin ingikendanziin:*** "I don't know it"; ***jiimaanens:*** "small boat"; and ***oshkanshiin:*** "someone's fingernail(s)." Long vowels after a nasal consonant *m* or *n* are often nasalized, especially before *s*, *sh*, *z*, or *zh*. It is often difficult to decide whether to write these as nasalized vowels or not. For example, while we write the word for *moose* without indicating the phonetic nasalization, many prefer to write it with an *n* — ***mooz*** or ***moonz:*** "moose."

HURON/OUENDAT GLOSSARY

For a Huron Talking Dictionary, see
www.firstvoices.com/en/Huronne-Wendat-EN/
word-query-form.

Achie	White Ash
Anue	Bear
Attigouatan	Georgian Bay
A-yagh-kee	I go to war
Ohskënonton' (*o-ski-non-ton'*)	Deer
Öndawa	Black Ash
Önenha'	Corn
Otawindeht (*o-ta-win-dat*)	Otter
Ouentironk	Beautiful Water (Lake Simcoe)
Skenhchio (*sken-shoe*)	Red Fox
Tindee	Two
Tsou'tayi (*sou-ta-he*)	Beaver
Waughshe Anue	Bad Bear
Yatie' (*sha-tip*)	Bird

Lakȟóta Glossary

The second Lakȟóta word is from the Lakȟóta
Dictionary of John P. Williamson.
For a Lakȟóta Talking Dictionary, please see
www.bearhawk.net/pages/wordsearch.html.

Aíčhimani	Journey
Akíčita (*ah-kee-chee-tah*)	Camp guards and/or warrior society responsible for hunting and war parties
Čhaŋkáškapi (*chon-kos'kay*)	Fence
Chaŋku Wašte (*chan-koo wash-tay*)	Good Path
Čhaŋnúŋpa Wakȟán (*chah-nuen-pah wah-kahn*)	Sacred pipe
Čhaŋpȟásapa wí (*can-pa'-sa-pa wi*)	July (Moon of Cherries Blackening)
Čhiyé Tȟáŋka (*chee'-ay ton'-kah*)	Big Elder Brother
Ȟaȟátȟuŋwaŋ (*ha-ha-ton-wan*)	Anishinaabe, Ojibwe, or Chippewa
Ȟaŋté Čhaŋȟlóǧaŋ	Yarrow
Hokšíčala (*oke-shee-chah'-lah*)	Baby
Húčhiŋška (*hue-chin-ska*)	Milkweed
Hupák'iŋ (*hoo-pock-een*)	Travois, pole sled
Íȟoka (*ee-hoh-ka*)	Badger Society

Itázipčho (*ee-dah-zeeb-koh*) Sans Arc: Lakȟóta
sub-tribe translated as
"No Markings" or the
French name for them
Sans Arc ("No Bows")

Kȟaŋǧí Ȟupáhu Wakpá Crow Wing River
(*kohn'-gay hoo'-pah
wah-koh'-pah*)

Kȟaŋǧi Wakpá Crow Creek
(*kohn'gay wa-pa*)

Kȟaŋǧí Yuhá Crow Owners' Society
(*kohn-gay yue-hah*)

K'tay (*kat'á*) Kill

Matȟóȟota (*mah'-toh-ho-ta*) Grizzly bear

Mawátani Owl Headdress Society
(*mee-wah-deeh-nee*)

Mnišá Wakpá Red River, also known as
(*mnee-shah wah-koh'-pah*) Wine River to the Lakȟóta

Mníšoše Wakpá Missouri River
(*mini-so-se wa-pa*)

Nážiŋ Išnála Stand Alone
(*nah-zhee is-na-la*)

Oglečhe Kutepi Arrow shooting
(*oh-glay-say kue-day-pe*)

Ógleiglúzašá (*oga-lee-sha*) Wears a Red Shirt

Oȟ'áŋkȟo Nape Swift Hand
(*oh-hon'-koh nah'pah*)

Óta Heȟáka Many Elk
(*oh'-tay he-ha-ka*)

Pȟáŋžela Napé Soft Hand
  (*pohn-zah-lah nah'pay*)

Pispíza (*peace-piza*) Prairie dog

Psáloka (*sa-ah-loo-ka*) Crow

Ptesáŋ Wí (*tay-san wee*) White Buffalo Calf
Woman

Pteyáȟpaya (*pa-tay-pay-ah*) Cowbird

SápA Maȟpíya Black Sky
  (*sah'-pah maii-hoh'-pee-ah*)

SápA Ziŋtkála Black Bird
  (*sah'-pah zint'-kah-lah*)

SnázA (*snee'-zhay*) Scar

Sotkàyuha Bare Lance Owners'
  (*shoh-dkah-yue-hah*) Society

Šuŋgmánitu Tȟáŋka Wolf
  (*shoon-gur'-mah-nee-tee
  tanka*)

Sutá Wičhášа Strong Man
  (*soo-tah wee-chah'-shah*)

Tȟáȟča Čiŋčá Deer Child
  (*tah-ka shin-sha*)

Tȟáȟčasaŋla Antelope
  (*tah-kchah'-sohn-lah*)

Tȟahúka Čhaŋgléška
Na Wahúkheza Hoop and spear game
  (*tah-ha-uka chan-glay-sh-ka
  na wa-hu-keza*)

Tȟamní Placenta

Tȟatȟáŋka (*tah-tohn'-kah*) Buffalo

Tȟatȟáŋka Katʼá　　　　Buffalo Kill
　(*tah-tohn'-kah k'tay*)

Tȟawíŋyela (*tah-win-yela*)　Doe

Tȟíŋta (*tin'-ta*)　　　　Prairie

Tȟíŋpsiŋla (*timp-sila*)　Turnip

Tȟokȟála (*tah–koh-la*)　Kit Fox Society

Waglékšuŋ　　　　　　Turkey
　(*wal-gay-leck-shahn*)

Wakȟáŋ Tȟáŋka　　　Great Mystery
　(*wakhan thanka*)

Wakȟáŋheža　　　　Children, sacred ones
　(*wak-han-hay-za*)

Wakhéya (*wa-kay'-ah*)　Lodges, teepees, dwellings

Wakpá Atkúku　　　Mississippi River
　(*wak-pa' at-ku-ku*)

Wasná (*wah-snah*)　　Pemmican

Wawátʼečala Iȟá　　Gentle Smile
　(*wah-wah'-tay-chah ee-'hah*)

WičákȟA (*wee-chah-kah*)　Speak True

Wičháȟpi (*wee-chalk-pee*)　Star

Wípazukȟa-wašté-wí　June (Moon When the
　(*wi-pa-zoo-ka-*　　　Berries Are Good)
　wash-tay-wi)

Wókpȟaŋ (*who-kpah*)　Parfleche-rawhide bags

Wóphiye　　　　　　Medicine bag

Yapízapi Iyéčheča　Dandelion
　(*ya-pee-zapi eye-che-ca*)

Lakȟóta Pronunciation Guide

Vowels

Character We Use	IPA Symbol	Lakȟóta Pronunciation
a	a	Like the a in father.
e	e	Similar to the a in gate.
i	i	Like the i in police.
o	o	Like the o in note.
u	u	Like the u in flute.

Nasal Vowels

Nasal vowels don't exist in English, but readers might be familiar with them from French (or from hearing people speak English with a French accent). They are pronounced just like oral ("regular") vowels, only using the nose as well as the mouth. To English speakers a nasal vowel often sounds like a vowel with a half-pronounced *n* at the end of it. You can hear examples of nasal vowels at the end of the French words *bon* and *Jean,* or in the middle of the word *Français.*

Note: The Sioux pronunciation of the nasal vowels *on* and *un* is exactly the same.

Character We Use:	Sometimes Also Used	IPA Symbol
an	an, ą, aŋ, aŋ, aN	ã
in	in, į, iŋ, iŋ, iN	ĩ
on	on, , oŋ, oŋ, oN	ũ
un	un, ų, uŋ, uŋ, uN	ũ

CONSONANTS

Character We Use	Sometimes Also Used	IPA Symbol	Lakȟóta Pronunciation
b		b	Like b in bill.
c	č, ch, ć, , ċ, j	ʧ ~ ʤ	An unaspirated, "soft" ch sound like the ch in filching or the t in vulture. Sometimes it sounds more like the j in jar. This character is also used to represent the aspirated ch (see aspiration below).
c	č, ch, c', ċ, c	ʧh	An aspirated, "hard" ch sound like the one in chair. This character is also used to represent the unaspirated ch (see aspiration below).

291

c'	c', č, ç, c'	ʧ'	Like ch in char but with a catch after it (like ch'ar).
d		d	Like d in die. Only used in Dakota pronunciation.
g		g	Like g in gate. Also used to represent the g in the Spanish word saguaro.
g	ġ, gh, ğ	ɣ	Like g in the Spanish word saguaro. Also used to represent the g in gate.
h	x	h~x	Like h in hay. At the end of a word or before another consonant, it is pronounced like the ch in the German ach.
h'		h'	Like h in hay but with a catch after it (like h'ay).
j	zh, ž, ź	ʒ	Like a French j. In English you can hear this sound at the end of words like garage.

k	, , g	k	Like the unaspirated k in ski. Also used to represent the aspirated k in key.
k	kh, k', , kx	kh~kx	Like the aspirated k in key. Sometimes it's pronounced raspier. This character is also used to represent the unaspirated k in ski.
k'	k', ḳ	k'	Like k in key but with a catch after it (like k'ey).
l		l	Like l in light. Only used in Lakȟóta pronunciation.
m		m	Like m in moon.
n		n	Like n in night.
p	, , b	p	Like the unaspirated p in spin. Also used to represent the aspirated p in pin.
p	ph, p', , px	ph~px	Like the aspirated p in pin. Sometimes it's pronounced raspier. This character is also used to represent the unaspirated p in spin.

p'	p'	p'	Like p in pin but with a catch after it (like p'in).
s		s	Like s in so. Also used to represent the sh in show.
s	š, sh, ś, s'	ʃ	Like sh in show. Also used to represent the s in so.
s'	s', ş	s'	Like s in so but with a catch after it (like s'o). Also used to represent sh with a catch after it.
s'	š', sh', ś', s'	ʃ'	Like sh in show but with a catch after it (like sh'ow). Also used to represent s with a catch after it.
t	, , d	t	Like the unaspirated t in sty. Also used to represent the aspirated t in tie.
t	th, t', , tx	th~tx	Like the aspirated t in tie. Sometimes it's pronounced raspier. This character is also used to represent the unaspirated t in sty.

t'	t', ţ	t'	Like t in tie but with a catch after it (like t'ie).
w		w	Like w in way.
x	, r	x	Guttural sound that doesn't exist in English. Like ch in the German ach.
x'	,	x'	Like ch in the German ach but with a catch after it.
y		j	Like y in yes.
z		z	Like z in zoo.
z'		z'	Like z in zoo but with a catch after it (like z'oo).
,		?	A pause sound like the one in the middle of the word uh-oh.

STRESS

Word stress in the Lakȟóta languages is significant. For example, *zica*, with the stress on the second syllable, means "squirrel," but *zica*, with the stress on the first syllable, means a kind of bird. Unfortunately, for language learners, native Lakȟóta speakers almost never mark where the accent falls in a word (any more than English speakers do). In texts written by linguists, sometimes we see a stressed syllable in a Lakȟóta word marked with an acute accent such as *zicá*.

Mi'kmaq Glossary

For the Mi'kmaq Talking Dictionary, please see
www.mikmaqonline.org.

Apalqaqamej (*a-bach-caw-a-mitch*)	Chipmunk
Apistanéwj (*a-bis-tan-ouch*)	Marten
Bootup	Whale
Eli'tuat (*el-e-do-what*)	Men with Beards
Elue'wiet Ga'qaquj (*el-away-we-it ga-ah-gooch*)	Crazy Crow
E's (*s*)	Clam
Gespe'g	Land's End
Jilte'g (*jil-teg*)	Scar
Ki'kwa'ju	Wolverine
Midewiwin	Grand Medicine Society
Na'gweg (*nah-quik*)	Day
Natigòsteg	Forward Land (Anticosti Island)
Nukumi (*no-ko-miss*)	Mother Earth, Grandmother
Tepgig (*dip-geek*)	Night

Mi'kmaq Pronunciation Guide

See also www.native-languages.org/mikmaq_guide.htm.

VOWELS

Character We Use	Sometimes Also Used	IPA Symbol	How to Say It
a		ɑ	Like the a in father.
á	a', a:	ɑ:	Like a only held longer.
e		e	Like the e sound in Spanish. In English the Mi'kmaq pronunciation sounds like a cross between the vowel sounds in met and mate.
é	e', e:	e:	Like e only held longer.
i			Midway between the vowel sounds in hit and heat.
í	i', i:	i:	Like the i in police only held longer.
i	', ê, ŭ	ə	Schwa sound like the e in roses.
o	ô	o	Like the o in note.
ó	o', o:	o:	Like o only held longer.
u	o	u	Like the u in tune.
ú	u', u:	u:	Like u only held longer.

DIPHTHONGS

Character We Use	Sometimes Also Used	IPA Symbol	How to Say It
aw	au	aw	Like ow in cow.
ay	ai	aj	Like eye.
ew		ew	This sound doesn't really exist in English. It sounds a little like saying the AO from AOL quickly.
ey	ei	ej	Like ay in hay.
iw		iw	Like a child saying ew!

CONSONANTS

Character We Use	Sometimes Also Used	IPA Symbol	How to Say It
j	c, ch, tj	ʧ~ʤ	Like ch in char or j in jar.
k	g	k ~ g	Like k in skate or g in gate.
kw	kw	kw~kw	Usually, it's pronounced like qu in queen, but at the end of a word it's pronounced more like a k with a puff of air after it.
l		l	Like l in light.

m		m	Like m in moon.
n		n	Like n in night.
p	b	p ~ b	Like p in spill or b in bill.
q	x, ĝ, kh	x ~ ɣ	Guttural sound that does not exist in English. Like ch in German ach or g in Spanish saguaro.
qw	xw	xw~xw	Guttural sound that doesn't exist in English. Usually, it is pronounced like a q and a w together. But at the end of a word it's pronounced more like a q with a puff of air after it.
s		s ~ z	Like s in sue or z in zoo.
t	d	t ~ d	Like t in sty or d in die (see voicing, below).
w		w	Like w in way.
y	i	j	Like y in yes.

SELECTED RESOURCES

BOOKS

Bennet, Doug, and Tim Tiner. *Up North Again*. Toronto: McClelland & Stewart, 1997.

Capps, Benjamin. *The Old West: The Great Chiefs*. New York: Time-Life Books, 1975.

_____. *The Old West: The Indians*. New York: Time-Life Books, 1973.

Clifton, James A., George L. Cornell, and James M. McLurken. *People of the Three Fires*. Sault Ste. Marie, MI: Michigan Indian Press, 1986.

Crowe, Keith J. *A History of the Original Peoples of Northern Canada*. Montreal and Kingston: McGill-Queen's University Press 1974.

Curtin, Jeremiah. Native American Creation Myths. Mineola, NY: Dover, 2004.

Drury, Bob, and Tom Clavin. *The Heart of Everything That Is: The Untold Story of Red Cloud, an American Legend.* New York: Simon and Schuster, 2013.

Hannon, Leslie F. *The Discovers.* Toronto: McClelland & Stewart, 1971.

Johnson, Michael G. *Native Tribes of North America.* 2nd ed. Richmond Hill, ON: Firefly Books, 2014.

King, Cecil. *Balancing Two Worlds: Jean-Baptiste Assiginack and the Odawa Nation.* Saskatoon: Saskatoon Firstprint, 2013.

Le Sueur, William D. *Count Frontenac.* London: Oxford University Press, 1928.

Mack-E-Te-Be-Nessy, Chief (A.J. Blackbird). *History of the Ottawa and Chippewa Indians of Michigan.* Ypsilanti, MI: Ypsilantian Job Printing House, 1887.

Mowat, Farley. *No Man's River.* Toronto: Key Porter, 2006.

Nichols, John D., and Earl Nyholm. *A Concise Dictionary of Minnesota Ojibwe.* Minneapolis, MN; University of Minnesota Press, 1995.

Raddall, Thomas H. *The Path of Destiny.* Toronto: Doubleday Canada, 1957.

Robson, Lucia St. Clair. *Ghost Warrior.* New York: Tom Doherty Associates, 2002.

Schmalz, Peter S. *The Ojibwa of Southern Ontario.* Toronto: University of Toronto Press 1991.

Trigger, Bruce G. *The Huron Farmers of the North.* New York: Holt, Rinehart and Winston, 1969.

Trumbull, Henry. *History of the Indian Wars.* Boston: Phillips and Samson, 1846.

Walker, James R. *Lakȟóta Society.* Lincoln, NE: University of Nebraska Press, 1982.

Warren, William W. *History of the Ojibway People*. St. Paul, MN: Minnesota Historical Society, 1984.

Weatherford, Jack. *Indian Givers*. New York: Crown, 1988.

Williamson, John P. *An English-Dakota Dictionary*. St. Paul, MN: Minnesota Historical Society Press, 1992.

Zu Wied, Prince Maximilian. *People of the First Man: Life Among the Plains Indians in Their Final Days of Glory*. North Saanich, BC: Promontory Press, 1982.

MUSEUMS

Akta Lakȟóta Museum (Chamberlain, South Dakota)

Assiginack Museum (Manitowaming, Manitoulin Island, Ontario)

Centennial Museum of Shequiandah (Shequiandah, Manitoulin Island, Ontario)

Dakota Indian Foundation (Chamberlain, South Dakota)

Lilian's Museum (M'chigeeng, Manitoulin Island, Ontario)

Manitoba Museum (Winnipeg, Manitoba)

Museum of Ojibwa Culture (St. Ignace, Michigan)

Old Mill Heritage Center (Kagawong, Manitoulin Island, Ontario)

Royal Ontario Museum (Toronto, Ontario)

WEBSITES

http://ojibwe.lib.umn.edu

www.bearhawk.net/pages/wordsearch.html

www.firstvoices.com/en/Huronne-Wendat-EN/word-query-form

www.freelang.net/online/ojibwe.php

www.hilaroad.com/camp/nation/speak.html
www.lakotadictionary.org/nldo.php
www.mikmaqonline.org
www.native-languages.org/algonquin_guide.htm
www.native-languages.org/mikmaq_guide.htm
www.thealgonquinway.ca
www.youtube.com/watch?v=OPnjDj3xR2g
www.youtube.com/watch?v=ysa5OBhXz-Q